Salon Affair

D A Latham

Copyright © 2014 D A Latham

All rights reserved.

No part of this book may be reproduced, scanned, or distributed in any printed or electronic format without permission.

Please do not participate in or encourage piracy of copyrighted materials in violation of the author's rights.

ISBN: 1500287563
ISBN-13: 978-1500287566

DEDICATION

With thanks to all the people who helped bring this story to life, and of course my dearest, darling Allan.

CONTENTS

Acknowledgments	i
Chapter 1	1
Chapter 2	18
Chapter 3	30
Chapter 4	43
Chapter 5	64
Chapter 6	78
Chapter 7	91
Chapter 8	107
Chapter 9	122
Chapter 10	135
Chapter 11	148
Chapter 12	167
Chapter 13	185
Chapter 14	199
Epilogue	209

Acknowledgements

With thanks to

Tomme Darlington

Dannielle Reed

Michael Harte

Tina Johnson

Amy Watton

And

Gemma Pinfield-Thomas

This is a work of fiction, and all characters, names and situations are purely illustrative and are the product of the author's imagination.

Any resemblance to actual persons, living or dead, business establishments, events, or locales is entirely coincidental.

Chapter 1

I finished up my last client, taking her through to reception to recommend her products, and hand her over to the receptionist to pay her bill. I said my goodbyes, and hot-footed it through to the staff room to claim my glass of wine, and a chair, ready for the staff meeting. The entire staff were there, with it being Saturday evening, and we just had to wait for the receptionist to lock the front door and join us, and we could find out the reason for the impromptu meeting.

Damien, the salon manager looked ill at ease when he stood to address us. "Guys, as you probably realise, the salon isn't doing quite so well lately. We've tried various marketing schemes, even a coupon offer to try and get new clients, but our accountants have told us that we're carrying too many staff for the revenue." *Well, if you stopped giving it away for next to nothing on Groupon, we might make a bit more profit,* I thought. I kept quiet. "So I have to inform everyone that we're having to make three people redundant. Everyone will be put into the pool, and scored based on performance over the past year, then the three lowest scored will be informed. The process will take around a month. I'm sorry guys."

I looked around the room at my workmates. They all looked uncertain. Personally, I felt quite safe. I'd trained there originally, and worked to the 'Gavin Roberts' method.

I also had an enormous clientele, and was usually the second biggest revenue earner in the salon.

"So who's gonna get the push?" asked Belinda, our newest, and dopiest stylist. *Probably you.* "I don't think it's fair, I haven't had time to build up properly yet, I've only been here a year." She seemed blissfully unaware that a year was more time than most stylists got when it came to building a following. I wanted to tell her it was probably her habit of talking non-stop about her boyfriend, and his various issues with commitment, rather than her client's hair, that was the problem. Her refusal to retail didn't help either, as she assumed everyone was too poor to afford anything, which was quite rude really. Damien ignored her.

"Next week, each person will have a meeting with me, and asked if they'd like to opt for voluntary redundancy, so give that some thought, and I'll see you all next week." Damien dismissed us, not meeting anyone's eyes.

I pulled on my flat boots and coat, ready for the walk to the station. "I bet it'll be you," sneered Holly, the über-bitch. She never wasted an opportunity to be nasty to me. Unfortunately, she was the most popular stylist in the salon, and the only one to make consistently more than me.

"I'm sure there's other people in the firing line in front of me," I pointed out, smiling at her bitchy, rather put-on, pitying look.

"Not on your pay scale. Just think how much they'll save sacking you, and sharing out your clients. At least my clients insist that they'll only have me, and nobody else. My clients are totally loyal, unlike yours," she pointed out. About two years previous, I'd broken my ankle and been off for three months. During that time, the other stylists had looked after my clients. She'd taken that as clients not caring who did them, rather than them being understanding of my predicament.

Matt was waiting for me at the station when I got off the train. "How was your day?" he asked. He only worked office hours, and seemed to think me working Saturdays was strange, even after a couple of years together.

"Busy, all fine, until last thing. Damien told everyone he's going to have to reduce the staff by three people. All those cheap deals he did have dented profits."

"Do you think you'll be ok? Or could you get made redundant?"

"I doubt it. I wouldn't mind changing salons though, somewhere a bit more creative and high end. He said we could take voluntary redundancy if we wanted."

"I don't know if that's a good idea Lil, you have certain protections due to long service. If you changed to another salon, they could just sack you." *Oh thanks, believe in me why don't you?*

Matt followed me into the semi I shared with my parents and younger brother. He made himself comfy at the kitchen table, and listened as I told my mum what had happened. "Why not start looking for another job, just in case," Mum advised, "if nothing happens next week, then all well and good, but at least you'll have a back-up plan."

"Mark, can you get off the computer for a little while please?" I asked my little brother. He sighed loudly, and slid off the wheelie chair, to give me access to the family desktop. I closed down YouTube, and googled 'hairdressing jobs, London'. There seemed to be pages of them, I flicked through, several catching my eye. "There's loads, look, Sassoon, Trevor Sorbie, and Gino Venti are all advertising for stylists. That's just on the first page."

"You should get Lisa to check over your CV, update it a bit," advised Mum. Lisa was my best friend, and was a secretary in a recruitment company. She was bound to know about CVs.

"Are we going out tonight?" I asked Matt, knowing full well that the answer would be 'no'. Matt was in the throes of buying his first studio flat, and was saving obsessively. As I predicted, he shook his head.

"Sorry Lily, even with a two for one coupon, dinner at Zizzi's would still be over twenty quid. I had to pay for the survey today. *There's always an excuse*, I thought, determined not to offer to pay. Recently, I paid for everything so that the tightwad could squirrel his money away for a flat that would be solely in his name. In his defence, we'd only been together two years, and I had an appalling credit rating due to not earning for those three months in a plaster cast, and a boob job that I'd struggled to pay for. "Your Mum's chilli is better than fancy restaurant food anyway," he asserted, as Mum plonked plates of chilli and rice down in front of us.

Matt borrowed my iPhone to see what was on telly that evening, announcing the programs that he wanted to watch through mouthfuls of rice. "I might give Lisa a call if you're just gonna be watching telly all evening," I told him. He looked a little hurt.

"These are the programs that you like to watch Lily, what would you prefer to do then?" he demanded, a little edge to his voice. If I was being truthful, I would've said that I wanted to go out clubbing in London, after listening to Holly all day, telling her clients about some fancy bar and club she'd visited, which had sounded impossibly glamorous and fun. *I bet she doesn't sit indoors watching x-factor on a Saturday night,* I thought. I knew it would be pointless expecting Matt to take me to the Kensington Roof Gardens. All that'd happen would be him asking for tap water, and bitching about the prices. Even Lisa, my very best friend, wouldn't go somewhere like that, claiming to be too uncomfortable about her weight to get dolled up.

She turned up that evening, wearing a onesie and slippers, repeating her delight that she didn't have to get 'dressed up' to visit, having been coming round to ours since she was three. We left Matt sitting with my parents watching Ant and Dec, and sat at the computer to write a killer CV.

Salon Affair

Between Lisa and I, we really jazzed up my résumé. I listed out all the courses I'd attended since graduating college, and Lisa thought up an excellent mission statement along the lines of me wanting to continue growing professionally. She even found a great photo of me on Facebook, efficiently cropped Matt out, and added it to the top corner.

Once it was all done, I sent it off to five salons, filling in their online applications as I went. "One of those has gotta get you an interview," said Lisa, "I can't see you having any issues finding a new job, what with being the best hairdresser in the world 'n' all that."

I smiled gratefully. Lisa had been my very first client/victim, patiently sitting for hours as I struggled through my first ham-fisted attempts at cutting. "Do you think I'm doing the right thing?" I asked.

"Course you are. You're way too good at your job to hang around in Gavin Roberts forevermore. I know it's near Victoria, but it's not true West End hairdressing. There's no way you should be doing groupon Tuesdays and student Wednesdays. You should be doing hipsters and celebrities."

The program must have finished, because Mum came in to make cocoa, and Matt came to see what we were up to, and remind us that Big Brother was just about to start. He read through my new CV, smiling at the photo, and agreed with Lisa that it was really good.

He stayed over that night, as was normal on a Saturday night. I snuggled into him, careful not to 'crowd him', which he hated. He had issues with intimacy, and although he enjoyed sex, it had to be on his terms, with everything staying the same, done in the same order. Thankfully, I quite enjoyed our little routine, and Matt often remarked that we shagged 'efficiently', both successfully reaching orgasm with minimum effort on his part, or disruption of sleep on mine. If I was truthful, I'd admit that it was a little 'pipe and slippers', but I couldn't muster up the enthusiasm to change it.

So there we were, lights off, fumble fumble, tweak tit, condom on, then a bonk that generally lasted around ten minutes. I'd come, then him, and he'd pass me a tissue. Afterwards, he'd roll over and doze off. Matt didn't do cuddling.

I lay awake in the darkness, trying to analyse what was bothering me. Nothing had changed, Matt was just doing what we did every weekend. Lisa was just being Lisa, my fat, funny, best friend. The problem clearly lay with me. *Maybe a new job will provide all the change I'm craving.*

The next morning, Matt went off to his usual Sunday morning football practice, and I joined Mum in a trip into Bromley for a mooch about. We were sitting in Café Rouge, having a latte and a sit down, when I pulled out my phone to check my emails, seeing straightaway that there was one from Gino Venti. I opened it, and read through it, skimming past the pleasantries. "I have an interview, Mum, and it's tomorrow!" I squealed, thrusting my phone into her face for her to read it. She took the phone from my hand, and read it through carefully.

"Tomorrow at three o'clock. Lucky it's your day off. Where is it?"

"Bond Street, well, South Molten Street. Right in the heart of the West End. It's a really glamorous salon, think they feature in hairdresser's journal on a regular basis. They win all sorts of awards. I'll have to look really trendy."

"Best we have a look in Karen Millen then. Just don't tell your father."

"You're the best," I beamed. Mum had always wanted to be a hairdresser, but had never realised her dream, mainly due to marriage and babies getting in the way. She was a great supporter though, and we enjoyed secret splurges on dad's credit card every now and then, usually when I needed to look the part for something.

Salon Affair

Two hundred quid later, I had a new outfit, and new shoes, ready for the following day. We smuggled it all into the house, past Dad, who was snoring on the sofa. I carefully cut off all the tags, and hung it all up to keep it pristine.

Mum and I nipped round to see Aunt Doris for an hour after dinner, taking a bag of food, and some Tupperware boxes of dinners that mum had made and frozen for her to heat up during the week. Strictly speaking, she was my great aunt, my Mum's father's sister. She hadn't had children of her own, and after her husband had died, relied quite heavily on Mum. She was a game old girl though, quite good company, and still had all her marbles, even though she was in her eighties. In recent years, she'd got a bit wobbly on her pins, so needed a bit more help than she used to.

Mum sorted out the kitchen, and put a wash on, while I quickly hoovered and dusted. It wasn't a large house, so we were able to get it freshened up quite quickly. I told Doris all about my interview, and my new outfit, while I carefully dusted all the knickknacks on the mantelpiece.

"You aim as high as you can Lily. You're going to be a long time sitting in front of a fire when you're old. Do as much as you can now, while you're young. I'm grateful for all the good memories I have." She gazed wistfully at her gas fire as she spoke.

"Out dancing on a Saturday night?" I prompted.

"Of course, and more besides. I was a bit of a girl in my day you know. The war was over, and all we wanted to do was have fun. So many people had been killed and maimed, that we felt as though we had to party even harder, you know, to make up for what they missed out on. Plus of course, we'd all grown up with the rationing and deprivation, so it felt wonderful to drink, eat and dance without a care in the world." She smiled to herself, before whispering; "of course, the men were all sex starved, and desperate. It was a great time to be a pretty girl."

"I bet. Mind you, it was all a bit more staid in those days, wasn't it?"

She laughed. "Not really, the only difference was that you had to get married if you got pregnant. Human nature never changes Lily, it's why you should grab life with both hands, and never settle for second best." She changed the subject when Mum came in bearing a pot of tea, and a plate of biscuits.

Matt was sitting watching telly with Dad when we got home. He smiled at the news that I had an interview. "That's great, at least if the worst happens, you won't be out of work. Your fares'l be a little more though. Bond street's a tube ride as well as the train, so don't forget to factor that in when you're discussing pay."

"I won't. Tell you what, shall I meet you from work tomorrow? Seeing as I'll be up there already. We could go for a drink before we come home."

"Nah, costs a fortune for a pint up there. Better off getting a pack of Buds in the supermarket." He went back to his telly program, not noticing me pulling a face at him, and slumping down onto the sofa next to him. I was getting seriously ticked off with his 'every penny counts' philosophy, which he'd always had, but had become magnified with his flat purchase. I couldn't really understand it, he earned great money, had loads of savings, and would still have plenty left after paying his new mortgage each month. He was behaving as though he'd be poverty stricken.

I was quite relieved when he went home, saying he needed an early night, in preparation for the week ahead. "Are you and Matt alright?" Mum asked, frowning.

I sighed. "Yeah, I'm just getting a bit fed up with how tight he is all the time. We seem to sit indoors every night. Feels like we're an old, married couple."

Salon Affair

"I'm sure he'll be better when he's actually got that flat, and got used to paying a mortgage. He's probably just a bit nervous about it," counselled Dad.

The next day, I awoke with a tummy full of butterflies. I spent an inordinately long time doing my hair, and was ready by mid-day, and pacing around, waiting till it was time to leave. My phone chirped, making me jump. It was only Lisa, wishing me luck, and saying she'd be round later to hear all about it.

I decided to leave early, just in case a train was delayed or cancelled, or I got lost. I checked my bag, making sure I had my purse, keys, phone, and travel card, and debated whether or not I needed to take my scissors. They hadn't said I'd be trade testing, but they also hadn't said I wouldn't. I slipped them in anyway, just in case. Satisfied that I was organised, and looked suitably fashionable in my new outfit, I set off.

I'd got used to the noise and dirt of central London during the years working at Gavin Roberts. Compared to the area around Victoria, South Molten street seemed quiet and genteel. I was still early, so found a little coffee shop to sit in, and watch the world go by, until it was time to impress. I sipped my latte, as my nerves really kicked in. As I watched impossibly groomed, beautifully dressed women wander past, carrying designer shopping bags, I felt gauche and provincial. *Snap out of it Lily, these women need people like you to keep their polished personas alive,* I told myself.

At five to three precisely, I walked down to Gino Venti. I hadn't been sure whether or not it would even be open on a Monday, but I could see that it was indeed open, and buzzing in there. A Mediterranean looking woman was behind the reception desk. She greeted me with a broad smile. "Hello, welcome to Gino Venti, how may I help you?"

"I'm here for an interview with Gray Parker," I said. She looked at her screen.

"Lily Hollins?" I nodded. "Gray's expecting you. Please take a seat, and I'll tell him that you're here. Can I get you a drink of anything?" I shook my head. I really didn't want to have to manoeuvre a cup and saucer as well as my handbag and my feet. She went off, presumably to get Gray. I sat down on the cream leather sofa, and looked around the reception area, checking out the products. There was only one product line that I wasn't pretty expert on, the rest I'd already done extensive product knowledge training with. The rest of the reception area was pretty swanky. The desk itself looked as though it was carved out of limestone, with a brushed steel G V logo mounted on the front of it. The magazines were all this month's Vogue and Tatler. Not an old or cheap one to be seen.

"Gray won't be a minute," the receptionist said, making me jump. I'd been so engrossed in checking out the salon, I hadn't seen her come back. A few moments later, a tall, lean, man walked though with a client. He reeled off a list of her services to the receptionist, and picked a few bottles off a shelf to place on the desk in front of the client. I watched as she kissed him on both cheeks, and turned to pay her bill.

"Lily Hollins? I'm Gray Parker, pleased to meet you." I stood up, and shook his hand.

"Nice to meet you too. Her hair looked lovely." I nodded towards the client.

"First compliment, and you haven't even left the salon yet, Maggie," he called out to the glamorous blonde, "that's an extra ten quid on the bill."

The client giggled. "You're such a tease Gray. Alright, I'll pop an extra tenner in your tip jar. Do you pay that lady to say nice things?" *An extra tenner? Jeez.*

"Seriously, your hair looks lovely," I told her, "the colour's beautiful." For all her cut glass accent, and designer clothes, the woman seemed really friendly and nice. She smiled and thanked me, and I followed Gray through to the main salon. There were two stylists working, and a few clients sitting with colour taking.

"I wasn't sure if you'd be open on a Monday," I said.

"Oh yes, we're open seven days a week. There's only so many clients we can fit in the salon in one go, so we have to open long hours to accommodate everyone."

I followed him through to a tiny office, taking a seat opposite him. He was one of those rather beautiful looking men, tall and lean, but not thin, with a crooked smile, and extremely stylishly cut, short hair. He was also wearing head to toe Prada. I guessed his age at around forty. "So, Lily, what made you apply to us?"

"I need to progress as a hairdresser, and your salon is pretty well known. I saw the article in Hairdressers Journal, and figured that this salon's where it's all happening right now."

"You've been at Gavin Roberts a long time? Trained there, and all that. It's a great salon, so why do you want to leave?" His eyes bored into me. I couldn't exactly say 'because I'm bored, because I hate Holly the bitch, because I'm doing five pound groupons due to my fuckwit manager accidentally selling two thousand of them to every tightwad bargain seeker in London'.

"My ambition is to be a top West End hairdresser, and I need to move out of my comfort zone to be able to achieve that." *Good answer Lil, pat on the back for that one.*

"I see. What's your specialism?"

"Cutting, but I vardered in both cutting and colouring. I can do all of it to an extremely high standard."

"I saw that on your CV. How come you vardered twice?"

"I had the opportunity, and took it. I wanted to be able to do every aspect of hair, not just one thing. It's also why I took on so many additional courses," I said.

He nodded. "It's very impressive. Must have taken up a lot of your spare time?"

"I didn't mind. Most of the courses were so interesting that it never worried me, doing them on my days off. I don't have kids or anything to worry about, so can purely concentrate on my love of hair." I slipped that in, in case he wanted to ask, but was wary of the rules governing asking about kids.

"I see. Have you got a portfolio?" I pulled the file out of my bag, and handed it to him. It held all my precious certificates, as well as photos of the work I did to achieve them. He flicked through it, pausing at a picture of a colour I did as my entry for Redken young stylist of the year contest. "This is good. What did you use?"

I reeled off the formula, and placement technique. He seemed quite impressed. "Did you win?" He gestured to the picture.

"Came second," I replied, feeling a blush rise up my neck. I wished I'd been able to boast being 'young hairdresser of the year', but I wasn't.

"So the judge was a blind arsehole then?" He smiled at me.

"The winner's style was beautiful. If I'm honest, he won fair and square."

Gray looked up, and regarded me intently. "He works here. The one that won."

"Really? He's fantastic." I remembered a bleach blonde, slightly tubby feminine boy, screeching when the winner had been announced.

"Don't tell him that, he's bloody impossible as it is. We'd need a crowbar to get his head out the door." Gray smiled. "So Lily, what about your expectations?"

"I don't really know what to expect to be honest. I'm a hard worker, a team player, and a good hairdresser. I can build a clientele pretty fast, and my client retention runs at about 90%."

Salon Affair

"Ok, let me tell you about how we work. It's fairly unique because we don't have strict hours as such. Everyone works on a 40% commission, so we all work long hours. There's no basic, so if you sit around in the staff room, or take an afternoon off, there's no pay. Bear in mind a cut and dry starts at a hundred quid, you can see why we all put the hours in. We all choose our two days off each week six weeks in advance, so that bookings can be made ahead."

"Is it busy?" I was beyond curious.

"Extremely. We turn people away every day, which breaks my heart."

"Sounds brilliant."

"A lot of people like set hours, set pay, and the same days off every week. It's not for everyone. I take it you can be quite flexible?"

"Oh yes. There's nothing holding me back."

"Good, now, trade test. I don't suppose by any chance you brought your scissors?"

"Yes I did. Would you like me to stay and work this afternoon? Show you what I can do?"

"That would be brilliant. I'll show you where to put your bag, and orientate you with the salon."

I stowed my handbag in a locker, and followed Gray back out to reception, where he introduced me to Paulina, the receptionist, and asked her to book me some clients. "What time do you need to get away?" He asked.

I shrugged. "I don't. Book what you like."

Paulina beamed at me. "Great. I've got a list of people waiting on cancellations. Anything I shouldn't book?" Gray shook his head.

"She's an all-rounder. A rare breed." He smiled at me, and wandered over to greet his next client, who was waiting patiently on the sofa.

Within half an hour, I was working on a head of highlights, then another client while the colour was taking.

I was painfully aware of the other stylists watching me closely, and Gray assessing everything I was doing. I just tried to relax into it, and work as if I was in Gavin Roberts. In total, I did three clients, each one getting a restyle, advice, and a bag of retail added onto their bill. By the time I'd finished, it was nearly seven, and the others were all finishing up too.

"Let's go over the road for a drink and discuss how you've done," said Gray, as I put on my coat, and said goodbye to the others. He spoke briefly to Paulina, before steering me out, and a few doors down to a swanky looking wine bar.

"I'm meeting my husband in about half an hour, so what would you like to drink?" *Husband? Oh, I geddit.*

"Could I have a white wine please?" I wondered if I should offer to pay, but Gray had gone to the bar before I could say anything. While I was waiting, I tried to tot up my takings in my head, but as I didn't really know their prices, it was impossible to work out.

Gray placed a glass in front of me, and sat down opposite. "So how was that for you?" he asked.

"Good thanks. I enjoyed it. The salon's lovely to work in."

"You looked comfortable. Your work's very good by the way. I think you're a bit wasted working for Gavin Roberts."

"Thank you."

"Your takings today were 440 services and 180 retail. You get ten percent of retail by the way." I nodded. "We take off the VAT, then you get 40%, so that's 140.80 plus 18 retail. I make that 158.80. Not bad for three and a half hours work." He pulled a wad of cash out of his pocket, and counted off a hundred and sixty quid.

"I didn't expect to get paid for a trade test," I spluttered. He shoved the money across the table to me.

"So, when can you start?"

"It depends. They might want me to work my notice, they might want me to go straightaway." I paused, "So does this mean that I've got the job?"

He smiled, "Of course. Quite a coup, getting first and second place winners of the Redken hairdresser of the year. Tomme, the winner, he's fantastic, but he's more of a princess than you'll ever be."

I sipped my wine, and looked around the bar. It was one of those achingly trendy places that I'd been desperate to try. The other patrons seemed wealthy and hip. I was grateful for my new outfit. Gray chatted about the other stylists, who were all male. I'd be the only girl. "Does Gino still work?" I asked.

Gray shook his head. "He retired a few years ago. Paulina's his niece, she looks after the salon for him, and I manage all the staff and clients, the actual hairdressing part really. Paulina just handles the money. She's quite good though, for a non-hairdresser, runs the reception really well."

I finished my drink just as a handsome, suited man approached us. He bent down to kiss Gray's cheek. "Chris, this is Lily, our new stylist." I shook his hand, and stood to leave.

"I'd better be getting off. I'll call you as soon as I know what date I can start."

"You don't have to rush off, if you'd like another drink?" Chris said. I glanced at my watch, it was nearly quarter to eight.

"I'd better get going, they'll all be wondering where I am."

As soon as I got on the train, I switched on my phone, to find various text messages from Mum, Lisa and Matt, all wondering where I was. I called Mum, and told her the good news, and see if someone could pick me up from the station. Apparently, Lisa and Matt were both round my house already, waiting for news.

Over a celebratory cup of tea, I told them all about my afternoon. Lisa and my parents were all made up for me, but Matt had to pour cold water over my triumph. "I don't think commission only is legal Lily, they need to fix proper working hours, and at least pay minimum wage. Are you expected to pay your own tax? Or do they put you on PAYE?"

I gave him a hard stare. "I just earned £160 in three hours Matt, I hardly think I should be whining about minimum wage, and Gray made it quite clear that there isn't fixed hours."

"You should be paid double time for Sundays," he said, rather sulky at my refusal to take his advice.

"Don't be ridiculous, I'm not on an hourly rate. Listen Matt, are you pleased for me or not?"

"Of course I am, I just don't want to see you exploited."

I exploded. "How can 40% of everything I do be exploitation? You once worked out that if I worked mobile, it'd only be 50% profit after the costs, so how on earth do you think that providing a salon in Bond street and a hefty price list, along with as much retail as I can possibly sell, and a steady stream of clients equals exploitation? Would you rather I carried on in Gavin Roberts at seven quid an hour?"

"At least it's pay if you're quiet."

"I slog my guts out. I'm never quiet, so your argument doesn't stack up."

"I just can't see you earning much, 40% of nothing is still nothing Lily, and I'm not having you sponging off me."

I stood up, feeling my fury rising. "I think you'd better go. Considering I've never asked you to pay for anything, and you're way too tight to even offer, I won't accept being called a gold digger."

"Lily, calm down," said Lisa, who was watching proceedings.

Salon Affair

"No I won't calm down. I put up with sitting in every night, so that he can save every penny for his stupid flat, and when I finally get the chance to realise my dream, he behaves as though I'm not good enough." I turned back to Matt, "I think you need to go and find a nice girl, who won't outshine you, and is happy to sit indoors counting pennies with you. This isn't for me."

"You're making a big mistake, nobody will ever care for you as much as me. I guess I didn't realise my affection was measured by how much I spend on you," he huffed.

"Just go, please. Take your stuff too. I've had enough Matt." I sagged into my chair, relief flooding through me at finding the excuse to end it. Mum and Dad stayed silent, rather wisely not getting involved. I knew they liked Matt, but seeing as they didn't try and talk me round, it appeared that they agreed with my decision.

Chapter 2

After Matt had stomped off, Mum had remarked that she didn't blame me for my decision. While Lisa typed out my resignation letter, Dad made another tea, and asked if I was ok, saying that I was best off finding a man who supported me, rather than put me down. With my new job, it all felt pretty life changing, and exciting. I didn't regret dumping Matt one little bit.

I felt a bit strange, going into work the next morning, my resignation letter in my handbag. I collared Damian, and asked for a meeting. We were both free at 12, so the time was booked out. It meant that I had all morning for my nerves to build. Even Holly the über-bitch loudly telling her clients about her Saturday night out at Mahiki failed to upset me.

The second client of the day was a cheapskate groupon, with big ambitions for her hair. My stomach sank as she declared; "I want a whole new look, something bouncy and full, but I don't want it puffy. I don't want any length cut, no layers, and I don't want a fringe." She looked at me expectantly, her silicon-coated, lank hair hanging in straggles. I sighed.

"So, let me get this right, you don't want anything cut, but you want a new look?" She nodded enthusiastically. "Am I allowed to trim the ends?"

"I want a restyle," she asserted, "that's the coupon I paid for."

"It's hard to do a restyle without cutting it."
"Oh you can cut it, but not the length or the layers." *Are you shitting me?*
"Right, so which bit can I actually cut? You just ruled out every hair on your head." Her face dropped.
"Can't you restyle it without cutting it short?"
"Of course I can, but I'll have to cut something, otherwise it'll just look the same."
In the end, I persuaded her to go for some long layers. It felt like a ridiculous amount of work for just five quid. The tight cow even refused a coffee, in case she had to pay extra. By the time I'd finished, I was at boiling point. "It doesn't look very different," tight cow remarked.
"Well, it's about as different as you're gonna get, taking off the minimum of hair, refusing a colour, and using cheap shampoo which weighs it down." I asserted.
"For five pounds, I would have thought a colour should be in with the price," she said. I laughed at her, much to her dismay. I couldn't wait to get out of that salon.
At twelve, Damian and I went into his office, a tiny, scruffy little cubby hole. The company didn't believe in spending money where clients couldn't see it. "So, Lily, you wanted to see me?"
"I'd like to opt for voluntary redundancy," I blurted out.
"I see. Why's that?"
"Because I'm sick of working on groupons, sick of Holly being nasty, and you asked for people to opt for redundancy," I said, "you could share out my clients, and save my wage."
"Are you sure? I wasn't trying to force you out."
"Very sure."
"Let me make a phone call to my accountant, find out what you're entitled to, and I'll let you know by the end of today."
Halfway through the afternoon, Damian called me back into the office. "I spoke to the accountant. He's told me that

you'd be entitled to five weeks pay as redundancy, but there's a problem with your notice period."

"What sort of problem?" I asked.

"In your contract it states that you're entitled to one weeks' notice for every year worked. Unlike redundancy, it goes back to the start, so that's ten weeks notice." My heart sank. "What he suggested, is if you want to go straightaway, that we agree to ten weeks pay in total. It would free you to get another job, and save us having to make you work another ten weeks. We just can't afford to lay out 15 weeks pay in one go."

"I'd agree to that," I told him, my stomach flipping.

"Ok, go tell reception to move everyone over to Belinda, and gather up all your stuff. I'll quickly type up the agreement." He couldn't meet my eyes.

I grabbed a carrier bag from the staff room, and, after informing Laurie on the desk, I started stuffing my brushes into the bag. "Been sacked?" trilled Holly.

"Me? Don't be daft. Opted for voluntary redundancy. Bigger and better things Holly." I beamed at her scowling face, staying tight lipped when she asserted that I'd never get another job. Disgruntled at not getting a reaction, she turned back to her client. When I'd made sure that I had everything packed, I went back to the office. Damian presented me with two copies of the letter stating that I'd forgo some notice in exchange for immediate release. I read through carefully, and satisfied, signed both copies, as did he.

"Your pay and P45 will be processed on your normal payday, which is Thursday. You'll get the full amount then. Lily, I'm sorry about all this, I would never have got involved with that coupon site if I'd known..." he trailed off.

"Damian, you didn't do it deliberately, and I need a change if I'm honest. Those clients....it's dragging me down...I need to move on, somewhere different."

"I understand. You should be somewhere that supports your creativity. I know a star when I see one. I fully expect to see you in 'Hair' magazine someday." He hugged me. "You take care Lil, don't take any shit eh?"

I said my goodbyes to everyone except Holly, and stepped out of the salon for the last time. For some inexplicable reason, I felt shocked, unable to believe that I'd actually done it, resigned from my steady job to begin an adventure.

While I was waiting for my train at Victoria, I called Gray to tell him that I'd be free immediately. "Excellent news. Do you want to start tomorrow? Or would you rather have a day off?"

"I can start tomorrow, if that's ok?"

"Fantastic. You need to bring a copy of your passport or driving licence for our records, your national insurance number, and your diary so we can program you a schedule. Need your bank details too. Can you get here for nine?"

"Yep, no problem." My head was spinning slightly.

"Great, I'll let Paulina know. She'll be delighted. Gotta go, client waiting." He rang off.

I hurried home, and sorted out all the documents I'd need for the next day. I even found time to nip into Bromley and get my nails done. I popped in to see Aunt Doris on my way home to tell her my news.

She clapped her hands together, and beamed as she congratulated me. "And what has Matt had to say about it?"

"I dumped him. He was horrible to me, thought that I'd fail, and should stay at Gavin Roberts."

"Good. That boy was tighter than a gerbil's arse. Not the right man for you dear. Never seemed to notice how lucky he was, to be with you."

"He was always careful, but since setting his sights on buying that flat, he just got impossible."

"I'm not really talking about that dear, he just never seemed....passionate about you. You should look for the man that desires you above all others, not someone who sneers at your achievements, and would rather spend Sunday morning on a muddy pitch than in bed with you."

"Well, he's history. Next time, I want an Adonis with a six pack and a generous disposition." Aunt Doris laughed loudly. I wasn't even joking, Matt had a serious case of moobs, and a pot belly.

Lisa came over that evening to keep me company while I got myself ready for the next day. She sat on my bed as I did my eyebrows, and applied a tan. "Have you spoken to Matt?" she asked.

"Nope," I replied, "and I don't intend to. We weren't in love or anything like that. I think we just settled down together too soon."

"I think he loves you, well, he stayed with you for two years, which is always a good sign," Lisa pointed out. "Do you want to try Internet dating? I've found some quite decent men on there."

"You've been Internet dating?" I asked, incredulous.

She grinned. "Yep, been on two dates so far, and got another one tomorrow night. All different men of course."

"Lisa Fitch, you dark horse! You never told me you were going on dates." I'd actually only known Lisa to have one boyfriend, and he turned out to be a bit of a loser, who tried to scam her out of money.

"Yeah well, I met them on that 'Voluptuous Venus' site. At least the fellas know that a twig won't turn up. I liked the one who took me out last week, Dave. He described himself on the site as a feeder, and took me for a carvery. Was a bit off putting having him watch me take every mouthful though."

"And this one tomorrow night?" I was struggling to keep a straight face.

"His name's Tony, and he just says in his profile that he likes bigger girls. He's a butcher, and lives in Orpington. Seems quite nice."

Salon Affair

"Where're you going?"

"Meeting in the Bell, then maybe go on from there." She picked up my tweezers and proceeded to work on her eyebrows, her tongue sticking out to the side, as she often did when concentrating. By the time she'd finished, her brows were bright pink. "They'll have gone down by tomorrow," she said confidently.

I was up extra early the next morning, and made the early train. I frowned at a text from Matt, wishing me luck, wondering how he'd found out I was starting my new job. I picked up a latte from Starbucks to take in with me, partly to kill a little time, and partly to warm my hands. I arrived at half eight, concerned that I'd be waiting outside, but the lights were already on.

"Welcome Lily, hope you'll be happy here," said Paulina, smiling widely. "All the others are in the staff room. I booked you from half nine, so we have time to fix your schedule after you've said hello to everyone."

I smiled back at her, and went through to the back of the salon, passing two juniors who were busy folding towels at the basins. Walking into the staff room, I heard a screech. "A stylist with a vagina!! I'm so excited!" It came from the youngest man in there, the same one I'd seen win the 'young stylist' crown. He was still bleach blonde, but had clearly been dieting since the last time I'd seen him. He was beaming at me, not in the least bit aware that I might be offended. "I adored that copper ombré you did for the competition. I was convinced you'd win," he gushed.

"If you hadn't blown that judge in the gents beforehand, she might've done," interjected a handsome, tanned Adonis.

"Shut your gob, bitch, I didn't blow anyone. I won fair'n'square." He turned to me, "Don't take any notice of that gobshite, I'm Tomme, pleased to meet you." He kissed both my cheeks. Gray stood to introduce me to the others. The tanned Adonis was Anthony, he gave me a rather awkward little hug. A tall, dark, rather serious looking man was introduced as Trystan, and finally, a muscular, shaven headed man as Michael. I'd met Trystan and Michael at my trial afternoon, so just nodded hello.

"I put you in the section nearest the basins," said Gray, " and organised a trolley for you. "I'm sure you'll be fine, but just ask if there's anything you can't find. Lottie and Tula are our juniors today, and they'll help you if you need it."

"You'll find Tula a bit more helpful than Lottie," said Michael, "ask that miserable little moo to do anything, and you'll get a dirty look and a half assed job done."

I laughed, "I'll bear that in mind. Have we got a busy day today?"

"Every days a busy day here," said Trystan. "Tomorrow's gonna be a bloody nightmare. It's the national telly awards, so all of us are rammed out. It'll be hell with all those dozy starlets demanding something 'unique', when we gotta churn out at least twelve each. Please tell me you can put hair up?"

"Yep, no problem. I'll try and come up with some different ones tonight. Do we carry fake hair in stock?" I looked at Gray.

"There's a full selection in the cupboard next to the colours. The prices are marked on them. Just hand the empty packet to Paulina at the end, so that she can re-order."

At nine, the others were called out to start their clients, and Gray and I completed the paperwork, signing my new contract, and sorting out payday details. Afterwards, I sat with Paulina, and went through the next six weeks, fixing my two days off each week. As I had nothing planned, I was able to work around the days that the others had already chosen. I also saw that I had rather a lot already booked in.

The day seemed to flash by in a blur, the clients being pleasant and easy going. Before I knew it, it was half seven, and we were all finishing up. I went to the staff room to get my bag and coat.

"Who's up for a drinky?" said Trystan. Tomme hooked his arm around my shoulder.

"Come on Lily, we're all going to the wine bar down the road. You've got to come, it being your first day. We need to find out all about you."

"He just wants to know if your tits are real or not," laughed Michael, "not that he's ever seen a tit in real life."

"I have. I'll have you know I saw my friend Julie in the nude once," said Tomme, affronted. "It was a bit gross though."

We were all given little printouts of our day's takings as we left, everyone calling out a cheery goodbye to Paulina and Gray on our way out. "How come they aren't joining us?" I asked.

"Gray'l be down in a bit, but Paulina's a bit iffy around gay men. Don't think she knows how to take all the tuna jokes," Trystan explained.

"I see," I replied, unsure whether or not I wanted to listen to tuna jokes either. I followed them down the street to 'The Bond Street Wine Bar', which was a delightful, and expensive looking place. We all settled ourselves at a table, and agreed to order a bottle of red, and one of white. Trystan perused the wine list, and ordered a bottle of Chardonnay and a Merlot, which he said was 'exceptional'. "Are you a wine buff then?" I asked.

He smiled at me, "Of course. I pride myself on my wide and varied interests."

"He only does it so he can chat up sophisticated men," Michael interjected, "he's beyond desperate for a husband."

"And you're not, bitch?" Trystan teased. "Michael hangs around gyms the whole time, thinks he's gonna pull a muscle Mary, and live happily ever after."

"Have you got a boyfriend Lily?" Michael asked. I shook my head.

"I was seeing someone, but I dumped him a few days ago. It just wasn't working. He was too suburban and staid for me." I felt a little disloyal discussing Matt with them, but as I had no intention of going back to him, I thought being honest with my workmates was the best policy.

"We have loads of single men come into the salon, you'll definitely meet someone nice," said Tomme.

"Oh, I don't date clients." I'd learnt that lesson the hard way, dating someone after cutting his hair, before I'd met Matt. It'd been a disaster, and I'd lost a client over it. Gray arrived, and pulled up a chair, while Tomme poured him a glass of red.

"We've got a heavy day tomorrow guys," he said, before taking a sip of his wine. "A few more rang this evening in desperation, apparently Pierre at Ten Hair is down with flu, so all his clients are scrambling around for a hairdresser tomorrow." The others all groaned.

"A day of dozy starlets then. Who drew the short straw for Helen Woodman?" Tomme asked.

"Paulina booked her in with Lily." He turned to me. "She's a bit high maintenance." The others all sniggered.

"I'm sure I'll be fine," I said, dismissing their smirks casually.

"Wonder how coked up she'll be?" Michael mused. "Mind you, she might be alright with Lily. It seems to be what she delightfully calls 'faggots' that enrage her. She's usually polite to Paulina."

While they were all discussing Ms Woodman's homophobia, I looked around the bar. The decor was a curious mix of old and new. Beautiful wood panelling on the walls contrasted with a huge, state of the art bar, with bottles of obscure spirits displayed on mirrored shelves, and backlit to create a futuristic display. I glanced across to see a handsome, fair haired man watching me intently. He was perched on a barstool, sitting alone. I smiled tentatively at him, and watched as he raised his glass to me.

"Looks like you won't need to chat up a client," said Tomme, who had noticed proceedings. "I do believe you're being ogled, and he's rather gorgeous. I'd do him."

"You'd do anyone, slut," teased Anthony. "I've cut his hair a few times. His name's Julian. I'm sure he owns this place."

"Hetero?" I asked.

"Sadly," Antony replied, "it's such a bloody waste."

The bar had filled up considerably by the time we needed more wine, so rather than hang around for the waitress, Anthony went up to the bar to fetch another two bottles. I watched as Julian greeted him warmly. They chatted for a few minutes, before Julian motioned to the barman, and leaned across the bar to say something.

"So, Lily, your tits, are they real?" Asked Tomme, taking my attention away from Anthony and Julian.

"No, had them done a couple of years ago. Do you like them?" I asked. I was quite proud of them personally, and liked to show off my investment.

"From a visual perspective, they look great. They suit you," he said, ignoring the sniggers from Michael and Gray.

"Tomme, are you sure you're gay? Ogling udders isn't in the remit you know," Trystan pointed out.

"Oh soreee," said Tomme sarcastically, "I didn't ask to touch them or anything, nobody said I couldn't look. I thought we were all meant to be getting to know her." He turned to me, "I quite like boobies. No idea why."

Anthony returned with a bottle of red, followed by a waitress bearing a bottle of champagne, and some flutes. "Compliments of Mr Alexander," she announced, smiling at me.

"Looks like you pulled," Gray pointed out.

"I'm going out for a ciggie," Trystan snapped, scraping his chair and looking furious as he stomped off. Nobody joined him.

"He's beyond jealous," said Anthony, "it's just the sort of thing he fantasises about a man doing for him. It's probably even worse being from someone like Julian. Trystan's cock was biting his leg off last time he came into the salon." The others all cackled.

I took a sip of the champagne, I was no expert, but it tasted as though it was the good stuff. The others all had some too. "You can come out with us again, if it means we get free champers," Michael said, smiling.

"It doesn't normally happen to me, men sending bottles of bubbly over." Inside I was thrilled. I glanced over to the bar, and seeing Julian staring back, I raised my glass and smiled at him, fully expecting him to come over and say hello.

Before he could make his move, a tall, slender, brunette strode up to him, kissing him on the cheek. She perched on a barstool next to him, blocking our view of each other. I watched as she stroked his arm, clearly on touching terms.

"Oh dear, looks like his girlfriend showed up before he could make his move," murmured Gray.

"Oh well, never mind, at least we got free champagne," I said, trying not to sound disappointed.

I left the bar at around half eight, a little tipsy from the alcohol, and lack of food. As soon as I was on the train, I fished out my phone to call mum to meet me at the station. I frowned at another text from Matt, asking how my day went, and speed dialled mum without bothering to reply to him.

Back home, I recounted all the details of my day, in between scarfing down the casserole mum had kept warm for me. I showed them my little printout listing my takings, and told them about being rammed out with starlets the next day, at which point my little brother's ears pricked up. He'd been studiously ignoring us, while playing on the computer. "If you do that little blonde one off Eastenders, can you get her autograph, and give her my number?" he called out.

"No I can't. Anyway, why would she be remotely interested in you, squirt?"

"In case you hadn't noticed, I'm 22 now. Plus I'm taller than you. You're gonna have to think of a better insult."

Hmm, fair point.

I ignored him, and flicked through the copy of Vogue I'd picked up at Charing Cross, checking out the styling and looks that had been deemed 'on trend' by the pundits. I was determined to be a credit to the salon, and turn out some cutting edge, paparazzi-worthy work. Unsure as to whether or not they stocked hair chalks, I tucked some of my own in my bag to take with me the next day.

Chapter 3

The next day at work was a total blast. The whole salon was a fug of hairspray all day, and we all bounced ideas off each other. It was everything I'd hoped West End hairdressing would be. Even the infamous Helen Woodward behaved herself, and seemed to get caught up in the vibe that we had going on, although she did come out of the loo sniffing loudly at one point.

Gray produced some of the most perfect, classic hair-ups I'd ever seen. I would've loved to have had time to just stand and watch, and drink in the perfection. He was also amazingly fast, managing a hair-perfect French pleat in just half an hour.

We sped through the day, with four juniors running between us, fetching pins, shampooing and pouring endless coffees, it made the salon buzz. We had to get everyone done by five at the latest, as the show started at seven, so it was a race to the finish, which involved all of us having to work together to get done in time. I ran ahead, so used the few spare minutes to double hand blow dry with Michael, who was running behind due to someone waltzing in late, then having a tantrum when she was told she'd missed her slot.

When the last starlet had left, we all slumped into our chairs. "Jesus Christ, that was manic," said Tomme.

"I need a fag, a coffee, and a wee," said Trystan, "and not necessarily in that order." He went off to have a ciggie out the back, joined by Tomme and Anthony.

"Can you make everyone coffees please?" Gray said to Lottie. She rolled her eyes, and sloped off to the staff room at a snail's pace, having forgotten that she'd had a lunch break, unlike all of the stylists.

Gray looked in the stock cupboard, "Hardly any hairpieces left. I'll make sure Paulina re-orders pronto."

"I used a lot of it," I told him. All bar one of my clients that day had a bit of fake hair added. Every actress had wanted their hair bigger and longer than nature had intended. It made up for the lack of retail that a day of styling caused.

"You did really well today Lily," said Gray, "a lot of stylists would've crumbled under that column. Your work was great, really on trend." I glowed under his praise.

Nobody was working late that night, so we were just packing up when we heard the door open. "Any chance of a quick cut?" Said a masculine voice. We all groaned.

"Hi Julian, I'll have to ask, see if anyone's willing to stay late. They've all finished for the day." Paulina came through to the salon. "Can anyone do Julian Alexander?" Five pairs of eyes stared in my direction. Everyone kept quiet.

"Ok, I'll do it. Suppose I owe him one for the free champagne." I heard myself say. It wasn't particularly late, only half five, so an extra forty minutes wouldn't kill me. I followed Paulina through to reception to greet him.

He was standing by the desk, six foot of pure, masculine man, with twinkly blue eyes, and a slightly crooked, boyish smile. "I was hoping it'd be you volunteering," he said, "sorry for keeping you late though."

"It's not a problem, and I need to thank you for that bottle of champers last night, so it's the least I can do," I replied, trying to keep my professional head on, and not go girly and stupid in front of him. *Don't flirt with clients,* I told myself. I led him through to my styling chair, and sat him down to discuss his hair. "So, what type of look are we going for today?" My standard opening line.

"I don't know, what would you suggest?"

I ran my fingers through his rather thick, blonde hair. It felt soft and pliable. "Do you like the style it's in, or would you like to try something different?"

"I'll leave it to you. Just make me look like the kind of man you'd agree to a date with." *Flirt.* I wasn't quite sure how to respond to that, so took him over to the backwash, and got Tula to stop her cleaning to shampoo his hair for me. While he was being prepared, I went out into the staff room. The others all had their coats on, apart from Trystan, who was nowhere to be seen.

"You have fun there babe," said Michael, "I'm off to the gym to get one for myself tonight. I need to blow off some steam after the day we've had."

"Where's Trystan?" I asked.

"In the loo, probably sobbing, and mopping his wet mussy. The sight of Julian flirting around you was too much for him."

"Mussy?" I had no idea what Michael was talking about.

"Man pussy. His bumhole." They all cackled. I pulled a face. *Ew.*

I'd just gowned Julian up, when all the others left, each calling out a cheery goodbye as they went. "So Lily, how are you enjoying it here so far?" Julian asked.

"It's great. Really busy and buzzy. I'm having a great time."

"And all the queens behaving themselves?"

"Yeah, they're fine, a lot of fun. It's Anthony who normally cuts your hair isn't it?"

"Sometimes, depends where I'm working when I need it done."

"I thought it was your bar down the road?"

"One of them, yes. I've got others too, and a few shops as well." I didn't really know what to say, so I concentrated

Salon Affair

on my cut, letting a comfortable silence stand. After five minutes, I felt him relax. He sighed. "I love getting my hair cut. Has anyone ever told you what a lovely touch you have?"

"Frequently." I paused, as I wanted to find a conversation that kept him talking. His voice was deep and mesmerising. Slightly posh, but not public school. "So, do you live local?" I asked.

"Yes, Gloucester Place. I often work very late, so need to be central. What about you?"

"Bromley, although I'd like to live up here. Have you had your bar long?"

"A few years." We lapsed back into silence. I concentrated on the cut, and noticed he was watching me intently in the mirror. His gaze unnerved me so much that I caught myself with the scissors.

"Shit." I examined the cut. It looked tiny, but would be bleeding profusely within minutes. "I'll just get a plaster, don't want to bleed all over you." I ran out to the staff room to grab a plaster out of the box. *How sodding embarrassing.*

"You ok?" He asked when I returned.

"Yeah, just a little nick, nothing really. I'm not usually clumsy. Sorry."

He smiled, "I'm sorry, am I making you nervous?"

"Not at all," I snapped, "I'm just a bit tired after all those starlets today. There's some awards thing tonight, so we were rammed out all day." I was a bit embarrassed about cutting a chunk out of myself in front of him, *not terribly impressive*, and cross that he'd been able to rattle me in such an obvious way.

"You should've said no, and I'd have come back tomorrow."

"It's fine. It won't take long." I chipped into the top, thankfully without losing anymore skin from my fingers. I quickly dried his hair, and styled it with some wax.

"That looks great. I really like it," he said, as I showed him the back, "so do I look good enough to date?"

I smiled, "You look very handsome. I doubt if your girlfriend would be happy with you looking good enough to date though."

He frowned. "Girlfriend?"

"The brunette, last night. I was going to thank you for the champagne, but you looked a bit busy."

He laughed. "That was Susie, she's a business associate, not my girlfriend. We're partners in a coffee shop in Shepherds market. I've known her for years."

I blushed slightly at having made a mistake. He hadn't really explained why she was stroking him though, so I was still on my guard. I brushed the hairs off him, and stood as Tula helped him on with his coat. Taking him through to Paulina, I placed some shampoo, conditioner, and the wax that I'd used, in front of him, on the desk. "These are the products I'd recommend. Shall I put them in a bag for you?" He smiled at me.

"Sure." I watched as Paulina rang them up, and placed them in the bag I was holding open. "Oh, and can you drop your card in there as well please? I'd like your number." *What?* I stood there, a little unsure. With Paulina watching, I didn't really want to scribble my number down for him. She'd assume I'd chatted him up as a client. "So that I can ring for an appointment next time, rather than just walk in." *Oh.*

I snapped out of my dream state, and grabbed a business card from the desk to drop into the bag. Julian looked amused at my slightly flustered appearance. He paid his bill in cash, and told Paulina to give me the change, before thanking me for his haircut and sauntering out.

Paulina and I watched as he strode off down the street. "I do believe he was hitting on you," she murmured, "be a little careful, because a jealous queen is a terrible thing."

"He was the one who sent over a bottle of champagne in the bar last night. Trystan did get a little snippy about it. Not my fault though, I didn't ask for it."

She clicked through with her mouse to cash up, and print off my takings. "You had a fantastic day, selling all those hairpieces. Shame they only go through as retail though. You'd have made a fortune if they were classed as services."

I read through my printout. At over two hundred quid a pop, I'd sold two grand worth of fake hair. Two hundred quid commission on that alone wasn't too shabby. Idly, I wondered how much the mark-up was. "Do you want me to wait while you cash up?" I asked.

She shook her head. "I'll be fine. I just lock the door while I do the till."

I went out to the staff room, and changed into my flats. Pulling on my coat, I grabbed my handbag, and scooted off home. I was exhausted, both from the pace of the work, and the stress of cutting Julian's hair. It had been a long time since anyone had affected me that much.

I told Lisa about him when she came over that night, describing him down to the smallest detail. In turn, she told me about her date with Tony the butcher, who sounded quite nice. He'd taken her to a steak house in Petts Wood, and they'd both discovered that they had a mutual love of enormous dinners. "He's certainly not a skinny minny, but then that suits me just fine. At least I didn't have to push a salad round my plate all evening, and get a McDonalds on the way home."

"He sounds nice," I told her. She had a tendency to be hypercritical of men, and expecting to date a Brad Pitt lookalike was punching somewhat above her weight. "When are you seeing him again?"

"He's asked me to the pictures Saturday night. We're seeing Wolf of Wall Street, then eating afterwards. Apparently the gourmet burger place there is really nice."

"That sounds lovely. At least he takes you out." It was a veiled reference to Matt-the-tightwad, who Lisa had championed from the start. I'd had another text from him that evening, asking why I wasn't replying to him. I'd ignored it, not wishing to open up a dialogue.

"Not made up with Matt yet?" She asked.

I shook my head. "I don't intend to either. Life's too short to sit indoors every night, and it's way too short to be with a man who doesn't love me. I deserve better than that."

"So you gonna hold out for this Julian then?" Lisa asked.

"Maybe. He hasn't asked me out yet though. I don't want to get my hopes up."

"Men don't send over bottles of bubbly unless they're interested. He'll ask you out, you mark my words."

I checked my bank account on the way into work the next day, to make sure that my wages from Gavin Roberts had gone in ok. With commission and holiday pay, it had worked out at just under three and a half grand. Not a huge amount, but a nice little windfall all the same. I could pay Mum back for my interview outfit, and have a bit of a clothes splurge on my next day off. All the others looked immaculate for work, so I had to follow suit, and invest in some designer wear. I worked out that it would only be eight days until I was paid by Gino Venti, as they had an end of the month payday, as opposed to Gavin Robert's 21st.

That day was a little quieter. Still busy by most salon's standards, but not as frenetic as the day before. I had a little time to chat to my workmates, and get to know them a little. My favourite was Tomme, as he was truly outrageous, and as funny as hell. He kept me fully entertained through a twenty minute tea break with tales of his drink-fuelled weekend in Brighton, cruising the bars, and finally picking up a young celebrity, who was playing a lothario in a popular soap.

"Where are you going this weekend?" I asked.

"Just local. It's my turn to work, so probably just a bar, then onto Manhunt for a few drinks. Nothing exciting. What about you?"

"Nothing yet. My friend Lisa's out on a date." It wasn't a lie, but I didn't want to have to admit that I'd sat in every Saturday night for the past year or so. "Do you all go out together?"

"Occasionally. Tryst prefers the more upmarket places. Hates the clubs that I love. We took him to Heaven once. That was a mistake. He danced with all the grace of a tasered bear, which was fucking mortifying. Michael and Antony both like the scene though."

"Have either of them got boyfriends?"

"Not really, well, Anthony has a fella he hooks up with sometimes, but it's not really a boyfriend as such. Michael likes the muscle boys at the gym. His gaydar's a bit wonky though, and he keeps getting bashed up by straight boys who don't like being ogled.

"Hmm, I can see why that would be a problem. What about Gray?" He was the one I knew the least about, mainly because he was always so busy, and had never had time to chat.

"He's an old married man. Been with Chris a long time. They have upmarket dinner parties, and invite their 'powergay' friends. All very tasteful and staid. I couldn't imagine him with his hand down a twink's pants in the Vauxhall Tavern."

I laughed, and shook my head. We were still giggling when Anthony walked in, carrying Paulina's iPad. "Who wants to see their hair on Heat's website?" We all crowded round. Quite a few of the actresses we'd done the day before had been photographed. I noticed that Helen Woodward looked entirely different to the pasty, sniffing mess who had turned up, being perfectly made up, and wearing a glamorous, shimmering, long dress. There was only one 'hair by' credit, and that simply named the salon, as opposed to Trystan, who had actually done the hair in question. Ten Hair, our rivals, hadn't even got a single mention, which pleased everyone.

"Next one is the Brits in February. That one is a bit more fashion focused. We got three mentions last year for the work we did," Anthony told me.

"So this year we aim for more than four?" I asked.

He looked at me a little strangely. "God, you're competitive. Yes, I suppose so." I blushed a little at revealing one of my faults. I'd always been over ambitious, and it wasn't always a trait that went down well with other people.

I popped in to see Aunt Doris on my way home, to tell her all about my first week, and see how she was. "So this Julian, is he handsome?"

"Yeah, really handsome. The type of looks that make you do a double take. From what I've been able to tell, he's got a decent physique too."

"A bar owner too. He sounds quite a catch, especially if you want your own salon later on." Aunt Doris was the only person I'd discussed my big ambition with. She fully supported my desire to have my name above the door of a salon one day, but had counselled me to wait until I was older, and more settled before tying myself down to a business. She'd also told me once that she had a few quid stashed away, which, when the time was right, she'd invest in a salon with me. In the meantime, I had to make a name for myself.

My first Saturday at Gino Venti was manic busy. It was Michael's day off, and the rest of us were scrabbling to keep up with the relentless flow of clients. I even had a few clients request me by name, recommended by people I'd done earlier in the week, which was a great accolade, and seemed to please Gray, as it confirmed his decision to hire me was the right one.

Salon Affair

I was finishing a head of highlights, when a woman walked in bearing an enormous bouquet of lilies. I could smell their heady scent from my station at the back of the salon. Paulina walked through, carrying them. "You had a delivery," she said, her face impassive. She put them in the staff room, and returned to her desk. I desperately wanted to go and see who they were from, but carried on with my client. "Ooo, who's sending you flowers?" She asked.

"I've got no idea, I'll go and have a look after I've got these last few foils in."

"How exciting. I hope they're from a man."

"So do I, as long as it's the right man." I fervently hoped they were from Julian, and not Matt. Sending flowers wasn't Matt's style, but he might have worked out that I wasn't speaking to him, and wanted his Saturday night shag. It had been two days since I'd cut Julian's hair, and I'd been thinking about him a lot, probably building things up in my own mind into something that they weren't.

I finished folding the last foil, and handed my client over to Tula for drinks and magazines, before trotting out to the staffroom, feeling four pairs of eyes follow me. The bouquet had been placed in a bucket of water on the floor. It was enormous, and consisted of white lilies and baby's breath, all wrapped in white paper finished with a huge, white satin bow. *Classy.*

I pulled out the little envelope, and slit it open.

I'd like to thank you properly for a great haircut, call me on 07956867596 if you're free tonight. Julian

"Lucky bitch. What're you gonna do?" Tomme made me jump. I hadn't heard him come in. He was reading the card over my shoulder.

"I don't know." The idea of me calling him was terrifying. I didn't do calling men.

"I thought you fancied him?"

"Yeah, but that doesn't mean I should call him. Women don't just phone men when they're commanded to you know."

"Oh for fucks sake Lil, just call him. There's no law against it you know. You're off tomorrow, so let him take you out tonight."

"I don't have time, my next client's waiting."

"Go consult, then get Lottie to do a slow shampoo, that'll give you time. Come on, no excuses. Do it." He propelled me back out into the salon where my client was waiting. Five minutes later, I was back in the staff room, nervously holding my phone. Taking a deep breath to calm myself, I punched in his number. He answered on the first ring.

"Julian Alexander."

"Hi, it's Lily, thanks for the flowers, they're beautiful."

He paused, I could almost hear his smile. "You're very welcome. I'm glad you called. Does this mean you'll let me take you out to eat tonight?" His voice was sultry, and seductive on the phone. I shivered slightly.

"Yes, ok....that would be nice."

"Oh I'll make it more than nice. Where shall I pick you up?" His question threw me a little. I couldn't ask him to pick me up from Bromley, and I didn't have any spare clothes at the salon.

"How about we meet outside the salon at say, half eight?" I'd just about have time to zip home, change, and zip back.

"I'll look forward to it," he purred.

"Great, listen, I'd better go, I've got a client waiting," I said, "I'll see you tonight."

I ended the call, and turned to see the five of them standing in the doorway, all listening. "God, you lot are nosy."

"The clients all want to know too," grinned Gray, nodding towards the salon, "so we sneaked in."

I shook my head at their beaming faces. "So you're seeing him tonight?" Tomme asked.

"Yep. Gonna be a hell of a rush though, getting home and back. I'd better tell Paulina not to book me any more today."

"You can get ready at mine, save you going home, if you like. I don't live far," offered Tomme.

"Thanks, but I don't have any clean clothes with me."

"Prada's only two doors down. They sell everything you'd need. Do you have your makeup bag?"

I nodded. It actually wasn't a bad idea. It would save at least an hour and a half, plus an interrogation from Mum. I quickly text her to tell her I wouldn't be home.

I finished at five, and nipped down the road to buy a dress and some underwear. One of the assistants was a girl I'd done earlier in the week. "Claudine! I didn't know you worked here?"

"Didn't I say? Been here a few years. What can I help you with today?" She replied in her sultry, French accent.

"I need a dress, for dinner tonight, some underwear, and maybe a pair of shoes. I'm going straight out from work, so don't have time to go home and change."

"Not a problem, let's put you in a changing room, and I'll bring a selection. Everyone loved my hair by the way." She led me through the shop, and into the changing room at the back. After instructing me to get undressed, she disappeared to fetch some dresses.

I loved the third one I tried on. It was very Audrey Hepburn-esque and fitted beautifully. I blanched slightly at the price, but told myself that it would be an investment purchase, which would last for years. Claudine appeared bearing a pair of high heels. "Here, try these on. They'll go perfectly."

I stared at my reflection. I looked grown up, and classy, exactly the image I wanted to project. I chose a new, lacy bra and thong set, and watched as Claudine rang up my purchases, gulping at the final figure. *This better be worth it.*

   Tomme's flat was small, but perfectly formed, and extremely stylishly decorated. It was also only a fifteen minute walk from the salon. He made a coffee while I quickly showered, then blow dried my hair into big, bouncy curls. When I'd dressed, and done my makeup, he cast an appraising eye over the total look. "You need more bronzer on your legs babe, and jooshe your hair up a bit." I complied, squirting on more extra-strong hairspray. "Perfect. If I was straight, I'd fancy you."

   Tomme promised to bring my work clothes into the salon for me, so that I only had to carry my handbag, which I dropped twice, before I managed to get it to stay on my shoulder. "Lily, are you nervous?" Tomme asked, amused.

   "Of course I am. It's a first date, I'm supposed to be nervous. I just hope I don't panic, and do something stupid, like order spaghetti, or drink till I'm sick."

   He laughed. "Why is ordering spaghetti such a bad thing? I like spaghetti."

   "So do I, but not on a date. Nobody can eat it without being messy. I'd look dead sexy with tomato sauce smeared round my gob wouldn't I?"

   "Blimey, the things women worry about. Makes me glad I'm a poof." He gave me an awkward little hug. "Go get him Tiger, and remember, we all want to know every detail, particularly cock size. Make plenty of notes. Better still, take photos."

   "Not on a first date. I don't do it till the third date."

   He looked disappointed. "Cop a feel at least then." I laughed as I pulled the front door shut behind me.

Chapter 4

I stood nervously outside the salon, hoping I wouldn't be stood up. It was an irrational fear, as Julian wasn't a stupid young boy, but it had happened to me once, and the humiliation had been overwhelming, especially as it had been a school disco, and all my classmates had witnessed it.

I spotted Julian strolling down the street, he smiled widely when he saw me. He was wearing fitted black jeans, and a white shirt, undone at the neck. A black jacket finished off the look. *Yummy*. I was really glad I'd splashed out on my outfit.

"You look lovely, I'm so glad you came tonight," he said. He kissed my cheek softly, sending a little shiver down my spine. "I thought we'd go up high to eat tonight." He stuck his hand out to hail a cab. One slowed down almost immediately, and pulled to a halt at the kerb. Julian grasped my hand, and pulled me over to it. He opened the door for me, and with his hand burning an imprint on the small of my back, guided me in.

"Tower 42 please," he said, before sliding the glass privacy screen across. He turned to me, "Have you eaten there before?"

I shook my head. "No, never even heard of it. Is it one of yours?"

He smiled, "I wish it was, but no, not one of mine. I didn't want to take you to a restaurant or bar that I own, as I'd only end up dealing with problems. You know what staff are like, they want you wiping their noses every five minutes." He smelt delicious close up, all citrus and mint, *probably due to the shampoo I'd sold him,* I thought. "I booked a table at Vertigo," he said, shaking me out of my reverie, "modern European bar food. I hope you like it."

"I'm sure I will." *I haven't got a scooby what modern European is.* "Have you been there before?"

"No. It'll be a new experience for me too." I looked out of the window as we sped towards the city. *This is the sort of Saturday night I dreamed of,* I thought gleefully.

We pulled up outside a vast skyscraper, which seemed to dwarf all the enormous buildings around it. "This is it, we're eating at the top. Hope you don't mind heights," Julian said, before helping me out of the taxi, and paying the driver.

We had to pass through security, airport style, to even get into the building. As my bag was searched, I breathed thanks for Tomme's offer to take my clothes into work for me. A guard pulling out my knickers would have killed me. We made our way to a small lift, which simply said 'floor 42', and got in. I could feel the sexual tension shimmer between us in the confined space. He seemed a touch nervous too, and shifted slightly from foot to foot, fidgeting with his pocket. It was rather endearing, and seemed to humanise him a little. I'd built him up in my mind to be a cocky, arrogant Lothario, who seduced women with champagne and flowers on a daily basis, so seeing evidence of his own nerves calmed mine a little.

The maitre'd took our jackets, and showed us to a table by a vast window. The view was spectacular. "The whole of London laid out at our feet," I mused out loud, as I gazed at the glittering lights below us.

Julian cocked his head to one side, and regarded me intently. "I suppose it does feel as though we have the world at our feet up here." I dragged my eyes away from the view, and beamed at him.

"This place is amazing, thanks for bringing me here."

"You're very welcome. It's lovely to see you so enchanted. Warms a cynical heart to see a smile like yours."

We were interrupted by the waiter bringing our menus. Julian waved away the wine list, and simply asked for a bottle of Krug. I read through the menu, and relaxed when I saw that it was all fairly straightforward. "We could have the sharing platter," I said, "looks like it has a little bit of everything."

"Good choice, then I can feed you seductively," he purred. Before I could flirt back, the waiter arrived with our champagne, which was deftly opened and served, and our food order taken.

"So, Julian, tell me about yourself..."

"What would you like to know?"

"We could start with where you're from, how old you are, that kind of thing."

"Ok, I'm 33, and I'm originally from Surrey. Now, your turn."

"I'm 26 and from Bromley in Kent."

"Are we speed dating? Isn't that what they do at those events? Grill each other as quick as possible."

I grinned at him. "I've got no idea, I've never been to one. Have you?"

He shook his head. "I've always found the sheer idea of them quite horrifying. I prefer to do my chatting up over a haircut." He smiled a cute, crooked grin to let me know he was joking. "So, how are you enjoying it at Gino Venti?"

"I love it so far. It's so.." I scrabbled for the right words, "creative. It's almost as though there are no barriers."

"In what way?"

"Well, the clients don't quibble about cost, so I'm not limited in that way, and they come to us based on reputation, so are more open to ideas."

"And how is it, working with all those men?"

"Oh, they're all lovely. They're all gay, so it's a different dynamic, more open and friendly, apart from Trystan, because he's got a crush on you."

Julian laughed. "It'll be an unrequited crush I'm afraid. Not my thing at all."

"Glad to hear it. I must admit, being around them all day does make me question if there are any men in the world who're straight, because according to the boys, every man in London's gay."

"I can assure you they're not. My clubs and bars are all straight, and every night I see the lengths men go to for a bit of skirt. It's what most of the bar fights are about."

"So how come you're not working tonight?" I asked

He sat back in his chair, spreading his knees wide. "Because I'm taking you out. I figured that hairdressers don't generally go out late on Friday nights, besides, I'm the boss, I get to do what I like."

"Have you been out with a hairdresser before then?" I was surprised by his statement, and convinced he must have previous experience, rather than being that insightful. He shook his head.

"No, never. You're the first. It's just common sense though, isn't it? Saturdays are the busiest day in your trade, and by the time we've finished this champagne, you might feel a bit ropey tomorrow. You're not working are you?"

"No, day off, although I'm planning to go clothes shopping. What do you do during the day, if you work evenings?" I was curious.

"It depends. I've got a couple of coffee shops, and two boutiques, so often travel round those to see how they're doing. I do paperwork and stuff, go to the gym, you know, the usual. I don't work every night, just when we have problems or things I need to sort out." He paused, "so how long have you been a hairdresser?"

"Ten years now. I started at sixteen."

"It's a growth market, a good trade to be in. People will always need their hair cut."

We were interrupted by our food arriving. It was delightful, served on a gigantic plate, a series of satays, tiger prawns, and other finger food, almost like a party buffet all to ourselves. "I love this concept," mused Julian, "like a sort of European tapas. "I'm thinking of introducing something like this in one of my bars." He picked up a tiger prawn, dunked it in sauce, and took a bite. He had the sexiest mouth. I could barely take my eyes off him. "Here, try this," he said, picking up another, dunking it, and holding it in front of my mouth. I took a bite, closing my eyes as the glorious lime dressing hit my palate.

"Mmm, gorgeous." I took the rest of it in my mouth. I watched as he sucked the dressing off his fingers.

"Gorgeous, like you." He stroked his other hand down my bare arm, sending trails of heat through me. I shivered. His eyes bored into me as he fed me some chicken satay. A drop of sauce must have touched my lip, as he leaned over to catch it with his finger, before sensually licking it off. I thought I'd combust on the spot. This was the most full-on seduction I'd ever experienced.

He let me feed him too, holding my hand to guide me. Even his touch was sexy, he exuded masculine gentleness in a way which very few men can, only the ones who genuinely adore women. I was transfixed by his attentiveness, his evident sex appeal, and his hypnotic blue eyes, which gazed into mine. In that romantic castle in the sky, I was thoroughly, totally, seduced.

He carried on until we'd finished the food, the pair of us oblivious to everyone around us as we teased and tormented each other with the promise of what was to come. All my previous thoughts of playing by the dating rules were well and truly forgotten, as he turned me on with just his actions and his touch. I was desperate to have his hands on me.

My eyes flicked over his body, he looked lean and muscular underneath his clothes, his shoulders firm and wide, his hands soft and neatly manicured.

"Do you find me attractive Lily?" He asked, smiling at my trance-like state, "Because I find you inordinately attractive."

I blushed at being put on the spot. "You're good at this, aren't you?" He pulled a quizzical face. "Seduction, you're good at it," I clarified.

"I think you've got that the wrong way round, I'm helpless around you, you have this..." he scrabbled for the words, "charisma, sex appeal, I don't know what to call it. You must have had lots of men tell you though." I shook my head, not quite believing what he was saying. He smiled his adorable crooked smile. "So, tell me how come you haven't already been snapped up?"

"I was seeing someone for the last two years, and split up with him recently. We wanted different things. What about you?"

"I never met 'the one' I suppose. I had a long relationship from my late teens into my twenties, but she wanted to see the world, and I wanted to build up my business, so we split. Last I heard, she was trekking around South America with a dreadlocked Australian. I work fairly unsociable hours, so although it's easy for me to meet women, it's not easy to sustain a relationship. I find most women want a nine to fiver." I smiled, thinking of Matt with his safe, boring office job. There was nothing about it that I'd found remotely attractive.

"I don't think that's true at all. Well, at least not for me. My ex hated the fact I worked Saturdays, and now that I'm at Gino Venti, Sundays as well some weeks. The nine to fivers are better off sticking with each other, and leaving us ambitious devils alone."

He raised his glass, "I'll drink to that." We clinked glasses, and I took a sip. I was getting to that stage of intoxication where my face was a little numb, I needed to slow down a bit. "So... you're ambitious?" I nodded. "Tell me, what's your ambition then?"

"I want my own salon. In the West End, mentioned in every magazine around." With the champagne loosening my tongue, I'd told him what very few people knew. I thought he'd laugh, but to his credit, he didn't.

"I think you'll get it. I could see you as a salon owner. You just need the right mentor or backer." He sipped his drink, and gazed at me, as if he could see right into my innermost psyche. I didn't answer, and turned my attention to the view.

"Is that the London eye over there?"

"Looks like it, right by the Oxo Tower. The Shard looks beautiful doesn't it?" He pointed to a glass tower which was lit up from ground to tip. "I love London. I think it's the greatest city on Earth. Full of opportunity and life."

"I'd like to move up here, live nearer the salon. Tomme, my workmate, lives in the cutest little flat just off Baker Street. I'd quite like something like that."

"Near me then, I'll keep my eyes open for you. There's always places coming up, but they're not often advertised, especially the better ones."

I drained my glass, and refused the last bit in the bottle, which Julian finished off. I was feeling a touch pissed, and rather horny, a dangerous combination. "Now, where would you like to go next? This place closes at midnight, so we can go on to a club if you like? Or I could make you a coffee?"

"I think I'd prefer a coffee, if that's ok. Champagne goes straight to my head. I'll need to see about getting a cab too."

"No problem, I've got an Addison Lee account. I can sort that for you easily." He motioned for the waiter, who came over bearing the bill.

"I thought we were having coffee?" I said.

"We are, I'll make you one back at mine." He pulled out a wad of notes, peeled off a few, and tucked them into the folder that contained the bill. "It's alright, I'm not an axe murderer, you're as safe with me as you want to be."

I was more nervous travelling down in the lift than I had been on the way up. Having been subjected to a full on seduction, I knew we'd end the night in Julian's bed, which terrified me. It was all very well sitting back, and letting him charm me, it was an entirely different thing getting naked with him. I felt provincial and gauche, my previous experience limited to 'efficient' or fumbling shags. I could tell I was way out of my depth.

He snaked his arm around my shoulder. "You're shivering, are you cold?" *No, I'm a bag of nerves.* I shook my head, he looked amused. "You don't have to do anything you don't want to do. I'm happy to be a perfect gentleman." He kissed my cheek softly, and whispered into my ear; "I can ravish you into explosive orgasms another time." As soon as the words were out of his mouth, everything south of my waist tightened viciously, my tummy doing that delicious squeezing thing. If I was being entirely truthful, I was desperate to see him naked, feel him inside me, taste him. I wanted to witness those intense blue eyes burning with lust.

I shook myself back to the present, and smiled at him, non-committal. I made the decision to go back to his for coffee, and play it by ear, mentally putting off my decision until later. He smiled a sphinx-like smile back, no doubt aware of the effect he was having on me.

The cold air hit me as soon as we got outside, sending my head spinning. I grabbed hold of Julian's arm to steady myself, as the combination of high heels, and champagne, made staying upright rather precarious. "Babe, are you drunk?" Julian asked, evidently amused.

"Bit light headed. I'll be ok in a minute," I snapped back. *Sober up stupid girl.*

Salon Affair

"I take it you're not a drinker then? You had less than half a bottle of Krug."

"I'm a bit of a lightweight with alcohol." *Don't be sick, don't be sick*, I repeated in my head. The very last thing I wanted to do was honk up in front of him, or worse still, in the taxi, which we'd be charged for. "Can we walk for a bit? Let me sober up a little." Even in my inebriated state, I knew not to get into a cab until my head had stopped spinning.

"Sure, let's walk towards the West End, just let me know when you feel ok to get into a taxi. Do you feel sick at all?" He seemed so kind, and caring, as he held me firm, and walked me along Old Broad Street, towards the Bank of England.

"The cold air just got to me, that's all," I said, embarrassed. He just smiled in reply, and squeezed me a little tighter. We walked in silence for a while. He didn't even seem mildly tipsy. Eventually we reached St Paul's.

"Do you think you'll be ok to get in a cab now? Only I'm sure your feet must be hurting by now." *Is this man for real?* In truth, I did feel a little better, although still too tipsy to make an informed decision about shagging him. He was right, my feet were killing me.

"Yeah, I'm fine now." We carried on walking while waiting for a taxi to come past. After a few minutes, Julian was able to flag one down.

"44 Gloucester Place please."

I managed not to throw up in the taxi, much to my relief. I concentrated on looking out of the window, so that the motion of the car didn't add to my general queasiness. Thankfully, the journey didn't take long, and we pulled up outside a stucco-fronted terrace, with a large '44' painted on the porch pillar. I swayed slightly, as Julian paid the driver, and had to clasp his arm to keep myself steady. "Come on you, let's get some coffee inside you," Julian said, amused at my inebriation. I expected him to lead me up the stairs to the large, black front door, but instead, he unlocked a gate in the railing, and carefully helped me down the stone staircase towards the basement flat, locking the gate behind him. *Oh great, a hobbit-hole.*

I was pleasantly surprised by his apartment. The hallway was neat and tidy, and quite spacious for a flat. He led me into the living room, which was, again, quite large, and furnished with two squashy sofas, and an enormous telly. The glass coffee table had a copy of GQ magazine, and a copy of Time Out. The only other furniture was a bookcase, which housed an assortment of books. Through my befuddled brain, it struck me that there were no feminine touches, no cushions, knickknacks, or pictures up.

"I'll go make us some coffee. Sit yourself down. Do you have milk and sugar?"

"No sugar, just milk, thanks." I plonked myself down on the settee, and watched as Julian put his phone into an iPod dock on the bookcase. The strains of Adele filled the room. He went off to make our drinks.

What with my foggy head, aching feet, and tired body, I felt my eyes getting heavier and heavier.

****

I snugged deeper into the duvet, enjoying the warmth, before becoming aware of daylight. My eyes snapped open, and I struggled up onto my elbows to find out where I was. Looking around, I was alone in a large bed, in a fairly stark, cream-painted bedroom. *Crap, I must've fallen asleep on him.*

I realised, at the moment I saw my dress on a hanger, that I was wearing my bra and knickers. He'd placed my shoes and bag on the floor, below where my dress was hanging. I cringed with embarrassment, debating whether I should just sneak out quietly, or brazen it out, and laugh it off. In the meantime, I needed a wee, and my mouth felt as though it was fur lined.

Salon Affair

I pulled my dress on, and picked up my shoes and bag. Stepping outside the bedroom door, I listened for sounds, but hearing nothing but the rumble of traffic, I crept down the corridor. I found the bathroom, and locked myself in. After a wee, I nicked Julian's toothbrush for a quick brush, and wiped under my eyes with his flannel. I looked rough, my hair looked like I'd been pulled through a hedge, and my skin was blotchy. I found a comb in my bag, and raked it through, wincing as it stuck in all the hairspray I'd used the night before. *It'll have to do.*

I tried to flush the loo quietly, and held my breath, listening at the door for movement, before opening it gingerly, ready to slip out unnoticed.

"Hi babe, sleep well?" I jumped out of my skin. Julian was standing in the doorway opposite, wearing just a pair of sleep shorts. He was shirtless, and barefoot, and judging by his damp hair, fresh from the shower. *Look at the abs....* "Sorry, did I make you jump? I've made a pot of coffee. No sugar wasn't it?"

I had no choice but to follow him into the kitchen. It was a surprisingly bright room, due mainly to half of it being comprised of a glass conservatory. I winced at the sunlight streaming in. "I'm really sorry about last night," I began.

"No, I'm sorry. It was my fault, plying you with champagne like that. I hope you didn't mind me putting you to bed, only I couldn't wake you up. I did try." He smiled tentatively. I blushed.

"I sleep like the dead, especially after a drink." I paused. "Where did you sleep?"

"In my bed. I put you in the spare room. Thought you'd freak out waking up next to a strange man." He grinned, clearly amused. He placed a coffee down in front of me. I took a very welcome sip.

"I didn't throw up did I?"

He shook his head. "Nope, nor did you snore, dribble, or anything else. You just went sort of floppy and dead." His grin got wider.

"I'm glad you find me so amusing," I snapped.

"Well, it was quite funny. I've never seen anyone go out cold like that. You didn't wake up at all, even when I was struggling to lift you off the sofa. How people manhandle dead bodies, I don't know. Still, you look alright today. Not too hung-over I hope?"

"I'm fine thanks. I'll just drink this, and get out of your way." I stared into my coffee, not wanting to look at him, especially when his bare chest was so distracting. *Nice smattering of chest hair going on.*

His face dropped. "I thought you were off today? Maybe we could do something together?"

"Well, yes, it's my day off, but I've got no clean clothes with me, and I need to do some shopping." I paused, and curiosity kicked in. "What sort of thing did you want to do?"

"I don't know, maybe something touristy. How do you fancy going up on the London eye? Or the Tower of London? I've not been there since I was a kid."

"I need to go home, shower and change. My Mum'll be frantic." I glanced at the clock, it was only half seven. I pulled my phone out of my bag, and quickly text Mum that I was ok, and had fallen asleep at a friend's. Julian was watching me closely, especially when I opened and read the four texts from Matt, asking where I was, getting increasingly angry as they went on. *Tough, I'm still not replying.*

"Why don't we go back to yours, and I'll wait while you get changed, then we can go out for the day?"

"I live with my parents. I doubt very much that you'll want to sit making small talk with my Dad in his dressing gown. Plus they might be a little suspicious that I've been out all night." I was interrupted by my phone chirping. It was only Mum asking if I was coming home that day, so she'd know numbers for Sunday lunch. I text back that I'd be home in a little while, not mentioning anything else.

"Come on, I'll take you home. It won't take long on the bike."

"Bike?"

"Yes," he smiled, "I ride a motorbike. We'll be in Bromley in twenty minutes or so." Before I could answer, he sauntered off, presumably to get dressed. Fifteen minutes later I was perched on the back of his enormous beast of a super bike, wearing a black helmet, and my stomach in my throat. I clung tightly to his waist as we zoomed through the traffic, barely stopping all the way to Bromley. He found my house easily from my directions, and pulled up into the drive. I noticed the nets twitch as I clambered off the saddle, my legs a bit jellified.

"Hi Mum, I'm back," I called out as I walked in. She walked out of the kitchen, "Mum, this is Julian, Julian, this is Linda." Mum shook his hand.

"Pleased to meet you Linda," he said, as smooth as silk. "Sorry Lily didn't make it home last night, only she fell asleep on my sofa. I hope you weren't worried."

Mum smiled, and to my horror, went all coy. "Oh I don't worry. She's a big girl now. Come on through to the kitchen, and I'll put the kettle on." Julian trotted behind her quite happily, and sat himself down at the kitchen table. "So where did you two go last night?" She asked, filling the kettle.

"Tower 42, in the city. The bar was on the 42nd floor. The views were amazing," I told her. She smiled indulgently.

"Nice to see you being taken to exciting places. Are you stopping for lunch?"

"No, we're going to the Tower of London. I just came home to get changed."

"Righty ho. So Julian," she turned to him, "What do you do for a living?" I left them to it, and went off for a shower, and a change of clothes. I debated throwing some work clothes into a bag, *just in case*, hovering over my extra large bag, which would have room. On impulse, I threw a pair of clean knickers, and a fresh top in. If I wore my black jeans, and boots, I'd get away with them at work. *I'm planning to sleep with him.*

It'd struck me as a little odd that he wanted to spend the day with me, despite my passing out on him. We barely knew each other, yet he seemed totally comfortable in my company. By the time I'd finished, and gone back downstairs, my mother was totally charmed, and my Dad was laughing at a joke. "You look lovely. All ready?" Julian said. "I must just use your bathroom before we go."

I directed him to the downstairs loo. As soon as he was out of the room, Mum whispered "He's lovely, quite a catch."

"Nice fella," Dad agreed.

"We'll see. I've got no idea what time I'll be back. I'll text you," I told Mum. She winked at me, which made me cringe.

We had a brilliant day, doing the tourist trail around London. The London Eye was romantic, despite the pod being packed with people. Julian seemed incredibly tactile, either holding my hand, or resting his arm around my shoulders at every opportunity. I laughed at how geeky he was at the Tower of London, buying a guide book, and examining all the exhibits in minute detail.

"I like history," he said, slightly affronted at my teasing as he read me an excerpt from his guide, detailing the various prisoners Henry the something had had incarcerated.

"So do I, but you're very.....thorough," I replied, smiling.

"I like detail, I suppose it's the businessman in me. With all my companies, I plan all the tiny details, all the little things that make the total experience. In the bars, for instance, I tested out hundreds of different glasses to find the ones which looked luxurious while keeping drinks costs down. That way I only have to buy a few different sizes, and can do it in bulk to lower costs." He stroked my cheek, sending a shiver of electricity through me. *Clever too.*

He must have seen the effect of just his touch, as he leaned towards me, and kissed me softly, pushing his hands into my hair. He pulled back slightly to look at me, before kissing me again, firmer this time, his tongue meeting mine for the first time. His lips felt soft, his hands gentle, as they caressed the back of my head. Breathless, I pulled away. "We're in the Crown Jewels," I murmured.

"I don't care where we are. I've wanted to do that since I met you," he breathed. "Come back to mine?"

I nodded. In truth, I was desperate for him. I'd been horny for him all day, just from his touch, and his gentle attentiveness. I swear he sped back to the West End at a hundred miles an hour. He pulled me into his flat, slamming the door behind him, pressing me up against the wall to kiss me again, his mouth claiming mine with an urgency borne of frustration. "Undressing you last night, it was torture, not being able to touch you. You have the sexiest body," he panted after pulling away.

"Seeing you in just those little shorts this morning was the same," I confessed. He led me down the hall to his bedroom door, a room I'd not yet seen. It was different from the rest of his flat, being more...finished. The walls were painted cream, with the exception of a feature wall, which was papered with an aubergine pattern. The bed was enormous, and sported a cream and aubergine duvet. There were even matching curtains, which Julian immediately pulled shut.

He wrapped his arms around me, kissing me hard. As his hand slithered down to feel my bottom, I shivered.

"Don't be scared," he whispered, "I'll never hurt you. I'll be gentle." I could feel his hot breath on my neck as he spoke.

"I'm not scared, just a bit nervous." *There, I've admitted it.* His hands slid round to cup my breasts.

"I'm a kind and gentle lover, Lily. I'd never hurt such an exquisite person as you." He paused. "Can I undress you? I really want to see you naked." His voice had taken on a purring quality. *So sexy.* He grasped the hem of my sweater, and pulled it over my head, before flinging it carelessly at a chair in the corner. His hands roamed over my bra-clad breasts, kneading gently.

Not to be the only one stripping, I undid his shirt, my fingers fumbling a little with the tiny buttons. He wore a T-shirt underneath, which he yanked off himself, before unclipping my bra, managing the task one handed, with a practiced ease. He pulled me into him, crushing his chest against mine, nipping gently along my shoulder, culminating in featherlight kisses up my neck.

I felt his hands hook into the waistband of my jeans, skimming around my hip bones to meet at the front, and pop the button, while his hot mouth travelled down to capture my nipple, and suck it hard. I arched into him, willing him to speed up, and salve the ache that was building inside.

He slid my jeans down far enough to be able to slip a finger inside me. It merely served to amplify the intense throbbing inside. I needed more than just his finger. I took a deep breath, and undid his jeans, feeling his rather impressive erection straining through his jersey boxers. I slipped my hand under the waistband, and grasped his cock. He took a sharp intake of breath. "Oh yes Lily, like that," he gasped, as I stroked him.

Acting purely on instinct, I dropped to my knees, and, after freeing him from his clothes, took his cock in my mouth. His breath hitched, as I licked and sucked him,

Salon Affair

holding him at the root. With my spare hand, I caressed his balls, which seemed to excite him even more.

"Enough," he barked, shocking me, "You'll make me come. I want to make love to you," he added in a softer voice. I let go, and with shaky hands, pulled off my boots and jeans. "Are you on the pill?" He asked.

"Yes, but I still use condoms."

"Very wise," he muttered, kicking off the rest of his clothes, and pulling open a drawer to find a box. I watched with feminine, carnal appreciation, as he unrolled a condom over his rather impressive dick. He pushed me back, onto the bed, then crawled up my body, sucking each nipple as he went. As he kissed me, he pressed into me, stretching and filling me completely. "Oh god, that feels so good," he breathed, before starting to move, every thrust hitting that perfect spot, easing the tension that had been gnawing at me.

I'd just begun to relax, and allow my orgasm to build, when he changed positions, pulling me on top. Impaled on his iron cock, I leaned forward, and kissed him deeply, as I worked myself into a frenzy. He must have felt the telltale quivering of my imminent orgasm, as he stopped me again, and pulled me into a new position, laying on my back, with him laying on his side, at a right angle to me. It allowed him to rub tiny circles on my clitoris, while he fucked me really deep. I couldn't hold back any longer, and came with a shout. The only way I can describe it is like my body detonated. A bomb went off inside, pulling my insides upwards viciously.

"That's it baby, just ride it. Go with it," he murmured, as I practically convulsed around him. It was a world away from the gently fluttering orgasms of my past experiences.

He rode me right through my orgasm, thrusting deep and fast, until he stilled, pressed in deep, and let go, his face screwing up, as if in pain, before relaxing. We lay there a few minutes, no sound apart from our breathing, to break the silence. Wordlessly, he pulled out, and grasped my shoulders, taking me into his arms. Eventually, he spoke, "I knew we'd be good together."

"Mmm," was all I could reply, in my post-coital daze. *Will sex always be like that?*

"Are you going to sleep?" He prodded me in the ribs. I opened my eyes, and beamed a smile at his beautiful face.

"I'm trying not to," I said, "but that was the biggest, most intense orgasm I've ever had. So forgive me for being a little dazed."

He grinned. His wide smile showing his perfect, white teeth. "The biggest orgasm you ever had? I'll take that as a compliment. Give me another half hour, and I'll give you another one." He leaned down, and kissed my breast. "Now, in the meantime, shall I make you something to eat?"

"I'm starving," I confessed. I watched as he pulled on his sleep shorts, and threw his shirt over to me. I pulled it on, surreptitiously sniffing his gorgeous scent. He led me by the hand into the kitchen, where I made us coffees, while he rustled up some cheese on toast. His fridge was pretty empty. "Are you a good cook?" I asked.

"Not great. I never have much in, and I usually eat in my restaurants, or at the gym. It's a bit pointless cooking for one."

"Don't you have a cleaner, or a lady who keeps house?" I asked. He shook his head, and pulled a bit of a face.

"It's not a huge flat, and it's only me here, so I manage alright. The only room that gets messy is my office, and I wouldn't want anyone rearranging stuff in there." He paused. "Can you cook?"

"Yes, I'm not bad at all. Mum taught me when I was little. I can't do really fancy stuff, but I can do family meals ok. Mum works at a solicitors as a receptionist, and book-keeper, so I often got dinner ready if I was home first. My

Salon Affair

Dad's useless, and my brother, Mark, can't even boil water."

"I'm not that bad," he laughed, serving up our snack still bubbling. I decided to let mine cool a little.

"How long have you lived here?" I looked around the slightly bare kitchen. It looked like a rental flat, one which had only been furnished with the basics.

"Ten years, yeah, I bought it in 2003, so just over ten years." *He owns it?*

"Oh, I thought it was rented."

He sipped his coffee. "Why?"

"Well, there's no pictures up, and not much furniture."

"No woman's touch? I suppose I'm a bit of a bloke. As long as I've got a telly and a sofa, I'm quite happy really. Women always want to clutter things up."

"So you've never had a woman live here?"

He shook his head. "No, never."

"How come?" I was intrigued. This gorgeous hunk of sexy man clearly wouldn't have trouble getting a girlfriend, and with sexual prowess like his, keeping her happy.

"I guess I don't really do domesticity." His voice took on an edge, "I told you before, women struggle with my work life. Talking of which, I'm gonna have to work tonight. I can go in a little late though," he winked suggestively, "gives us a bit more time."

One enormous orgasm later, I sat in bed, watching him dress. "So what do you have to do tonight?" I asked, fairly innocently, I thought.

"Bit nosy aren't you? It's just work. Staff stuff, money stuff, ordering, nothing sinister," he snapped, shocking me a little. Only five minutes before, he'd been murmuring sweet nothings, and calling his climax. The atmosphere between us switched to chilly in a nanosecond. I jumped off the bed, and scooped my knickers on.

"I'll get out of your way," I said, avoiding his eyes. I dressed in double quick time.

"You want a lift?" He asked in a more measured tone.

"No, I'll be fine. I can take the tube. Thanks anyway." I concentrated on keeping it together, even though I felt as though I was being dismissed. He'd had his way with me, and now wanted rid. *Player.* I couldn't get out of there fast enough. I grabbed my coat from the peg in the hall.

"Lily, what's up?" He called out. "Don't I get a kiss goodbye?" He wandered up to me. I gave him a chaste kiss, and pulled on my coat.

"I'll see you around," I said, avoiding his eyes. With that, I turned and walked out, closing the door behind me. I ran up the steps, and back into the world before he could follow me. I strode purposefully towards the tube station, angry with myself for overreacting, angry with him for his dismissal. I mulled over our weekend in my mind, re-thinking our conversations. By the time I was on the train home, I was certain I'd been played. I called Lisa.

"Can I come round?" I sniffed loudly.

"Course you can," She paused, "are you upset about something?"

"Yeah," I replied, in a small voice. "I'll be at Bromley South in ten."

"I'll pick you up."

I was so relieved to see Lisa's little Fiat outside the station. As soon as I hopped in, I let out the sob which I'd repressed all the way home. "Come on then, what happened?" She asked softly.

"I got played. He made out he was the perfect man, and was super-interested, then afterwards, went all cold on me, and almost threw me out to go to work." She stayed silent as she drove. Eventually, we pulled onto her drive. Her parents were away in Barbados, so we had the house to ourselves. She made some tea, and listened as I told her in elaborate detail about the events of the weekend, even showing her the pictures I'd snapped on my phone. *Julian*

Salon Affair

pulling a funny face, Julian up high on the eye, beaming a smile, one blowing me a kiss. Bastard.

"I think you've gotta wait and see if he played you. If he doesn't call, you'll know," she said, clearly not really getting the point.

"I don't want to just sit around waiting for my phone to ring," I whined, "I want to know why he changed."

"Maybe you gave it up a bit too easily," Lisa asserted, "men like a bit of challenge." I felt even more despondent. She was probably right, and I'd dropped my knickers a bit too quickly. Julian clearly wasn't the type to settle down, and was bound to be chatting up the next woman already.

Chapter 5

The boys were waiting to pounce when I strolled into work the next day. "Morning everyone," I called out.

"Cut the crap, did you shag him?" Tomme demanded. Anthony and Michael sat looking expectant. I switched the kettle on.

"I take it you're on about my date? I had a very nice time, thank you. Who's in today?"

"Just us four. Gray'n'Tryst are off. Paulina's out too, so we have to cover reception ourselves. Come on, did you shag him?"

"Not on Saturday night, no."

"Riiiight, when then?"

"Sunday. Then he dumped me." As soon as the words were out of my mouth, there was a collective gasp.

"Bastard. What happened?" Tomme had his 'sympathy face' on, the one he usually reserved for clients when they told him their bad news.

"Had great sex, then he told me to go, as he had to go into work. Went a bit icy."

"How is that dumping you?" Michael asked. "If he had to work, he had to work. I sent my hook up home this morning. Woke him up to send him home. Didn't want him in my flat alone." They all began discussing the etiquette of getting rid of lovers who outstayed their welcome. I tuned out, and made a coffee.

The only excitement that morning, was a package arriving in the post, clearly marked 'L'Oreal Colour

Salon Affair

Trophy'. Anthony opened it, and read the contents out. "So are we entering?" I asked.

"Of course. We got to the finals last year. Gray was talking about this the other day. He suggested using your copper ombré idea, but on a more geometric cut."

"Hmm, that'd work. I'm just concerned that the coppers are a bit passé now. I've got a client in next who I discussed doing a form of ombré with, but a purple to pink one. I'll do some experimenting."

"It's gotta be L'Oreal though, and they don't do a pink." Anthony pointed out.

"Oh I made one using 10.1 and red mixtone. Added a touch of blue mixtone too once, and got a pretty, silvery lilac. At least it doesn't fade to green like the crazy colour lilac. You can also add a load of clear to a 4.20, if you want the exact same tonal quality, as long as you pre-lighten." They all gaped at me. *Yeah, ok, I experiment..*

"Purple and lilac sounds fab."

Three hours later, they all gathered round my client, to snap photos, and discuss whether it would be a contender for the colour trophy. She adored her new colour, and was excited that we were considering using the same formula for such a prestigious competition. I'd done her hair in a kind of 'boho chic' look, which was one of my signature styles.

"I love the long, loose look, but this colour would work brilliantly on a geometric bob, as long as you can really blend the fade," Michael pointed out.

"It's all tint, so blending's not an issue," I replied, excited that my colour formula was being considered.

I bounced into the staff room, once my client had left, pleased at such a productive morning. I'd asked Tomme to arrange the lilies from Saturday in a vase, and put them in reception, so they weren't sitting on the floor of the staffroom as a reminder of my humiliation. I planned to finish fairly early, and go over to Selfridges after work for the shopping trip that I'd missed the day before, so didn't want to be lugging a bouquet.

My good mood was short lived, after I checked my phone, only to see two texts, one from Matt, berating me for ignoring him, and telling me that he'd heard I was seeing someone else behind his back. I rolled my eyes, and ignored him. The second text was from Julian, asking how my day was, and why I'd gone so arctic on him the previous evening. My tummy flipped. I showed the text to Tomme, and asked what he thought I should do.

"It depends if you want to see him again," he said. I thought about it, and knew deep down I did. Julian ticked every box I'd ever thought of, and a few more besides.

"Ok, so if I do want to see him again, what should I do?"

Tomme grinned, a knowing look on his face. "Very little. Let him sweat a bit. In about an hour's time, answer 'mad busy', then wait for his next move."

"Ok, will do. What about Matt? He really isn't taking a hint."

"Tell him to piss off. Be upfront, and don't leave him any hope." I turned back to my phone, and composed a text to Matt, telling him to leave me alone, and re-iterating that I wasn't going back to him, mainly because I'd met someone else. It was brutal, to the point, and would leave no ambiguity. Satisfied, I pressed 'send', and watched as the text showed first as delivered, then read. He didn't respond.

Later that afternoon, I followed Tomme's advice, and replied to Julian's text. Almost immediately I got a reply, asking what I was doing after work. Again, I left it a while before replying that I had plans. He went quiet.

Anthony decided to come to Selfridges with me after work, declaring that he loved shopping, and could almost be a fashion stylist. He picked out a load of stuff for me to try on, and between us, we managed to spend a thousand quid of my hard earned money on making me look the part. I had to admit, he was extremely talented, and had a good

Salon Affair

eye for fashion, picking out items I'd have dismissed. When we'd finished, I treated us both to a glass of wine in a little bar round the corner.

"So how long have you worked for Gino?" I asked. Anthony was probably the least outspoken in the salon, so I hadn't really got to know him.

"A few years now. I left the Northeast about a year before that, after being targeted for being gay. It's not as easily accepted on a rough council estate up there as it is in London. I didn't know anything or anyone when I first got here, so got a job in a ropey part of Hackney, until I twigged that the West End was where it's at. Gino was still working back then, and gave me my big break."

"What's he like?"

"Nice, talented. There's not a head of hair that Gino can't do to perfection. Gray was his protégé, and even with all the years of training, still looks like an amateur in comparison. Gino always kept his feet on the ground though, helped young hairdressers. He was a great teacher." Antony became misty eyed at the memories.

"Gray's hair-ups are amazing," I said.

"Yes, he's good. Gino just had this..." he paused, "eye for balance and detail. Everything he did was another level. It's why he won so many awards. We're just riding on his coat tails really."

"Why did he retire?" I couldn't imagine ever giving up doing hair.

"He's sixty. His hands were giving him gyp, and he developed bad veins in his legs. Even after just a few hours on his feet he was in a lot of pain. He went back to Florence, where his family were from originally, and lives the good life. Deserves it really after all the work he's done."

"I didn't realise he was that old," I said, "so Paulina's his niece?"

Antony nodded. "She's alright, a bit uptight, I think she wanted to be a hairdresser, but couldn't do it. Gino tried to teach her at one time, but she was useless, so he taught her the business instead."

By the time Anthony and I parted company, we were firm friends. His quiet reticence had concealed a thoughtful and fun personality. While he wasn't as outrageous and loud as Tomme, in his own way, he was just as entertaining.

By the time I got home, it was fairly late, and after quickly showing Mum my purchases, I was able to escape to bed without any questioning about Julian. I really didn't want to discuss him, as it seemed to appear that Lisa had been right about me blowing the whole thing out of proportion.

I skipped into work the next morning, dressed in a cute MuiMui top, with skinny Versace jeans, feeling like a million dollars. The day got even better when Gray announced we were all having a drink after work to discuss our entry into the L'Oreal colour trophy. I prayed to the hairdressing gods that my purple/pink ombré would be the chosen theme.

Gray seemed a little preoccupied all day, so much so that even Tomme, who was usually fairly oblivious, asked if he was alright.

"Just got a lot on my mind," was all he said. He certainly didn't seem like his usual cheerful self.

Tomme and I finished first, so went down to the wine bar to bag a table. I was a little disappointed that Julian wasn't there. He hadn't text me all day, so I was a bit concerned that he'd given up, the thought of which was surprisingly painful. Tomme had just launched into a funny story about a fella he'd met at a bar the night before, when my phone chirped with a text.

Hi beautiful, just come by the salon, they said you done for the day. R U nearby?

Salon Affair

"Sorry Tomme, but Julian just text to ask if I'm around. What do I reply?" I interrupted, before showing him the text.

"Tell him you're here, but won't be free for another hour," he advised, "we really need to get our work stuff sorted before you go off shagging again." I smacked his arm, which made him laugh.

The others all arrived together, and once the wine was poured, began to discuss ideas for our entry. Both Tomme and Anthony championed my purple/lilac idea, and, after the pictures were discussed, we took a vote. It was unanimous, my colour would be used to represent the great Gino Venti at the colour trophy. I was giddy with pride.

"So, I'd suggest that Lily and Michael produce the colour, Trystan the cut, Tomme the finishing, Anthony can style the model and direct the makeup artist, and I'll organise all the admin, photographer and stuff. Is everyone in agreement with that?" Gray swept his eyes around the table expectantly. Everyone nodded and murmured their agreement.

"How come we all do different bits?" I asked. I could understand one person doing the colour and another the cut, but involving all of us seemed a little over the top.

"It gives the impression we're a larger salon than we are, with a full sized artistic team. Toni and Guy will send a team of at least twenty stylists, even if half of them only fetch the coffees. It also means we all get to claim the accolade of winning the colour trophy," Gray explained. We went on to discuss ideas for the theme, the cut, and the vibe, deciding collectively on the title 'Ethereal Ombré'.

We'd just started on another bottle of wine when Julian walked in. My tummy jumped at the sight of him. I watched him scan the room, then smile widely when he found me. He came straight to our table, summoning the waitress as he strode over. After bending down to softly kiss my cheek, he said hello to all the boys, who seemed unusually quiet. *Probably nosy to hear what he has to say.*

"Meeting all finished?" He asked nobody in particular. They all nodded in reply. "Good. I've got about half an hour's work here, I just need to sort out some inventory, then I'm free. Back in a bit." He spoke briefly to the waitress, then disappeared through a door beside the bar.

"That man could get anyone he wanted. Why he chooses to stick his dick in a fishy stinkhole's beyond me," mused Trystan. I slapped his arm.

"Hey, I'm not fishy, thank you very much. Besides, you trying to say that your shitter's minty fresh?" I bit back. The others cackled.

"Well, he does douche with mouthwash, so there's always that possibility," sniggered Anthony. "Anyway, time to spill about old Hottie McGorgeous over there. What's he like in bed?" They all leaned in closer for privacy.

"Sexy as hell, biggest dick I ever saw," I blurted.

"I knew it!" Tomme exclaimed. "I thought you were walking bandy yesterday. What's his house like? He must be loaded, so I bet it's something else."

I shook my head. "Quite ordinary really, nothing special. I don't think he's that rich, well, I don't think he's hard up, but his flat is pretty basic."

"I wonder what he spends his money on then. Maybe he's a secret gambler or something," sneered Trystan. A cloud of doubt flitted through my head. Julian should be wealthy, he owned enough businesses. Apart from a pretty ordinary flat, albeit an expensively situated one, and a bike, there was no evidence of him being well off. *Hmm, maybe Trystan's got a point.*

We were interrupted by the waitress bringing a bottle of Lanson, courtesy of Julian, which pleased my workmates. She shared it out, then disappeared.

Salon Affair

"Changing the subject from Lily's love life, did any of you hear that Ten Hair has gone over to Sugar Cube? They're closing next week for their refit," said Gray.

"Really? So they won't be in the colour trophy then?" Tomme exclaimed. Gray smiled and shook his head.

"How come?" I asked.

"Sugar is a bit like Aveda in that you give them exclusivity. In return, they refit your salon, make it part of the 'Sugar' network of salons. Alright if you like their stuff I suppose. Seems too restrictive to me. They've been badgering Paulina for a meeting, but she's not interested, and we don't really need a refit."

"Do you have to pay for the refit?" I asked.

He shook his head. "No, they front the cost, but you have to agree to only stock and use their products. I think you're tied in for a certain number of years. Probably great for a start-up, but I'm surprised that George, the owner of Ten, went for a deal like that."

"Their styling range is ok. I've got their putty, and their heat protect, but their shampoos are bit shit, certainly not the same standard as Kerastase or Pureology," I mused.

"Exactly, and if I understand correctly, you have to use everything Sugar under the agreement. Like I said, great for a start-up, but not for our type of clients. Their colour range is a bit limited too. Makes me wonder if Pierre'll want to jump ship. It'd be a squash, but we'd fit him in somehow."

"I'd squash against him anytime," Anthony stated, "he's sex on legs."

"And a total slut. He was blowing some guy in the toilets in Manhunt a few weeks back, drew quite a crowd. Good technique too," said Tomme.

"Sounds classy," I replied, much to Tomme's amusement.

"Who's Miss Priss-pott now that she's told us all about Julian's dick? I'm sure you'd blow him in the loos given half a chance." Trystan said, rather bitchily.

"True," I agreed, mainly to diffuse any nasty atmosphere that could be brewing. It did the trick, as the others all laughed. Gray wrapped his arm round my shoulders in an awkward little hug.

"Poor Lily, they're such bad influences. You're so outnumbered aren't you?"

By the time Julian returned, we'd decided on doing our entry on a Sunday, two weeks away, which gave Gray time to sort out models, and the photographer. Julian pulled up a chair next to me, and asked if we were all done, before gently tucking my hair behind my ear in a tender gesture. I swear I heard Trystan whimper.

"Yep, two week's time, we're doing our entry for a big hair competition," I told him, trying to ignore the way my body instinctively responded any time he was near.

"Using the colour that Lily invented," Tomme chimed in.

"Wow, you think you have a chance of winning?" Julian asked, looking genuinely interested.

"I think we do. It was us against Ten Hair last year, and they just pipped it. They're not entering this year, and I don't think there's another salon in London able to take us on." Gray puffed his chest slightly as he spoke. *Yep, we're the 'A' team, and I'm part of it.* I thought proudly.

"So what do you win?" Julian asked.

"Publicity mainly. We all get interviewed, the salon gets a shedload of free publicity, and we get another trophy for the glass case. Gino won the colour trophy three times, as well as hairdresser of the year twice. He put us on the map," Gray replied.

"Sounds great, listen, I came by earlier to tell you that a friend of mine has an apartment available near me. It's only one bedroom, but he's just put in a new bathroom, and said he'd keep the rent reasonable for you. I've got the keys if you want to have a look, see if it's suitable."

Salon Affair

"Great, thanks for asking for me." I pulled my coat on, before saying ciao to the boys, and following Julian out, admiring his arse from behind.

He held my hand as we wandered towards Oxford Street. "No bike tonight?" I asked.

"No, I knew I was going to the wine bar, and had to do some tasting, so I walked," he explained. "Why did you race off the other night? Did I say something wrong?"

I hesitated. It felt a little juvenile to complain that he'd called me nosy. "I don't know," I told him, " I just felt....dismissed I suppose. I thought you'd had your way, and wanted me to go."

He turned to give me a quizzical look. "You really thought that? I'll admit I was pissed off at having to go into work, but that wasn't directed at you. It's just my routine, collecting the takings on a Sunday evening, so I can bank them on Monday morning. If I hadn't shown up, my managers would've been worried."

"You could've phoned them," I replied, trying not to sound petulant, although I suspect, I failed.

"True, but I wouldn't have been able to bank until today, and I had other stuff I had to do. I'm sorry if you thought I was being a bastard, it was never my intention." He grasped my hand a little tighter, and swung round to face me, stopping us both. I gazed up at him, as he leaned in to kiss me, softly and chastely, before he pulled back, and scanned my face. "I'll just have to remind you how good we are together," he whispered. I turned to mush. *Bastard knows exactly what he's doing to me.*

We turned up Baker Street, past Tomme's place, and stopped outside a modern portico, numbered 27. "This is it," said Julian. I looked around, noting that I was almost opposite George Street, the home of Daniel Galvin, and a host of wannabe salons, which had sprung up around him, mainly due to ex-staff of his, trying to compete.

"Looks good," I smiled. Julian punched a code into the keypad, which opened the door. We walked through a roomy foyer, and into the lift.

"Third floor, nice and safe," he muttered. He seemed a little nervy. I wondered why.

The flat itself was delightful, a large sitting room, open plan with the kitchen area, a roomy bedroom, and a lovely, freshly fitted shower room. It was furnished simply, but modern, the sofas the oatmeal colour so beloved of landlords. "How much is it a month?" I asked.

"Fifteen hundred, but I negotiated him down to twelve for you, if you want it, that is." I looked out of the window, it was high enough up to have a great view, but I still got the feeling of being at the heart of the action.

"How does this work then, if I say yes?"

"You'll have to pay a month's rent deposit, and a month's rent in advance. Sign a tenancy agreement, and it's yours. Most people do six months at first, to test out whether or not they like it. Once you move in, register for council tax. The heating is included under your rent, and the electric is on a key meter, so it's pretty simple. There's no parking space provided, but you can buy a resident's permit."

"I share a car with my Mum, so I wouldn't need it up here," I told him, my mind swimming with possibilities as I took in the size and shape of the living room. It was larger than Tomme's place, and better situated. He'd told me that he was paying 1400 a month for his. "Thank you for finding this. It's better than I'd hoped for," I said.

"So you're gonna take it?"

"Of course, it's lovely."

He beamed, before pulling me into his arms, snaking his hands under my jacket to crush me against his chest. His kisses became urgent, almost fierce, communicating his desire for me. He pulled back a little. "I'm so glad," kiss, "you're going to be near," kiss, "and won't be spending hours everyday," kiss, "commuting." Kiss.

Salon Affair

Breathless with need, I pulled away to scan his face. "Me too," I replied, watching his face soften into a smile.

"I want to take you, here, now," he breathed, his hands cupping my breasts through my clothes, his thumbs finding my nipples, and rubbing them rhythmically. I felt a rush of heat between my legs. "We have a bed, a sofa, a kitchen counter, you can take your pick."

"All of them," I breathed, running my hands over his firm chest, feeling the warmth of his body through his shirt. I felt the button of my trousers get popped, and his hands snake around the waistband, easing them off my hips. I pushed his jacket off his shoulders, and watched as he hurriedly shed it, letting it drop to the floor, keys jangling loudly in the silence.

"I don't think we want an audience," he muttered, before striding over to the doorway, and turning off the lights. The buildings opposite would have a perfect view. I made a mental note to buy blinds.

In the half light of dusk, illuminated only by the neon of shops below, he took on an ghost like quality, a perfect creature, created out of warmth, hot breath, and shameless desire. I shivered as his hands roamed over me, ridding me of clothes, desperate for my skin.

Within moments, we were both naked, pressed up against each other, kissing as though we each had a hunger that could only be satisfied by the other's mouth. He slipped a finger inside me, then two, teasing my wildly twitching clitoris. I grasped his cock, feeling it straining against the skin, hard and engorged. He groaned, and in one smooth movement, lifted me onto the kitchen work top, and plunged into me.

He held my waist in an iron grip, as he rode me, over and over, pushing my body towards an ecstasy I'd never experienced before. I felt each thrust push me further down an abyss, from which I'd never emerge the same again. "Harder," I heard myself beg, the slapping of his body against mine, and our combined heavy breathing the only sounds in the room. I felt his hand move from my waist, leaving a bereft little patch of skin craving his touch.

I jumped when his thumb appeared on my clit. In the darkness, every movement was unanticipated, and somehow more intense. With the pressure on my bud, waves of white heat washed over me.

"Come for me," he commanded. I complied, my body stiffening, before the intense pulsing began, re-arranging my insides with a delicious intensity. I simply lay there, letting my nervous system take over, revelling in the pleasure I'd only recently discovered my body was capable of.

He followed with his own orgasm, calling out as he poured himself into me, pressing in deep. After a few moments, I felt him relax, and flop forward to kiss me.

"Lily, I'm so sorry," he began. As soon as he said it, I twigged. *No condom.* "It went out of my head. I got carried away. I'll get you the morning after pill."

"It's ok, I'm on the pill. I just use condoms for protection against nasties," I told him. I hadn't given it a thought either in the heat of the moment. We'd both got carried away.

"I don't think I've got anything. What about you?" His voice was gentle.

"No, I doubt it."

He stroked his finger down my face, leaving a trail of heat. In the faint neon glow, I could see him smile, then lean in for another kiss, his strong, muscular arms wrapping around me, as he held me close, crushing my chest to his.

After helping me down, we dressed quickly, so we could put the lights back on. With my desire for Julian temporarily sated, I was able to pay more attention to the apartment, checking out the cupboards, and making notes of what I'd need to get. Blinds were at the top of my list.

Salon Affair

"I can get the contract off John tomorrow, and bring it to the salon if you like. Do you have the money for the deposit and rent?"

I nodded. "If you bring a laptop, I can do it via Internet, save waiting for a cheque to clear."

"The deposit goes into a scheme, so pay that one by cheque."

"Ok. After all that, when can I get the keys and move in? Any idea?"

"It's yours as soon as you've signed and paid."

"Don't I have to meet this John?"

He shook his head. "He's a professional landlord. Normally a letting agent would do all this for him, he doesn't usually have anything to do with his tenants. You'll deal only with a maintenance company, if there are any problems."

"Oh right. I didn't realise it would be so easy."

"Sometimes it's who you know Lily, that's what counts," he said, rather cryptically.

Chapter 6

Telling my parents I was leaving home was harder than I envisaged. They were ok in front of me, but I heard Mum crying in her bedroom, and my Dad comforting her, telling her that it was normal, and to be expected at my age. Mark had just grunted, and asked if he could move into my bedroom, which was larger than his, and had an ensuite. Lisa had thrown a bit of a strop, and had stomped off home, so I ended up spending the evening doing my grooming rituals alone in my room, dreaming about my new apartment.

I was busy the following day, with clients booked back to back right through the morning. I text Julian that I'd be free around two, and got on with my work, which unfortunately involved the fussiest old bat I'd ever encountered.

"The girl got my ears wet," she complained, throwing a look at Lottie, who rolled her eyes. *Yeah, she washed your hair. Hard to do without water,* I thought. I handed her a tissue, which she used to spend a good five minutes elaborately drying her ears. By the time I'd finished her hair, following her micro-managed instructions to the letter, I was drained and a bit cheesed off.

"That hair goes across more, and my old hairdresser did it a little higher," she pointed out. "I'm sure you want to get it exactly right."

Salon Affair

"Can I ask," I said, "why you didn't just stick with your old hairdresser rather than try and find a new one who does your hair exactly the same?"

"I fancied a change," she replied. *Kill me now.*

There must have been something in the air that day, as I heard Trystan repeatedly ask his client to lift her head up straight, and keep it still. I glanced over to see his client hunched over a magazine, her head flicking from side to side, as Trystan attempted to cut her hair. Frustration written all over his face. "Hun, I'm not gonna ask you again. I simply cannot cut your hair properly in this position, with you moving your head. You're gonna be wearing this cut for the next six weeks, so can I suggest you put the magazine down, and join in?"

"It's the only time I get to read magazines," she protested weakly, before looking up to see Trystan's annoyed face.

"They sell them in the little shop across the road. Now, head upright, and look straight ahead please. You can read during your blowdry, if you're that desperate." I suppressed a smile.

Julian arrived promptly, and followed me out to the staff room. I made him a coffee while he sorted out the papers that I'd need to sign, and set up his laptop. I quickly read through the tenancy agreement, and, spotting the clause about tenants needing credit checks, paused. "Do I need to pass a credit check?" I asked.

He shook his head. "No, John isn't too worried. I vouched for you. Told him you had a good job." I breathed a sigh of relief, and signed both copies. Julian handed one to me, and placed the other in a file, along with the deposit cheque. I logged into my bank, and transferred the first month's rent, noting that my pay from Gino Venti had gone in the day before, so I was quite flush.

"Congratulations," said Julian, handing me two sets of keys, and a thin file, which had instructions for the door code, and information regarding rubbish collection and council tax. "You're now a West End girl." He kissed me softly, a chaste, but prolonged kiss, only broken when we heard someone coming. We sprung apart moments before Tomme walked in.

"Put him down Lil," he said, no doubt noticing my flushed face, and guilty look.

"I've got a flat, right by you," I told him.

"Great. That'll make life easier. When you moving in, so that I can borrow stuff off you all the time?"

"Well, I'm off tomorrow and Friday, so I'll probably move in straightaway. There's a few things I need to get though."

"Is it furnished or unfurnished?"

"Furnished, but basic."

"You could go after work and make a list, then pick up what you need in the morning," Julian suggested.

"Are you around this evening?" I asked him. He shook his head.

"I've got to work. Sorry. Already promised I'd attend some meetings."

"I'll come with you," Tomme piped up. "I can help you measure up."

"Great, thanks. I don't suppose there's a tape measure here in the toolbox?" Tomme rooted through it, and triumphantly held one aloft.

Despite being mad busy, the afternoon dragged. Both Tomme and I were scheduled to work until seven. Thankfully he finished first, and had time for his fag and wee, as well as getting my coat, bag and flats ready for us to make a quick getaway.

He took in the foyer with a critical eye. "Been painted in the last year. Could do with some flowers or some art though, make it look posher." At least the lift didn't smell of wee.

Tomme was really impressed with the flat. "It's huge, and I love the open plan kitchen thing. You'll be able to chat while you cook me dinner," he stated, rather optimistically, I thought. He raked through the cupboards, checking out the cooking equipment, and crockery. "You need cleaning stuff, some vases, and there's no iron," he called out, after opening a drawer containing a built in ironing board. *Nifty*.

"Does Julian own this place then?" He asked.

"No, a friend of his. I had to pay the rent to Beta Limited." I called out as I noted down the window measurements.

The next morning, I went straight into Bromley to buy the items I needed. Mum had taken the car to work, so I phoned round the various man with a van adverts, and found someone free the next morning to move all my stuff. After packing up all my clothes and things, I decided to pop round and see how Aunt Doris was.

"So how's the new salon?" Doris began, after I'd made a pot of tea.

"Going great thanks. I designed a colour we're using for a big competition. My workmates are all lovely. It's all good."

"And how's that young man? Julian isn't it? Your Mum said he was a real dish."

"He's great. Found me a lovely apartment to rent near the salon."

"So you're moving up to town?"

I glanced up from the teapot, expecting to see an angry, or disappointed face, but Doris was beaming. "Yes," I replied, "tomorrow."

"Fabulous," she declared, "I'm jealous. I lived in Chelsea as a young girl. Loved it. Had a blast. Every youngster should live in the West End for a while."

"I don't think Mum's happy," I murmured.

"If you moved two doors down she'd still be upset about losing her baby girl, so don't take any notice. It's natural and normal to strike out on your own. She'll get over it soon, and be excited for you. She didn't take any notice of her parents when she went to live in Camden with some musician chap at just 18. Her Father was distraught at the time. All turned out alright though. People have to have their adventures before they settle down."

"I didn't know about that," I laughed, intrigued.

"Oh yes. Her Father was furious, convinced she'd end up in the white slave trade or something. I had to calm him down. Part of the problem was him making her do secretarial college. She wanted to be a hairdresser, as you know, and he wouldn't allow it. By the time she'd rebelled, it was a bit late really, as she'd met and married your Dad. That's why she always told you to follow your dreams."

"I knew Granddad didn't approve of hairdressing as a trade, and wouldn't allow her to do it. She'd have made a good hairdresser."

"Which is why you need to be successful. Don't forget I've got the money to back you when you're ready."

"You don't need to do that. Spend your money on yourself."

She laughed, "I couldn't spend it all if I tried. I've barely touched the last twenty years of royalties, let alone all the pensions Harry invested in."

"Royalties?" I knew her late husband had been a musician, and songwriter, but didn't know what he'd written. Doris didn't often talk about that side of him.

"Oh yes. I get payments twice a year or so. Whenever they use one of his songs, I get a payment. His music publisher called me yesterday to say that some company wants to use one of Harry's songs in an advert. I got quite a chunk last time that happened." She smiled, lost in her memories.

"So how come you live in a small house?" I asked.

"We used to live in Farnborough Park, but it was way too big for just the two of us, and not terribly convenient for the station, so we sold it, and downsized to this bungalow. Far easier to maintain as we got older."

I reeled with the news. I vaguely remembered being in a huge garden as a toddler. "Was I about four when you moved?" I asked.

"Yes, you weren't very old. We used some of the money to buy your Mum and Dad their house. Better than them having to pay a mortgage, especially when Mark came along, and your Mum had her hands full."

I was a little shocked. I knew my parents owned our house outright, and were fairly comfortably off, but I didn't know it was down to Doris. I began to regret being so secretive about my money troubles, and not allowing them to know how much of a muddle I'd got myself into. I'd hidden all the letters, and dealt with the collection agencies in secret. Thankfully, I'd paid it all off, and could breathe again.

Clutching Doris' frugal shopping list, I made my way to the big Waitrose at Bromley South to get both hers, and my own shopping for the week. With a basket perched on top of the trolley, I whizzed round quickly, before getting a taxi, first to Doris', then home.

We had a special family dinner that night, with Dad opening a bottle of bubbly to 'give me a good send off', as he put it. "I'm only twenty minutes away," I pointed out. "The way you lot are behaving, anyone would think I was off to Australia."

"It's a big thing, leaving home," said Dad, "something that should be celebrated properly."

"I'll celebrate when she's moved out," muttered Mark, prompting a clip round the head from Mum.

We'd no sooner finished eating when there was a knock at the door. I answered it, starting in surprise on seeing Matt standing there. "What are you doing here?" I demanded. "I've told you it's over." He had the grace to look a little sheepish.

"I know. I just wanted to see you before you left tomorrow, to wish you well."

"How did you know?" I demanded.

"Lisa told me. She's upset about you moving away."

"I can understand that, but why would that involve you?" *So that's how you've been keeping tabs on who I'm seeing and what I'm doing.*

"She asked me to try and talk you out of it, see sense if you like. Renting is just money down the drain Lily. If you really want to leave home, you could have moved into the new flat with me."

I stared at him, incredulous. "Matt, get it through your thick skull that we're over. I'm seeing someone else. I'm not moving in with him, because I want my own space, near my work, and in the middle of all the action. There's no way in God's green Earth I'm ever gonna live in a one room flat in the arse end of Orpington with you sitting in every night counting pennies."

"Well, the offer's there," he stated, ignorant of the stupidity of his proposal.

"Which I won't be taking up," I spat. "Goodbye Matt." I slammed the door in his face, and stomped back into the kitchen, my mood somewhat soured.

"What a silly man," Mum began, "he really never knew you at all did he?" They'd clearly heard every word of our conversation.

"I can't believe what a traitor Lisa's been. Telling him all my movements."

"She always liked him. Probably thought that if you ended up with him, you'd stay local and lonely forever," said Mark, astonishing me with his perception. He'd hit the nail on the head.

"Put it out of your mind, and look forward to tomorrow," soothed Mum. She'd got the day off too, so was helping me with the move. I couldn't wait to show her my new place. I knew she'd approve.

Salon Affair

The man with the van turned up early the next morning, and didn't take long to load all my bags and boxes. I gave him the address, and my number, and watched as he set off. Mum and I got the train, as it was quicker and easier than driving, and meant we'd get there before him.

She oo'd and ah'd over the flat, when we arrived, telling me it was far better than she'd imagined. She checked out the bathroom, declaring it 'lovely', and managed to introduce us to two of my new neighbours by leaving the front door open while she snapped pictures of the inner hallway.

Van man arrived at the same time as Julian, who helped him with all the bags and boxes, while Mum went off to find a Starbucks for a round of coffee and cookies. I watched his muscles bulge as he carried a box of shoes into the bedroom. "Like what you see?" He asked, smiling at the wanton desire clearly evident on my face.

"You really are sex on legs, but you know that already don't you?" I replied. His grin got wider.

"I could say the same about you. Is your Mum planning to stay all day?"

"Fraid so. At least long enough to help me unpack. I need to do it today, as I've got a run of six days from tomorrow. She won't be here this evening though," I smiled seductively, "do you have to work tonight?"

"Nope. I can earmark this evening for providing a takeaway, and several orgasms." *Belly squeeze*.

The mood was broken by Mum returning with drinks and snacks. She fussed over Julian, giving him an extra cake and the biggest cookie. "I think you're spoiling him," I told her as Julian happily worked his way through a chocolate brownie.

"Well, all that heavy lifting he's done, he deserves a treat." *Yeah, I know what sort of treat I'd like to give him...*

After he'd left, with a peck on the cheek, and a promise to be back by seven, Mum and I began the task of unpacking. It was quicker than I'd envisaged, and soon enough we were done, the boxes disposed of in the rubbish area downstairs, and the new kettle christened. The new blinds were up, and worked perfectly, and the flat had taken on a more homely feel.

Mum hugged me hard before she left. Satisfied that I had everything I needed, she tried to say a cheery 'take care', but her voice cracked slightly, betraying her. I hugged her again. "I'll be fine. Don't you worry," I told her.

"I know, I'm just being a bit silly. Ignore me," she said, her eyes glossy.

I watched her walk down the street from my window, dabbing her eyes with a tissue. I made another tea, and sat on my new sofa. The enormity of what I'd done crashed over me. *I live alone, in the West End, with a great job, gorgeous boyfriend, and a bit of cash in the bank.* It had only been a few weeks since I'd sat in my parents' house watching Saturday night telly with my fat, boring ex.

I was fresh out of the shower, wearing only a dressing gown when Julian arrived at seven, bearing bags of Chinese takeaway, and a bottle of bubbly. I'd lowered the blinds, and switched on the uplighters, to make the room intimate, and I hoped, romantic. With some background music playing, we ate sitting cross-legged on the sofa, chatting about the area, the salon, and our jobs. I found out that Julian had seven bars, three nightclubs, and three shops.

"So how come you live so frugally?" I probed. Trystan's comment had been bothering me.

"I plough all the money back into the business," he replied. "Did you expect me to live in a penthouse and bathe in champagne or something?"

"Well, yes, I suppose so."

"I will do someday, but right now, I'd rather be starting more businesses. I'm barely home, so it seems a bit pointless spending cash on a huge place. As long as I've got a comfy bed, and a big telly, I'm happy. I don't really do 'flash'. I'd rather buy another wine bar than a Ferrari."

"What do you want from life?" It was a bit of a deep question, but I thought I'd take advantage, if he was in the mood to open up.

"I want to be filthy rich," he answered without a pause, you?"

"You know mine. I want to be a rich and famous hairdresser."

We were interrupted by his phone ringing. He glanced at the screen, then answered it. "Hi, what's up?" A muffled male voice said something I couldn't make out. "Not tonight I can't," replied Julian, "I'm with my girlfriend." The muffled voice garbled something else. I wasn't listening any longer, too busy processing being called his 'girlfriend'. I smiled to myself, relaxing back onto the sofa, while Julian waffled on about a maintenance issue. *The gorgeous Julian Alexander calls me his girlfriend.*

I watched him talking, no longer listening to his conversation, caught up in the vision of his lean, relaxed body, a man comfortable in his own skin. His strong, talented hands gesticulated as he spoke, before scrubbing at the day old stubble on his jaw, and raking through his soft, dark blonde hair. *This Greek God of a man is mine.* The snarky voice inside my head jumped in to caution me, *for tonight at least. He'll get bored with you soon enough.*

He ended his call, and put his phone onto the coffee table. "Sorry about that. Rashish, the manager of one of my bars, thought it'd be a good time to discuss some changes we're planning to make to the kitchen area. I told him about Tower 42, and we decided to trial the concept." He popped the last bit of prawn toast in his mouth. I watched his Adam's apple bob as he swallowed, the movement inexplicably adding to my arousal. He really was all man.

He saw me looking, his eyes gazed into mine, betraying his lust. Without breaking eye contact, he undid the tie of my robe, pulling it open to expose me. "I want you in the bedroom," he rumbled, his voice low. He stood, pulling me up with him, and led me into the bedroom.

Slipping the robe off my shoulders, he stood back to gaze at my naked body. "You really are exquisite," he murmured, sending a thrill through me. "I really, really want to taste you. Lay down."

I complied, lowering myself down onto the bed, watching as he kicked off his clothes, hastily flinging them on the floor. He knelt at the foot of the bed, and slowly kissed his way up the inside of my leg, until he reached the apex. I shivered slightly as he pressed a featherlight kiss there, before stopping, and repeating the routine up my other leg. He flashed his movie star grin, as he nestled in between my legs, and began a slow, sensuous torture of my sex, running his tongue in a figure of eight between my lips, before holding me open to tease my clit with long, slow licks.

As the sensations intensified, I grasped at the sheets, my back arching off the bed, his mouth causing white heat to course through my body. He was merciless in his ministrations, each lick and suck pushing me further and further out of my body. He hummed with pleasure as he lapped at me.

Just when I thought it couldn't get any more intense, he slipped a finger inside me, curling it slightly to rub my spot, sending me into the stratosphere. With the softest little flick of his tongue over my clit, I fell.

He watched me come, unable to take his eyes off my pulsating sex. Under his gaze, I felt incredibly sexy, as opposed to the embarrassment and self consciousness I'd felt with former lovers, who hadn't made it as abundantly clear how much they'd adored my body.

"You are so juicy," he declared, as my orgasm began to subside, "and I really need to fuck you." He slammed into me, rearing up to look between us as his cock rammed me repeatedly, pushing my body towards another, even bigger climax. Abruptly, he stopped, and pulled out. "On your front," he growled. Shakily, I rolled over, letting him pull up my hips, and thrust back into me.

He held my waist in an iron grip, as he pummelled into me, his fingers digging into my flesh in a show of barely restrained animal passion. I moaned as I felt my orgasm begin it's unstoppable rise. He must have felt it too, as he sped up, his balls slapping my clit over and over again.

I came with a scream, my arms giving way, leaving me face down on the pillow. He followed suit, sounding like a wounded animal, as he stilled, gave one final buck, then collapsed onto my back, pressing me into the mattress.

For a few minutes, we both lay silent, the only sounds, our combined heavy breaths. I felt his heart hammering in his chest, as his delicious weight held me.

"Wow," he muttered.

"Yeah," I agreed.

More silence.

"Am I squashing you?" He asked in a more normal tone.

"Yeah, a bit," I admitted. He rolled off me, leaving me instantly bereft. "Drink?" I asked. I needed some water for my parched throat.

"Please. Something cold. Water's fine."

I cleaned up in the bathroom, and grabbed two bottles of water, before turning off the lights, and wandering back into the bedroom. He looked delicious, all post sex, and mussed up. I could've eaten him alive. I handed him a bottle, and watched as he glugged it down, clearly as thirsty as I was. He held his arm out for me as I slipped into bed beside him, initially careful not to crowd him. He wrapped his arms around my shoulders, and pulled me in close.

"Are you staying the night?" I asked.

He pulled away to look at me. "Of course, unless you preferred me to go?"

"No, of course not," I replied, before yawning, and snuggling back into his chest.

"Why did you think I wouldn't stay?" He murmured. I just shrugged, too comfortable and sleepy to reply.

"You have no idea how gorgeous you are, have you?" Was the last thing I heard him say before I dozed off.

I awoke early the next morning. Strangely excited at waking up in my new flat. I glanced over to see Julian fast asleep, his face relaxed and boyish, his sensual mouth slightly parted. I slipped out of bed silently, so as not to wake him. It was only six am, and without my commute, I wouldn't need to leave till about half eight.

Keeping quiet, I put a pot of fresh coffee on, and had a quick shower while it was brewing. Wrapping my wet hair in a turban, I wondered how I'd dry it without waking him up. I needn't have worried, as he padded naked into the kitchen while I was pouring my drink.

"Morning beautiful," he beamed. *How can he look so good first thing in the morning?*

"Good morning beautiful yourself," I trilled, returning his grin. "Ready for some coffee?"

"Some coffee first would be good," he murmured, glancing down at the morning erection that I was trying to ignore. *Shame to waste it though..*

An hour later, I poured two, rather stewed coffees. I grimaced at mine, and made a fresh pot. My poor hair had dried into a rather knotty mad-woman style, and I was, for want of a better description, sore.

Chapter 7

The next couple of weeks passed by in a blur. Work was manic, we submitted our entry to L'Oreal, delighted with our efforts, despite Gray being poorly on the Sunday we had the photo shoot for it.
"Which one of you bitches thought my Sunday off'd be the best day to do this," grumbled Tomme, arriving wearing dark glasses to disguise his bloodshot eyes.
"I," cough, "did," Gray answered through another coughing fit.
"Thought I looked rough," growled Tomme, "you look like you should be in bed Gracie."
"I think I've come down with a cold, that's all," snapped Gray. "I've worked with worse."
The pictures were phenomenal. Our model was a dancer, and had the long limbs, and innate grace that only a professional ballerina can project. The camera loved her. Anthony had dressed and accessorised her in a silvery grey Ghost dress, with delicate silver and amethyst jewellery he'd 'borrowed' from a hook-up of his who ran a concession in Selfridges.
I had to admit, as much as I loved the stretch root look on my long, loose cuts, it worked exceptionally well on Trystan's precision cut, as Michael and I had worked hard to balance and blend the colour fade perfectly. When the photographer showed us all the images he'd captured, I felt

a swell of pride. Even Gray seemed to perk up a little, when he saw what we'd all created.

I was still buzzing from it when Julian arrived at my flat to pick me up. We were going to one of his bars to test out the new 'European tapas' idea that they were trialling. "You look happy, I take it all went well today?" He asked as I opened the front door.

"It sure did. Seeing the pictures, I really think we're in with a strong chance this year."

"Excellent. I'll keep my fingers crossed. You ready?"

We caught a taxi over to Chelsea, to a bar I'd never seen before. It was reminiscent of the one in South Molten Street, insofar as the interior was similar, and the bar area almost identical. A stylishly dressed Indian man came out to greet us as we walked in. "Julian, how nice to see you, and who is this?" He asked, smiling at me.

"This is my girlfriend, Lily," Julian replied, "Lily, this is Rashish, he manages the bar for my business partner and I." *Business partner?* I kept quiet until we were seated at a little table, and handed the menu. Julian asked Rashish for a bottle of Lanson, which he scurried off to get.

"I didn't know you had a business partner?" I said. "I thought all the bars were yours."

He laughed. "I'd never get a moment's peace. No, all of my businesses have a partner involved. A different one for each. I front the money, and lend my expertise, and they gradually buy me out over five years. That way I don't work too hard, but still make decent money." *Hmm, that's not the same as 'owning' businesses,* I thought, rather disappointed. He must have seen my thoughts reflected in my face. "Lily, I make a great living, and get to keep my life in balance. Don't think I'm not ambitious, I am, it's just that I'm good at setting up businesses as opposed to running them. Talking of which, my partner just walked in. I'll introduce you." I glanced up to see a glamorous blonde make her way over to our table, beaming a smile at Julian.

"Hey babe, nice to see you. Who's your friend?" She flashed me a fake smile. *Bitch*.

"This is Lily, my girlfriend," he said, "Lily, this is Gemma." I was grateful to him for putting the insincere bitch in her place. Gemma extended a hand out to me.

"Nice to meet you," she said, clearly through gritted teeth.

"We're here to test out the new food line," Julian told her. "If it works, I'll introduce it in all the bars."

"So is Lily another aspiring bar owner?" She asked.

"No, I'm a hairdresser," I told her, puzzled by the question. She seemed to relax a little. *Maybe she thinks I want to take over her bar..*

"Lily isn't work related," Julian snapped at her.

"If you say so Babe, but we're all creatures of habit," she purred, a wolfish smile on her face. "Enjoy your meal, you'll be paying for your champagne next week." With that cryptic remark, she sashayed off, giving a little fingertip wave over her shoulder as she went.

"What on earth was all that about?" I asked Julian.

"It's her last payment to me this weekend, then ownership reverts to her. I think she's a little jealous of you."

"Certainly seemed that way." I buried my nose in the menu, my mind racing. *Was she an ex? Or did she harbour an unrequited crush? How am I gonna wheedle that information out of him without being a jealous bitch? Hmm*.

We ordered our food from a nervous Rashish. Julian was as cool as a cucumber as he sipped his champagne. "What's up?" He demanded.

"Is Gemma an ex of yours?" I blurted, cringing slightly at how juvenile I sounded.

He nodded. "Yes, a very long time ago, for a very short time. Enough to discover that we were better as friends, and business partners, rather than lovers. I found her way too high maintenance, she found me rather boring and tedious. Her words, if I'm honest."

"You're neither boring, nor tedious," I retorted. "What a bitch."

He laughed. "Thank you, that's high praise, coming from you. Want to know what I think?" He leaned in close, looking round to make sure we weren't overheard, "I think I'm not big enough, or black enough. That's what she really likes." I snorted with laughter, successfully breaking any tension between us.

"You're such a bitch," I sniggered. "I'm meant to be the hairdresser round here. You'd give the salon queens at work a run for their money." He flashed his movie star smile.

I barely saw Julian the rest of the week. I was working like a demon, and so was he. I cooked a meal for three of the boys from work one evening, so that they could criticise my decor choices.

"What possessed you to buy brown cushions Lil?" Anthony demanded. "You need some splashes of colour in here, and some texture. Purple fur would've lifted this room completely."

"I thought leopard skin would've worked great," Michael butted in, "make it a bit edgier."

"You bitches have no taste," declared Tomme. "I told her she needed taupe cushions. Then she goes and buys brown. I do my best to help, but goodness knows what we're gonna do with her."

"I'll supervise any further shopping trips, can't have that delicious man of yours thinking you've got awful taste," Anthony told me, helping himself to more chilli and rice.

"At least she can cook for him," Michael said, cleaning his bowl with some bread. "Most women have no idea how to look after a man. Lucky bitches still get the best ones."

"I am in the room you know. You're gonna have to stop talking like I'm not here. I like my brown cushions, thank you very much. Julian liked them too," I paused, "especially when he stacks them under my hips to get me in the right position for a good, hard shag," I added, rather mischievously.

"Ew, that's gross," said Tomme, pulling a face. The other two made gagging noises, for effect. I poured them some more wine, pleased with myself.

"So what've you got planned for your day off tomorrow?" Anthony asked.

"Gonna go meet my Mum, have a bit of lunch, visit my aunt, then seeing Julian in the evening," I said. I was really looking forward to going home to Bromley, as I'd barely been there since moving out.

"I just hope Gray makes it in. He really doesn't seem to be shaking off his cold," Michael mused, "it's not like him to be ill so much. Him and Chris are health freaks. Wheatgrass smoothies and shit like that."

"He's been run down since he had that terrible flu last year. Needs a holiday somewhere hot," Anthony chimed in.

"That won't happen. You know what a tight bitch Chris is. Makes Gray work like a dog. Poor fucker never gets a break," Tomme revealed. "All Chris is interested in is posing amongst the gay glitterati, pretending he's someone special, when we all know he's just a PC Plod, who got lucky."

"I didn't know he was a copper. I thought he worked in an office." The others all laughed at my statement.

"Works in the diversity department. Drives a desk. Being quite the special snowflake, he complains loudly about the smallest perceived slight against the gay community. Think they stuck him in that job because he was a shit copper." Michael was scathing.

The following night, Julian came over bearing an Indian takeaway, and bottles of beer. I told him about the boy's opinions of my decor, and my response. "God knows what they'd say about my place then, I don't even own a cushion," he laughed, "How come only three of them came round?"

"Gray's still poorly, and Trystan had a date."

"I saw Gray yesterday evening, leaving the salon. He's lost a hell of a lot of weight. What's wrong with him?"

"Dunno. Keeps catching colds. Think he needs a break, but the others said his partner won't let him. Costs us a fortune, taking a holiday, as we don't get paid."

"No paid holiday? Blimey, your boss has it easy. Sixty percent of everything you lot do, plus almost no employment costs. I think we need to start a salon, don't you?"

I stared at him, incredulous. "I don't think it's that easy..."

"Of course it is. We find a premises, fit it out, and Bob's your uncle."

"Nowadays, we don't even pay for fit-outs, there's a haircare company that does it for you, in return for using their products," I told him, Gray's opinion of Sugar popping into my head. *Great for a start-up.*

"I'll ask around, see if anyone's got a suitable retail unit. In the meantime, maybe you should explore this product company."

"Okay, are you sure about this?"

"Of course, I mean, we're great together, aren't we?" His eyes probed mine. He seemed to want my approval. We were great together, I really enjoyed our time together, and we had a fantastic sex life. If I was being truthful, I'd fallen in love with him, not quite able to believe that, just maybe, he felt the same way about me.

"Yes, we are," I confirmed. I watched the tension of the moment leave his shoulders, and he beamed a smile.

"Good, that's settled then, now, how about that early night you promised?"

The sex that night was intense, cementing our plans to have a future together. It seemed that we found a new

Salon Affair

closeness which hadn't been there before. Afterwards, I lay sated in his arms. "Do you have any kinks?" I asked.

"Everyone has a kink," he replied. Surprised, I propped myself up on my elbow to look at him.

"So what's yours?"

He blushed. *Adorable.* "It's a bit embarrassing, but there's something I've always wanted to do, since I was a teenager, in fact, and I've never had the opportunity....until now."

"Go on."

"I'd like a topless haircut."

I snorted with laughter, and fell back onto the bed. *Topless haircut? Is that the worst you can come up with?*

"Why is that so funny? I'm sure it's quite a common fantasy." His blush deepened.

"Is it? I've never come across it before. Where did it come from?"

"When I was a teenager, a woman called Tricia used to cut my hair. I was always mesmerised by her boobs. So near, and yet so far." He had a misty eyed expression as he recalled the memory.

"Anything else part of the fantasy? Stockings and suspenders? High heels?" I was curious.

"Oh god, no. She used to wear a pinafore, and Dr Scholls."

I howled with laughter at the thought of Mr Gorgeous getting all hot and bothered over a Sweaty Betty*.

*Note. A Sweaty Betty is the common term for a post-menopausal, old fashioned hairdresser, who works in a salon which caters for elderly ladies. It is always derogatory, and is used as a sneer by hipster, fashion conscious stylists. Nobody knows who the original Sweaty Betty was.

"So you want me to wear a pinny and orthopaedic sandals for your kinky haircut?"

He laughed. "No, some high heels and stockings would be very nice though."

"I'll bring my scissors home from work," I said, before kissing him.

The next day, I stopped off at an Ann Summers on my way home from work. I perused the sexy dress-up outfits, eventually finding what I was looking for, as part of a sexy maid's ensemble. With a pair of black fishnet hold-ups, and some black lace crotchless knickers in my basket, I scurried over to the checkout, rather furtively, hoping I didn't bump into any clients in there.

Back home, I laid out a cutting square, my comb and scissors, and a neck razor, and placed the stool from my dressing table in the kitchen, as well as the large mirror. After a quick shower, I dressed in just the knickers, stockings, the pinny from the maid's outfit, and my Prada stilettos. Satisfied, I slipped my dressing gown on to cover it all up, and made a cup of tea while I waited for Julian.

He arrived, freshly showered from the gym. I took his hand, and led him into the kitchen. "Welcome to my salon sir," I said, playfully. He looked delighted. I sat him down on the stool, in front of the mirror, and wrapped the cape around him. Throwing my robe over the back of a chair, I stood beside him, in just stockings, heels, and a tiny pinafore. I watched as he took a deep swallow.

"You look sensational," he rumbled, his voice deep and hoarse, as he drank in the sight before him.

"Thank you. Now, what are we doing with your cut today?" Inside, I was thrilled at the effect I was having on him. I needed him to crave me, as much as I craved him. This approach was clearly working.

"Just a trim, actually, we could scrap the haircut, and just go straight to the massive fuck I'm going to give you," he said. I smiled.

"Now now, that's not the fantasy. You have to sit and wait while I do the cut." I paused. "I think I'll just do a light trim." I began to work on his now familiar hair, grasping it firmly as I worked, concentrating to avoid taking a chunk out of my fingers. I looked up, and saw him watching me intently in the mirror, his eyes darkened with lust.

As I moved around him to cut the sides and front, I stood closer than normal, so that my nipples bobbed about six inches from his face. He growled, actually growled, before sliding his hand up my leg. "No touching the staff," I admonished. I was turned on too, and already soaked. It wasn't easy to do a haircut as foreplay, and I'd only done half, so I couldn't leave him lopsided. He dropped his hand back into his lap.

"Is it nearly done?" He whined.

"What are you? Twelve years old?" I laughed. "No, I've only done half. Be patient, and stop fidgeting."

"You haven't seen the effect this is having on me," he murmured, before pulling the gown across to show me the tent in his jogging bottoms.

"He sure seems perky tonight," I quipped, before resuming the haircut, moving with practised ease around Julian's head. I worked on the other side, checking that I'd levelled it up by standing behind him, and watching in the mirror as I ran my fingers through to feel the weight. My eyes caught his, as he stared intently, with a slightly pained expression. I could feel the heat radiating from him. A film of sweat formed on his skin, beading slightly on his forehead. He whimpered quietly, evidence of his erotic torture.

I cleaned up the neckline before moving to the front. I stood directly in front of him, holding his fringe firmly as I chipped into it. I knew my nipples were within capturing distance of his talented mouth, and I was definitely starting to crave my own release. Just the strength of his own arousal was an enormous turn on.

"Lily, stop, now.." He seemed in pain. I dropped the piece of hair I was holding, sweeping it back off his forehead quickly with my fingers.

"Shit, fuck," he proclaimed, leaning forward.

"What on earth is wrong?" I asked, worried that I'd hurt him or something. He put his head in his hands, worrying me further.

"This is so fucking embarrassing."

"What?" He stayed silent. I pulled his hand away from his face. "Tell me what's wrong? Did I hurt you?"

"No, you didn't hurt me," he sounded pained, "but you made me....come."

"Sorry, I'm not with you." I didn't have a clue what he was on about.

"I came in my pants. Like a fucking teenager. Sooo fucking embarrassing." He raised his head, his face burning red. I wanted to laugh, but I kept a lid on it. Inside I was high fiving myself. *I just caused this beautiful man to completely lose control. Wow.* "Don't look so fucking pleased with yourself over it, it's mortifying," he snapped.

"I'm just wondering if I've had that effect on anyone else while I've cut their hair," I mused.

"Probably." He sat back up, and I finished off his fringe. When I removed the cape, I saw for myself the evidence of his premature ejaculation. There was a dark stain on his grey joggers, and his erection was back to full strength.

"You can touch now," I murmured, desperate for him to relieve some of the pressure building within me. He simultaneously captured a nipple in his mouth, and slid his hand up between my legs, discovering that my lacy knickers were crotchless. He caressed my clit with featherlight strokes, rhythmically sliding his finger over it, lubricated by my own arousal.

He lifted his hips slightly to help me pull down his joggers, releasing an iron hard erection. Without further preamble, I lowered myself onto it, grateful for the crotchlessness of my knickers. I sank down to the root, feeling the wide crest hit my sweet spot, sending white heat coursing through my veins. He gasped as I began to move, holding onto his shoulders to steady myself as I slammed down repeatedly onto his cock.

Julian pinched and rolled my nipples as I lost myself in the sensations that only he alone could inflict. I went into a trance-like state as my body centred in the space that he was invading. We came together, me with a shout, him with a primal grunt which reverberated through me as I slumped onto his chest, my face buried in the crook of his neck.

"You. Are. A. Goddess," he said, rather forcefully. I hummed with satisfaction against his skin.

"Well, that makes you a sex god then," I purred.

"I can't believe you did that to me, made me lose control like that."

"I'll take it as a compliment," I murmured, before pulling back to give him a big kiss on the lips. He pulled me closer, deepening the kiss, clinging to me like a drowning man. I'd never felt so connected to another human being as I did in that moment.

****

The next day, I'd just finished a client, and was in the staff room making a coffee, when my phone dinged with a text from Julian.

Have found the perfect shop to rent. What time are you finishing, we can go view

I quickly text back that I wouldn't be done until six, thinking it would be too late. He replied immediately that six would be fine, and he'd pick me up at the salon.

All afternoon, I hugged the secret to myself, hardly daring to dream that it would become a reality. The day got even better when we received word that we'd been chosen as semi finalists for the colour trophy. "Drinks on me after work," Gray proclaimed.

"I'm out tonight straight from work, but I might join you a bit later," I said.

"Where're you off to?" Trystan asked.

"Just meeting Julian after work," I lied, "I won't need long." I realised as soon as I said it, that it had come out wrong.

"I'll give him some tips on lasting a bit longer," laughed Trystan. *Bitch.*

I was antsy all afternoon, counting down the clients until six. When I waved off the last one, I breathed a sigh of relief, and quickly changed into my flats.

Julian was waiting at the desk for me, charming a very doe-eyed Paulina. She was all coquettish as she printed off my takings slip, ignoring me, and talking to Julian about Florence. I grabbed it out of her hand, checked it briefly, before shoving it in my handbag, and practically dragging Julian out of the door.

"Hey, what's up?" He demanded, as I stomped down the road.

"You were flirting," I seethed.

"No, she was flirting. I was just being polite," he pointed out, before pulling me into a kiss. My anger melted immediately. "I can't help it if women find me irresistible." He grinned as he said it, to let me know he was joking with me.

"As long as it's only me that you find irresistible back, then I suppose it doesn't matter," I told him, waiting for his assurance.

"I think I demonstrated that last night," he murmured, before pecking my cheek. I'd been a little surprised that he'd insisted on going home afterwards, telling me he needed to be up early for a meeting, but I'd accepted it gracefully, as he'd worn me out, and I'd really needed to sleep.

Salon Affair

   We walked in silence for a while. "Where're we going?" I asked eventually. He grasped my hand.
   "Mayfair."
   I gasped, "Won't that be really expensive?"
   He shook his head. "Not necessarily, it's a small unit, and sometimes it depends on who you know. This unit's 30 thou a year, which isn't much, for the area. Remember you'll be able to charge a lot round there." We carried on, up North Audley Street, until we reached a small turning. Julian led me down there, and we stopped outside a small salon. I took in the pretty, arched shopfront, blown away by the location. He pulled a set of keys out of his pocket, and a scrap of paper with the alarm code written on it. While Julian busied himself unlocking the door, I stepped back to take in the whole view of the frontage. Remnants of the old sign remained, a ghostly reminder of someone called Roland James' dream of owning a Mayfair salon.
   I followed Julian inside. He flipped on some lights, and went over to a cupboard to silence the bleeping alarm system. After a few moments, the noise stopped. I cast my eyes around the room. It felt a little eerie, gazing over the remnants of what might have once been a vibrant, busy salon. The mirrors were of a style popular in the 80's, strangely shaped, with little points in the centre, and right hand edge. There were five in a row along one wall, with a single shelf running underneath all of them, in a sort of communal styling shelf.
   The chairs were grey, scruffy from years of use, the backs coated in thick crusts of hairspray. I walked further into the room. The basins were peach coloured, and set into a solid bar type arrangement, with what looked like more styling chairs underneath. The floor was tiled with grey ceramic tiles, which looked like they'd seen better days. "What do you think?" Julian asked softy. He was watching my reaction closely.
   "What happened to the previous owner?" I asked.

"Apparently he died. His estate was left to charity, who put the building up for auction. A friend of mine bought it. I gather it's been empty about a year or so, while his estate was sorted out. Come look over here." He grasped my hand and led me through a door to the left of the reception area, and up a flight of stairs. At the top was a small landing, and two doors. He opened the first to reveal what had once been a beauty room, with a hand sink in the corner. The other room was identical. "You could rent these out, get extra income from them, or even run them yourself," he enthused.

We went back downstairs, where I checked out the small staff room, and utility area. Everything was scruffy, and fairly old, but beautifully laid out. *So much potential*, I thought.

"How much will this cost?" I asked.

"There's no premium, just three months rent deposit, three months rent in advance. Standard stuff really." *Fifteen thousand pounds. I can ask Doris to help.* I walked over to the reception desk. There was an elderly computer sitting on it. I switched it on, and waited for it to grind through its boot-up. Julian watched as I clicked through to find the old records, discovering a client list of around 1600 names, complete with addresses and numbers.

"A decent start of a marketing list," I said, before closing it all down again, and switching the computer off.

"So what do you think?" He asked again.

"I think it's amazing," I told him, "with so much potential. Needs a refit though. I don't think the fittings reflect the location, and certainly don't make the most of this building."

"I'm happy to back you. I think you'd do fantastic here, and this building is a real find."

"I might not need it, let me talk to Sugar hair, and see what they're offering," I replied, ignoring the slight scowl crossing Julian's face. I carried on wandering around, mentally imagining working there.

"I want to help you," he said softly, pulling me into his arms. "I want the best for you, to make you happy, see you achieve your dreams." He kissed me, a passionate, loving kiss. He poured so much emotion into that kiss, I believed that he was as in love with me, as I was in him. The salon could be the shared endeavour that tied us together.

Reluctantly, we locked up the salon, and headed back to South Molten Street to meet the boys at the wine bar for our celebratory drink.

"That was quick Lil, it doesn't take him long does it?" exclaimed Tomme, clearly a bit pissed already. "I hope you're giving him a proper workout. Don't want him switching sides now, just to get some decent lovin."

Julian just grinned, and went off to pick us up some more wine and glasses from the bar. Trystan pulled up two more chairs, squeezing them around the small table. I sat down. "Gurl is working those jeans," he said, gazing at Julian's rear as he leaned over the bar to talk to the barman.

"He's not a 'gurl', and get your eyes off his bum. It's strictly one way traffic, besides, it's mine," I told him. The others all cackled. Trystan ignored me.

"Almost a bubble butt, and I bet it's as juicy as a peach," he mused.

Gray led a toast to our success at reaching the regional finals. London was the most fiercely fought of all the regions, and the London winner was usually favourite to win the national final. Julian sat quietly as we planned our approach for the next stage of the contest. We were keeping everything the same as our photo session. Michael and I would retouch the colour the day before, and Trystan would check the cut. At the contest itself, Tomme would just do the finish. Anthony decided he'd look for a new outfit for the styling, but if not, he'd use the same dress with new accessories.

"I'm thinking more chiffon, so she can dance down the catwalk, swooshing a filmy dress around," he told us. We all nodded in agreement.

"How on earth do you guys come up with all these ideas?" Julian asked, "I wouldn't have a clue where to start."

"We're creative beings, darling," said Gray, "it just flows out of us. We can't help being fabulous." He raised his glass, "To the greatest hairdressers in London." We all clinked and drank.

Chapter 8

I called the Sugar headquarters the next day. I was put through to a woman with a strong northern accent. "Hi babe, what can I do for you?" She drawled. I explained that I was planning a new salon in Mayfair, and wanted to explore the products and services that Sugar offered. As soon as I said Mayfair, she seemed a lot more interested, and suggested we meet for lunch so she could run through the concept. We arranged mid-day the following day, my day off. In the meantime, Julian had contacted his friend, and told him we wanted the salon. I also had to find a solicitor to check through the lease, which was easy, as my Mum's firm would do it quickly for a good price. I rung her from the loo, and told her about the new salon, to be greeted with a stunned silence.

"Hello, Mum, you still there?" I whispered, so that I wasn't overheard.

"Yes, yes, I'm still here. It sounds....fantastic. Are you sure about wanting this?"

"Totally sure," I replied. I'd already mentally decorated it, staffed it, and done my first celebrity hair interview for the hairdressers journal.

"Ok, I'll text you the office details that you'll need to pass onto the freeholder. Maybe come to dinner tonight? We can discuss this a bit more."

I went over there that evening, partly to enjoy one of Mum's roasts, and partly to tell them about the salon. Both Mum and Dad sounded cautiously pleased for me, and offered to help in any way they could. "And how's things with Julian?" Mum asked.

"Great thanks. We're getting on really well. He's a million miles away from Matt." I thought back to the previous night, Julian taking me to a little bistro after we'd left the wine bar, the fun bistro owner entertaining everyone with operatic songs while we ate fabulous Italian food. We'd had a great time.

"He seems very enamoured by you," Mum pointed out.

"We're enamoured by each other," I told her, a bit embarrassed by the conversation, "and he really believes in me. He's in no doubt that I can do this. He even offered to back me."

"Sounds like you can't go wrong," said Dad, before changing the subject to asking about my new flat. Mum had already filled him in on a lot of details it seemed.

"Seen Lisa?" my brother piped up.

I shook my head. "Not even spoken to her since I found out she'd been telling Matt all my business. I should make it up with her, but life just seems so busy right now, and I don't think she'd want to get 'dressed up' and meet me in town." I made air quotes around the words dressed up.

"Maybe it's best to leave things to blow over for a little while," Mum counselled.

"She's probably cross because your life's exciting right now, while she's sitting getting fatter every night in that hideous romper suit she wears," Mark pointed out. We both sniggered, rather nastily.

"Don't be so mean, you two," Mum scolded, which made us both snigger even more.

The next day, I met with Charlotte and Charlie Sugar at noon in a little coffee shop in Shepherds Market to discuss the new salon. Julian wouldn't be able to get there till half twelve, so we had a coffee, and discussed the Sugar Concept.

Salon Affair

"Basically, we become your partners, help you through the fit out, initial start up, and all that. We guide you on staffing, and we even train staff on the Sugar methodology. We set you up a website, handle your PR, sign writing, and even the printing. In return, you agree to stock and use our products for the term of our contract. It's really quite simple and straightforward." Charlie was persuasive as he spoke in a curious accent, a mixture of American and Northern English. He was a funny looking little man, with a revolting pencil moustache, skinny, but with a paunch, in direct contrast with his fairly attractive wife.

"Because it's such a prestigious location, we'd be able to offer you a choice of furnishings from our premium brochure." She pulled out a folder and handed it to me. I flicked through it. It was fairly ordinary REM salon stuff. I'd seen it at my local wholesaler for sale. The pictures all looked ok, mainly because the salons had been staged, and were new. My experience at Gavin Roberts had shown me how quickly stuff got wrecked in a salon. The fittings in Gino Venti were a whole other level. I was still looking through when Julian arrived. I introduced everyone, and ordered more coffees from the rather surly Polish waitress.

I outlined the deal to Julian, who frowned slightly when I handed him the folder. "So when you say 'contract', what exactly do you mean?" He demanded. Businessman Julian was new to me, a side of him I'd not seen before. It was sexy.

"Well, we front all the set up costs, so we require a contractual agreement that you'll purchase our products exclusively for a set amount of time," said Charlotte, smiling warmly at Julian. "We've now got fourteen salons operating under the Sugar label in London, customers look to it as an assurance of quality, rather like Anthony Mascolo did in the eighties with Toni and Guy. The difference is that we front the cost, they don't. It means we get behind talented people who wouldn't be able to afford a Toni and Guy franchise."

"I'd like to see a copy of the contract," Julian snapped.

"Certainly. I'll email one to you. In the meantime, you can read reviews from other salon owners on our website. We have over thirty salons in and around Leeds. We're aiming to become the biggest players in London too. We're currently in talks with some of the biggest and best known salons around, Nicky Clarke, Trevor Sorbie, Gino Venti, all of them are hoping to become Sugar Salons." *Liar.*

"Really? I didn't know Gino Venti was becoming part of Sugar." I hadn't mentioned that I worked there.

"Oh yes, they've been begging us. It'll raise their profile enormously. They know they can't compete with Ten Hair otherwise. Ten start their fit out next week. Charlie's done an amazing job planning their salon," Charlotte gushed, gazing with adoration at her ugly husband. "He's so talented at salon design, a real expert. People can't believe how wonderful their salons look when he's worked his magic."

"I'm sure," muttered Julian throwing a rather disdainful look over at the gormless Charlie. "I'd need to see the contract first before we go any further."

Charlotte wasn't deterred. She handed me a product brochure. "You'd get the grade A package to start up. It has three of each colour and six each of the products in our range, plus everything you need for back bar. We provide Sugar branded towels, gowns and dryers. Basically everything you need to begin trading. Supplies are easy to re-order from our warehouse, and are delivered within three days."

I looked through the brochure. It listed out their colour range, which only consisted of forty colours. The packaging of the products was rather garish and cheap looking. It just didn't look right for a Mayfair salon. "How come there's only forty colours?" I asked.

"You intermix. Just use a different developer to make them semi permanent as opposed to permanent. Great grey coverage," Charlie chimed in. "It makes them the cheapest, most cost effective colours on the market, and we're adding new colours all the time."

"I see." The thought of only having a cheap, basic range at my disposal filled me with horror. Even Gavin Roberts had carried a couple of different colour ranges, despite being a bit on the tight side. At Gino Venti, we had a whole room full at our disposal.

We had a light lunch before going over to the salon to let them see the space. Seeing it for the first time in daylight showed off even more potential than I'd realised. The area was busy, quirky, and there was an NCP car park just up the road. It really was a prime site. Charlie and Charlotte were impressed as well.

"Lovely space. I think we could do a real spectacular job of this. I'm thinking lots of black and dark wood," Charlie announced.

"I was thinking more creams and taupes, keep the space light and open," I contradicted.

"Charlie's the expert, let him guide you," warned Charlotte, "he always knows best." I gave her a hard stare. Neither of them were even hairdressers, but were dismissing my opinions as if they were the experts. I worked in a salon every bloody day. I knew what worked and what didn't.

Julian must have sensed my unease. "I'm sorry to interrupt, but I'm gonna have to wrap this up as I have a meeting in half an hour." He gave Charlotte his card. "I'll need you to email me the contract, price lists for re-ordering the products, payment schedules, and terms of trade please." He sounded so authoritarian. Businessman Julian was definitely sexy.

We locked up, and after a peck on my cheek, and a handshake with the others, he left to get to his next meeting. We went back to the coffee shop. "You make a really handsome couple," said Charlotte, shooting Charlie a look that I didn't understand.

"Thank you." I didn't really know what else to say.

"The two of you should join us one evening, we know this great club in Chelsea," she began. Charlie interrupted her.

"Depends how adventurous they are. They might be totally vanilla."

Charlotte smiled at me. "I doubt it. You don't strike me as boring or suburban. I'm sure you and Julian are fun, interesting people. Both of you are good looking too." She ran her fingers down my face. I shuddered slightly at the contact, telling myself that Northerners were always more tactile than Londoners. She took out a business card, and scribbled something on the back of it. "Tomorrow night, the Chelsea Review Club. I'll leave your names at the door. You have to be vouched for to get in," she told me, "so until tomorrow..."

"See you soon," Charlie promised, a sly smirk on his face. I smiled back rather weakly.

I watched as they left, relieved that they'd gone. Something about them unnerved me, and it wasn't just that I thought they were scammers over the salon business. I tucked their card and brochures in my handbag, and went back to my latte, dreaming about the salon. *I'm definitely having cream and taupe, stuff them.*

"Can I get you anything else?" I was interrupted from my musing by the same striking brunette who I'd seen stroking Julian's arm that night in the wine bar. He'd told me her name was Susie.

"No thank you. I'll be off in a minute." The coffee shop had filled up somewhat, and I could see that people were looking for tables. I drained my cup, and headed back to the flat, thankful that she hadn't recognised me, and hadn't been there earlier, when I'd been with Julian.

Salon Affair

After a little shopping, I returned home, fully expecting him to call. By eight, I'd resigned myself to the notion that he was probably working, so occupied myself with my grooming rituals. I'd just finished painting my toenails when he turned up, carrying his laptop, and a file of papers. "Sorry it's so late, but I wanted to check out this Sugarcube company. Took me a while."

"No problem," I said, "what were you checking?" I was curious.

"Scammers, the pair of them. She emailed me over the contract, and other documents. Load of rubbish really. They put about thirty grand into the business, take fifty one percent ownership, and tie you in for five years. I worked out that the minimum you'd pay back would be a hundred and eighty thousand."

I gasped. "For thirty thousand quids worth of equipment?"

"Yep. It's a great scam, almost wish I'd thought of it myself." I made us some drinks while he powered up his laptop, and sorted out his papers. "The furnishings are cheap, I found the prices individually online. The plumbing and electrics are all in place, so that cost is minimal. The flooring is debatable, depending on what you go for. The printing they'll do, works out about a hundred quid online, and the products they package for you add up to about twelve hundred, from their price list.

The contract states you have to buy a minimum three thousand pounds worth a month, which isn't too bad until you find out there's only ten percent profit margin on everything."

"Which I'd be paying the stylist selling it," I interjected, catching on.

"Exactly, now, the worst part is at the end of the five years. In the small print, it says you can buy them out of the business at fifty percent of the current value, so in other words, if, despite having them like an albatross around your neck, you manage to show a profit, it's gonna cost you one and a half times your annual profit to get shot of them."

"That's outrageous," I said, "why on earth would anyone go for a deal like that?"

He sat back. "They probably don't read the small print, don't check the details, and don't understand mark up, as opposed to margin. I checked those two out too. They both had a fraud enquiry over a beauty company, although nothing was proven, and they weren't convicted."

I gazed at him in awe, he really was impressive. "They asked us to some club tomorrow night," I told him, handing him the card Charlotte had given me. He read it, his face impassive.

"I doubt if it's the sort of club you'd be seen dead in. It's a fetish place in Chelsea. People dress in rubber and shag in public, that sort of thing."

"How do you know?" I blurted it out before my brain had gone into gear.

He pulled a face. "Some woman took me there once. Half an hour was all it took for me to realise what kind of place it was, and what they got up to in the fetish rooms. In the spirit of all the best tabloid journalists, I made my excuses and left." I giggled at his disapproving pout. "Well, do you want to look at fat old men with sweaty bollocks from all the latex, getting off on being whipped by equally fat old women in pointy-titted basques?"

"Sounds delightful," I laughed, "who took you there?"

"Gemma." His face was deadpan. "She hooked up with some black fella, leaving me standing there like a prat, then when some old bat, who was at least as old as my mum, started feeling me up, and showed me her shaven pussy, I ran for it." I watched him shudder at the memory. "I can guarantee you wouldn't last ten minutes in there, especially with the pair of Charlies. Wonder which one of them's the perv?"

Salon Affair

"Both probably, although it was her that came on to me, not Mr Gormless."

His head whipped round. "She came onto you?" I nodded. "That's kinda hot, even though it's also a bit gross," he murmured. I smacked his arm playfully.

"Didn't think you'd be the type to want to share, Mr Alpha Businessman."

He grinned, "not usually, but two women together is sexy. As long as I could watch, that is."

I stared at him, aghast. It felt to me like confirmation that he didn't feel as much for me, as I for him. Up until that moment, I'd been dismissing my own insecurities which whispered that I wasn't good enough for such a gorgeous man, and convinced myself that we were in love. A little piece of my heart broke. "You'd be happy to watch someone else touch me? Kiss me?" I needed him to say no, that he'd hate even the thought.

"In the context of a sex club, it'd be a bit strange to be faithful now, wouldn't it? Couples don't go to those places to get off with each other, they go there to be adventurous, and try stuff out. So, if you wanted to try out sex with a woman, I'd rather you did it in front of me, out in the open as it were, than sneak around in secret."

"I see." I wasn't quite sure what to say to that. Julian was being logical, but it still stung like a slap round the face. "What if it's you she fancies, and her ugly old man has the hots for me?" I knew I was pushing, but I didn't care, I wanted him to be jealous. He mulled it over for a moment.

"Well she looks like a tranny, not my type, so I wouldn't be remotely interested, and I know for a fact you find him repulsive, so we'd make our excuses and leave."

"What if it was someone good looking?"

"For god's sake Lily, it's not even happened. I don't know why you're looking for problems where none exist." He was getting exasperated.

"I just need to know what I'm getting myself into, before we do this," I whispered, pointing at the pile of spreadsheets and notes on the coffee table.

"People are usually in business together without a sexual relationship. The business will be done legally, and if this doesn't work out between us, we simply have a professional, mutually beneficial business arrangement." He spoke softly, in a soothing way, trying to assuage my fears. He stroked my face gently, before slipping his index finger under my chin to tip my face up towards him. "I think this will work between us. Don't you?" He asked.

I responded instinctively to his touch, leaning in to him. "Yes, yes I do," I agreed, trying to push my niggle of doubt into the darkest recesses of my mind.

"Excellent, I'll put together a business plan tomorrow, and in the meantime...." His hands slid down to cup my breasts, as his mouth demanded a deep, lush kiss. His body felt muscular and strong as he lifted me off the sofa, and carried me to the bedroom. My robe fell open shamelessly when he put me down on the bed. "Beautiful," he breathed, in carnal appreciation of my naked body.

I watched as he shed his clothes, admiring his sculpted pecs, with their fine dusting of fair hair, testament to the testosterone that he barely restrained when it came to sex. His thighs were powerful and thick as he slid his jeans down. I licked my lips at the moment he revealed his erection. His gloriously large penis sprang free, as hard as steel, encased in silky soft skin. My body began to hum with anticipation. "I think we need to take this one slow," he purred, "remind you of how great we are together, and stop you worrying. Have you got any baby oil?"

"In the drawer," I told him, intrigued. He found it, and came over to the bed, flicking off the overhead light on the way, so we were only lit by the bedside lamp.

"Roll over onto your front," he commanded. I complied immediately. *A massage!* I felt him spread some oil over

Salon Affair

my back, his strong hands working it into the stress knots around my shoulders. I groaned with pleasure.

"Hmm, seems as though we've found something you like," he crooned. I sighed happily, just letting the sensations wash over me. I felt his hands move lower, between my bum cheeks. I jumped slightly. "Just relax," he murmured, sliding his hands down further, between my inner thighs. "I want to touch every part of you."

My body came alive as his hands roamed over it, trailing sensuous lines up the inside of my legs, barely brushing the apex, which screamed out for his touch. By the time he'd commanded me to roll over onto my back, my clit was pulsing wildly, desperate for his attention. Instead, he concentrated on my breasts, gently caressing them, rolling and pinching my nipples. His face bore an expression of intense concentration. He seemed as lost in the moment as I.

When he eventually touched my soaked sex, I thought I'd climax immediately, but he studiously avoided my clitoris, gently stroking the outer lips, teasing me beyond endurance. "Please Julian," I pleaded.

"What is it you'd like?" He murmured.

"You please." I glanced at his straining erection, a bead of pre-cum glistening on the tip, and wondered how come he had so much self control.

"I like hearing you begging for it," he said softly, stroking the skin of my inner thigh. I whimpered.

"Please, I really need to come, I don't know how much longer I can stand it."

"Roll onto your front. Doggy style." I complied.

Instead of the expected fuck, he carried on his sensual torture, only stroking over my anus as well as my vulva.

Just when I couldn't take any more, he slammed his cock into me at the same time as delivering a resounding slap on my arse. Whether it was shock, or the noise, I don't know, but I know I came, having the orgasm to end all orgasms.

Like a tightly coiled spring, suddenly released, my body came apart in a blast of white heat.

I was barely aware of Julian as he continued to pound me at a punishing pace, his body slapping against mine, pushing me further and further into my own private sexual oblivion. Another hard slap across my buttocks brought me to, shaking me back into the present. When he did it again, the sharp pain seemed to contrast with the pleasure he was inflicting, in a dark, and carnal way. I felt the quivering of another orgasm begin.

"Don't stop," I pleaded, desperate for another release. His thrusts sped up, as did the frequency of the slaps. It was wrong, and opposite to everything I ever believed I'd enjoy, but as he stung my backside, I found myself turned on beyond anything I'd experienced before.

I came with a scream, collapsing onto the mattress, as my arms gave out. Even face down in the pillows, I willed him to carry on a few moments more.

"Argh, Jesus," he called out, as he first swelled, then let go, emptying himself into me. We both held still for a few moments, before he pulled out, and slumped down beside me. I rolled onto my side to face him. He was slicked with sweat. I fought the urge to lick it off him.

He pulled me into his arms. "God, that was intense. Who'd have thought you liked a good spanking eh?"

"Certainly not me," I purred, sated. "Not something I've ever tried before. Maybe I enjoyed it because it was with you."

"Maybe."

We stayed in our embrace until we'd both cooled down, and got our breath back. I was beyond thirsty. "Would you like some water? Or juice?" I asked.

"Water please."

I clambered out of bed, and turned towards the door. "Lily, put the light on a minute please?" I switched it on.

"Your arse is the most glorious shade of red," he said, "did I hurt you?"

I looked at it in the mirror, twisting round to get a better view. It was indeed glowing. "It is a bit. I can't say as I noticed at the time," I smirked, before trotting off to get our drinks.

We woke up the next morning tangled together in a mass of limbs. As I peeled myself off him to make some coffee, he stirred and opened his eyes. "Good morning beautiful," he murmured. He looked so gorgeous, all sleepy and mussed up, that my heart lurched.

"Morning beautiful yourself," I replied. "Are you ready for a coffee?"

"Mmm, please," he mumbled. I skipped through to the kitchen, and fixed our drinks. After taking them into the bedroom, I perched on the side of the bed to drink mine.

"What time do you have to be in?" He asked.

"Nine. I've got plenty of time. What are you up to today?"

"Business plan for you mainly. Would you like me to email the pair of Charlies and politely decline for you?"

"Please." I was relieved. I hadn't felt comfortable with them, and Julian's analysis had proven why. He clearly had great business sense, and a lot of experience. "Anything else you gotta do?"

"Not much. Bit of paperwork. Gemma made her last payment to me at the weekend, so I've just got to check that everything is fully in her name, then drop it all over to her. That's my involvement finished."

I frowned. "So how do you actually make any money?"

He sipped his coffee. "Say if I fronted fifty thousand for your salon, I'd take a fifty percent share of the company, plus a loan payment. So in your first year, you'd pay me back ten thousand, plus fifty percent of profit, which wouldn't be much. Second year twenty thousand, plus half of a better profit, third year, twenty thousand again, and a half share of a very healthy profit. The fourth and fifth years, there's no loan payments, so just my share of profit. After five years, I sign it over to you for no further payment. You get a well set up, and profitable company, using my expertise, and I get my money back, plus a healthy dose of profit. It's win win, unlike those scammers."

I processed the information. It sounded fair, and would still leave me plenty of freedom to choose my own suppliers. It also meant that Julian would be in my life for at least five years. He broke my reverie, "I'll do some projections for you, so that you can see the type of figures we're talking about. I don't suppose you have any records of your personal takings? I know you get a printout each day." *You don't miss a trick do you?*

I rummaged around in my chest of drawers to find the clip of printouts, which I'd religiously kept since starting at the salon. I placed it on the bedside table. "Bear in mind I've not been there long, so I take the least at the moment. The others are all better established than me."

"That's fine, I just need an idea of the figures involved. I'll be able to do a projection based on the increases I can see over the months."

"What if we don't make a profit?" I asked. It was actually my worst fear, failing and letting him down.

"We share the risk on this Lily. I wouldn't do it if I didn't think we'd succeed. I'll be there too, remember, so you won't be on your own. I'll be very hands on with the business side, helping you with the paperwork, management, that type of thing." He smiled at my frowning face. "I think we'll make a great team, and without the bar and the coffee shop in my stable, I'll have a lot of time to really push this project." He pulled me into a kiss. "You, my darling girl, will be the toast of the West End."

Salon Affair

I gazed into his eyes. He appeared sincere and earnest. "I just don't want you making a mistake, you know, backing me to do this," I said.

"How could anything that joins me to you be a mistake?" He murmured. "I waited a long time to meet you Lily, to feel what I feel for you, to connect to someone in the way we connect. I just know how much this means to you, and I want to be the one to help make all your dreams come true."

I processed his words, convinced that they were a declaration of love, albeit in a rather awkward, blokeish way. It made me inordinately happy though, and I flung my arms around him. "Thank you."

"For what?" He frowned.

"For believing in me, for telling me what I needed to hear," I replied, beaming at him. He flashed me his movie star smile, and hugged me tight. With nothing between us, I could feel his strong heart beat steadily. I breathed in his lovely scent.

"Don't ever doubt what I feel for you," he whispered, "I couldn't breathe if I needed you any more than I do."

Chapter 9

I skipped into work, happy, after my romantic morning, and looking forward to the day ahead. Julian had promised to work on my business plan, and come over with a takeaway after I'd finished. I picked up a Starbucks on the way, and bounced into the salon early, saying a cheery 'good morning' to Paulina, who was on the phone.

It all changed the moment I stepped into the staff room. I was confronted by the sight of Gray, in Trystan's arms, being held tight. I heard a sob. "Lily, can you give us a minute?" Trystan asked, with none of his normal snarkiness. I retreated back into the salon.

"What's up with Gray?" I asked Paulina. She shrugged.

"No idea. Nobody ever tells me anything."

Five minutes later Tomme and Anthony walked in. They too only spent a second in the staff room before joining us at the desk. "Any idea?" Anthony asked, nodding towards the door, which was now firmly closed.

"Nope. Gray seems upset about something," I said. I sat on the sofa to change into my heels, even though we had another half hour until clients. Tomme took a swig of my Starbucks. "Hey, leave it alone," I snapped.

"Gotta have coffee to get moving," he said, "can't cut hair without some caffeine in my system, and god knows how long they'll be in there."

"Wonder what's up?" Anthony mused, "it's not like Gray to be a drama queen. He's normally quite steady."

Salon Affair

"Maybe Chris tore his caftan," Tomme said, before stopping the two juniors from going into the staffroom. Just as Michael arrived, Trystan came out to see us.

"Charlotte, Tula, please stay on the desk, this doesn't concern you. Everyone else, staff meeting." We all trooped behind Trystan into the back room, and sat down. Gray looked red-eyed, and distraught. My stomach lurched at the prospect of something being wrong with the salon. He stood up to speak to us.

"Guys, you all know I've not been well for a while. All the colds I've had since I had that terrible flu last year.." He paused. I breathed a little sigh of relief that it didn't seem to be an issue affecting the salon. "But I've had some tests, and it wasn't flu, it appears I sero-converted." *Eh?*

"Nooo," screeched Tomme, jumping up to hug him tight.

"How?" Michael demanded. I looked around at the boys, they all seemed shocked and distraught. Trystan was wiping at the tears streaming down his face. I handed him a tissue. Paulina seemed as clueless as I was. She caught my eye, and gave a little shrug.

I took a deep breath. "What's sero-converted mean?" I asked. I knew I sounded a bit thick, but judging by the boy's extreme reactions, I figured it was something serious.

"It means that I've contracted the HIV virus Lily," said Gray. My hand flew up to my mouth. I watched as all the boys took turns hugging him, telling him how sorry they were at his news. There was a real, genuine outpouring of love and affection. In turn, I hugged him, sad that this beautiful, talented man now had such a cross to bear.

"So how?" Asked Michael.

"Chris was cheating, apparently. He admitted to trawling Hampstead Heath for rough trade. Bastard let me think we were monogamous and safe. He knew. Let me believe we both had flu. Lied and lied over it. I got the news yesterday, and confronted him. Even then he wouldn't admit it straightaway. It was only when I checked out his 'vitamin pills', that he confessed, and confirmed that he'd already begun drug therapy." Gray seemed quite calm as he spoke, although I was certain he was anything but.

"Hope you've kicked the lying bastard out," Michael said. Gray shook his head.

"He's asked me to leave, on the basis that I earn more than him, and can afford a place. I need to get a lawyer. If we sell the flat, we can both afford a smaller place each. I need to find out about the rules in divorcing a civil partner."

"The bastard needs to die in a grease fire," spat Tomme, "let alone taking half your property. What a lying, cheating little slut. Can't you report him to his bosses for deliberately infecting you? It must be classed as attempted murder..."

He was interrupted by Paulina, "So does this mean you have to give up work? If you're infectious?"

"Don't be daft Paulina, he's only infectious if he blows a load up your arse, which I think is highly unlikely," snapped Trystan, his snark back to full force. He shot her a disdainful look. I was pretty ignorant about the whole HIV/aids thing, and even I knew you couldn't catch it from normal contact.

"I gather it's only in blood or semen babe, so don't worry, you won't get it," I told her, trying to diffuse the situation. The last thing Gray needed was her panicking over sharing utensils, as she was a bit odd over the whole gay 'thing' at the best of times.

"What if you cut yourself?" She demanded.

"Then I'll put a plaster on it," Gray told her, exasperated. "How many times have I got blood on you? Let me see....that'll be never then."

"I'm worried. You can't blame me for being concerned. I don't want to catch anything," she said.

"You won't. I'm more concerned with how much I'm gonna be off. I'm starting drug therapy straight away, and the doctor warned me that it may take a while to get the doses right."

"We'll all help, cover when you're off, won't we?" Tomme said, glancing round at all of us. We all nodded.

"What do we tell the clients?" Paulina asked, "They might not want someone with a disease doing their hair." *Fucking bitch.*

"We don't tell them anything." Gray glared at her.

"We didn't tell the clients when I caught the clap from that Italian waiter, so why would you tell people about Gray?" Tomme challenged.

"How did you catch clap from a bloke?" I was curious.

"In my throat. It was gross," he replied, nonchalant.

"His breath stank like he'd eaten a shit sandwich for breakfast," added Michael, helpfully. I wrinkled my nose.

"At least make sure you don't use my cup. I'm frightened of this disease." Paulina's voice wavered. *Fucking drama queen.*

"Why are you trying to make this all about you?" I asked her. "It's poor Gray who has to deal with this, not you or I. Can I suggest you read up on the facts, and stop being so dramatic. Would you worry about catching cancer off someone too?" It came out a little more forcefully than I meant, but seemed to hit home. She shook her head, and stared at the floor. *Silly cow.*

"We're gonna make you an honorary gay man at this rate Lil," Trystan said, nodding towards a sulky Paulina. I managed a weak smile.

"I'll give you the number of the Terrence Higgins trust," Gray told her, "they can acquaint you with the facts, and put your mind at rest. In the meantime," he glanced at his watch, "we need to get our salon faces on, and get ready for these clients." We all stood up, and I filled the kettle. Tomme pulled Gray into a fierce hug.

"Don't worry Gracie, we'll all help you. Forget Chris, he's just the cuntiest cunt who ever cunted."

Paulina left the room with a face like a slapped arse. She hated swear words, of which Tomme had an impressive repertoire, which he used quite freely.

"She's something else, isn't she?" Observed Anthony. "Needs to get her head out of her fanny."

"She's just led a sheltered life," I replied, "once she gets all the facts, I'm sure she'll calm down."

Gray went out to start his client, which of course meant we could all talk about him. "Poor sod, he'll have to take pills for the rest of his life. If Chris had told him he wanted an open relationship, it would've at least given Gray the opportunity to play safe," said Anthony.

"He seems quite calm about it," I observed.

"He's not. He's totally in bits. Cut up over Chris cheating on him, then all the trauma of being diagnosed poz, he just hides it well," Trystan told us. "His life has been totally ripped apart, and it will be until he can get shot of the skanky bloodsucker. Let's pray there's no alimony in gay divorces, as that would just be insult to injury."

I listened to them all expressing their outrage at Gray's situation, admiring their solidarity. Despite their somewhat fruity language, they were all kind and caring men. I felt a pang of sadness that I'd be leaving them, and their world behind. Taking a deep breath, I went off to begin my first client.

We were all a little subdued all day. Paulina spent most of the morning on the phone, jabbering away in Italian, before going out at lunchtime to purchase a salad and coffee, and, rather annoyingly, making a show of using the plastic utensils to eat it in the staffroom. Anthony and I had to stifle our giggles when her plastic fork snapped on a particularly hard bit of radish, and she had to resort to eating it with her fingers.

Julian had text me to ask which product companies I wanted to use, so, hiding the screen from the others, I quickly text back that I preferred Redken and Kerastase. I

Salon Affair

wondered how he'd found out about product houses, considering he had no experience in the hair world.

The afternoon was so busy that it passed in a blur, our little salon family putting on our brave face, and giving the clients the happy show that they paid good money for. In truth, I don't think any of us were really feeling it. Nobody wanted to work late, instead, we all gathered in the wine bar after work, primarily to bitch about Paulina. We'd left her in the salon with the juniors, escaping under the excuse of a stylist meeting. She hadn't reacted, and I doubted whether she'd have joined us if we'd asked. She really was being a bit of a prick about the whole HIV thing.

"Maybe it's because she's foreign," Michael suggested.

"No, it's because she's a puritanical, sex negative arsehole," Trystan sneered. "Maybe she's a secret lesbo, and is jealous because we're out and proud, while she's a sad closet case. I mean, I've never known her to have a boyfriend, have you?" He asked Gray, who shook his head.

"Is Gino gay?" I asked. They all laughed.

"No, Gino was a tart. He had affairs all over London. Couldn't help himself. He was good looking when he was younger, and women just threw themselves at him. His poor wife gave up in the end, and left him, which gave him free reign. He was never homophobic or judgemental though, and was very gay friendly. It wasn't really an issue for him, and he's just as Italian as Paulina," Gray told me.

"Sex negative closet lesbo it is then," I said.

"Do you get a lesbo vibe off her? I mean, has she ever accidentally on purpose brushed against your tits?" Tomme asked.

"Not that I've noticed," I laughed, "the only person who does that is you Tomme."

They all cackled while Tomme blushed. *Sooo croote.*

We poured out more glasses of wine, and I settled back into my chair to listen to the conversation, and just enjoy the hell out of being with the boys. They were all urbane and fun, and clearly cared deeply about each other. "Lot of blue lights out there," Trystan said, indicating through the window. "I'm going out there for a ciggie and a stickybeak. Anyone coming?" Anthony got up, and the two of them trotted out of the bar to be nosy.

Thirty seconds later, Anthony ran back in. "It's the salon," he screeched. *Shit.* We all jumped up, and followed him out, to be faced with several police cars and an ambulance parked directly outside. Trystan was already in there, holding Paulina's hand, as the paramedics worked to stop the blood pouring from a wound on her head. I watched it spreading over the sleek, cream, salon floor, numb with shock. A pale, shocked looking girl was helped into one of the police cars, and driven off. She hadn't appeared big enough to inflict that much damage.

"What the hell?" Gray asked the nearest copper.

"Are you all employees here?" He asked our group.

"Yes, I'm the manager," said Gray, we all work here. What happened?"

"Robbery sir. Looks like the door was kicked in, and the lady attacked. Do you have CCTV?"

"Yes, yes we do," he confirmed. "Paulina, she's not, you know, dead....is she?"

The paramedic glanced up, "No sir, but it's a serious head injury. We need to get her to hospital as soon as we can. Looks like she's been hit with a bar or bat."

We all watched as Paulina was moved gently onto a stretcher, and loaded into the ambulance. Trystan got in with her, and promised to keep us all updated from the hospital.

Forensics then made their start, taking boot prints from the floor, photos, and blood swabs. They couldn't find any fingerprints though. After half an hour, they finished, and packed up.

"I knew she should never have cashed up on her own," Gray said, but she was so bloody stubborn about it. Seemed

Salon Affair

to forget we're in the middle of London, with all the associated dangers. Mind you, I suppose because we don't get much cash, she figured nobody would target us."

With Gray busy helping the police with the CCTV, and working out how much cash was taken, and Anthony calling the shopfront company to come and secure the place, Tomme and I began to clear up. It was beyond gross, watching him mop her blood off the floor, and I cringed as I wiped blood spray off the desk. "Bet those sodding juniors skipped off home early, that's why she was alone," Tomme muttered.

We watched the footage of the attack. Saw two African men burst in, popping the lock as easily as just opening the door. "Probably used a battering device," said the younger copper. The remnants of the door frame plain for us all to see.

We watched Paulina's terrified face, as the men rounded on her, one holding out a gloved hand for the contents of the till. The daft woman tried to refuse, holding the wad of cash behind her back, which prompted the second one to attack her with a baseball bat, bringing it down on her head with a sickening ferocity. "Why didn't she just throw the cash on the floor, and make a run for it?" I said to nobody in particular.

"That would've been the wisest thing to do madam," said the copper.

The first man simply snatched the cash from her lifeless hand, scooped the change out of the till, and the pair of them legged it.

"There was only three hundred and twenty in cash," said Gray, after checking the computer. "Not worth getting your skull smashed in for."

A passer-by had witnessed the scene, and called the police. We watched her lean over Paulina as she lay motionless on the floor, the girl trying to check her pulse while on her mobile, taking instructions. She'd been taken to the police station to give her witness statement, and probably lots of hot, sweet, tea. *Poor girl, seeing all that*, I thought.

I was interrupted by Julian calling. "Hi babe, I'm at your flat. Thought you'd be home by now," he said, sounding happy.

"I'm at the salon. We were robbed, Paulina's......" I couldn't get the words out in any sort of comprehensible form.

"Paulina's what?" I could hear the concern in his voice.

"She was attacked. We don't know how bad. Can you let yourself in? I don't know how long..."

"Sure, but do you want me to come and get you? I can throw our food in the warming drawer and be there in ten."

"Please." I needed his strong arms around me, and his quiet fortitude. Julian was one of those rare people who always seemed to know the right thing to do.

"I'm gonna have to phone Gino," said Gray. "Not a call I'm looking forward to, but it's gotta be done. This has got to go down as the worst week in living memory." He went out to the staff room to make the call, while the rest of us, and the police stood around, us checking for blood sprays, the police checking to make sure nothing had been missed. Gray had given them a copy of the footage, so after a final look around, they left.

"I wonder if the poor bitch'll die," mused Tomme, "who do you reckon will get all her stuff if she does?"

"Family probably," said Michael, who was sweeping up the splinters from the door frame. "I doubt if they'll give it all to you."

"I'm only after her iPad, possibly her phone. She's the same size as Lily though, and it'd be a shame to waste all those designer outfits."

"I'm not scavenging second hand clothes," I sniffed, "anyway, she'll probably recover. Hospitals are pretty good at trauma wounds nowadays."

Salon Affair

"You saw the amount of blood I mopped up," said Tomme, "she must've been drained dry."

I glanced up at the large salon clock, it was nearly half eight. It had taken nearly two hours to clean up, and deal with the police. Despite the salon being almost back to normal, there was a strange chill present, and it wasn't just because of the splintered doorframe. In just one day, two people's lives had changed irrevocably, despite both of them being completely innocent and unaware. I pondered the unfairness of it. I heard the poor, battered door open.

Julian broke my reverie. "Hey babe, you ok?" He asked, before wrapping his arms around me. I breathed in his familiar Julian-scent, and sighed.

"Yeah, just a bit shocked. It's been a rotten day." He squeezed a little tighter.

"Can I have one of those lovely man-hugs too? I'm shocked as well, and I had to mop up the blood," Tomme said to him, breaking the sombre mood. "I'm probably more traumatised than she is."

Julian lifted an arm, and smiling, pulled Tomme into our hug. "Group hug time then," he muttered. I smiled as Tomme rested his head on Julian's shoulder, and gazed at him in adoration. I could feel Julian stiffen uncomfortably at the contact, but to his credit, he didn't shove Tomme away.

We peeled apart when Gray returned. "That was grim, telling Gino. He's gonna try and get a flight either tonight or tomorrow. Paulina's his only niece, his late sister's only child, so he's distraught. I tried to call Trystan, but it just kept going to answer-phone. I don't even know which hospital they took her to." He raked his fingers through his carefully combed hair, mussing it up. Rather randomly, I realised it was the first time I'd ever seen Gray look remotely untidy.

"Listen, why don't you lot all go home? The shopfront people will be here any minute. I can wait for them," Gray told us all. "I'll let you all know as soon as there's any news."

"I'll wait with you," Michael told him, "I've missed the gym now, so don't need to be anywhere."

With that settled, Julian, Tomme, Anthony and I said our goodbyes, and walked towards Baker Street. Tomme gave Julian a blow-by-blow account of the events of the day while we walked, which I was grateful for. I hadn't been sure whether or not I should share the news about Gray's HIV status with anyone outside our salon family. Anthony chimed in too, so it was clearly deemed ok to discuss.

When the two boys left us to go to their own flats, Julian and I walked along in silence for a while.

"You ok?" He asked, eventually.

"Yeah, I'm fine. It wasn't me all those things happened to today. I feel so sad for Gray though. Imagine finding out that the love of your life was lying through his teeth, must be devastating."

"Mmm, must be," he agreed.

"I'm surprised he hasn't had a meltdown, especially with what happened tonight. Tomme was more traumatised than him," I said.

"Tomme's just a drama queen though. Gray's a bit older, steadier. I'm just glad you weren't present. That'd give me sleepless nights."

I leaned into him, grateful for both his warmth and his words. He instinctively wrapped his arm round my shoulder. "I wouldn't have fought them, I'd have given them the cash," I blurted.

"Very wise," he muttered, "it's not worth getting beaten up over. Cash is insured, it's replaceable. A person isn't. Promise me you'll never put yourself in that position.....please?"

I glanced up at his earnest face. "I promise."

Back at the flat, Julian pulled a rather dried up curry out of the oven, while I changed into yoga pants and a vest, before pulling on my warmest, thickest robe. I just couldn't shake off the chill that had permeated my bones. "It's a bit overdone," he said, looking at the gloopy heap on his plate mournfully.

"I'd make you something else, but I've not got much in," I confessed. I wasn't hungry at all, and just picked at mine. I managed to glug down half a bottle of wine though, which made me feel a little better, although it left me struggling to concentrate on the business plan Julian spread out in front of me. He tried to explain it all, pointing out how he'd arrived at the figures, but the spreadsheets swam in front of my eyes, and it seemed like he'd thought of every detail, so I couldn't think of anything to add.

"I need to go through this when I've got a clearer head," I confessed. It was half ten, and I was exhausted from the emotion of the day.

"Poor thing," he murmured, "I'll leave it all here, so you can go through it all when you feel more alert. Now, would you prefer me to go home? Or would you like me to stay?"

"Stay please." It was out of my mouth before I'd even had a chance to engage my brain. After Paulina's attack, I really didn't want to sleep alone. *That sounded really needy.* Julian didn't seem to mind. He just switched off the lights, and followed me into the bedroom. For the first time in ages, I didn't feel remotely horny, I just needed a cuddle.

I concealed my lack of enthusiasm for our lovemaking that night, even though it seemed to take me ages to come. Unlike my usual speedy orgasms the moment he touched me, my mind was clouded and preoccupied. Mr Sex-god really had to work for it, employing every trick in his considerable arsenal to coax a climax out of me. It wasn't until he dug his fingers into my hips, squeezing hard, that I was finally able to let go, quickly followed by himself. Think he was a bit relieved by then.

I still struggled to sleep, the events of the day racing through my mind with an intense ferocity. I could only lay there, trying not to disturb Julian as he fell into a deep slumber. In the sparse light from the streetlamps, I could make out his perfect lips, slightly parted, and his extraordinarily beautiful face relaxed and serene. I was glad he was there.

Chapter 10

Trystan and Gray both looked rough the next morning in work. Tryst had stayed at the hospital while Paulina had been in surgery, and hadn't slept. He rooted through my makeup bag for some concealer and bronzer to cover his dark circles and grey pallor.

The shopfront had been repaired, a new metal plate covering the splintered doorframe. There was no evidence left of the drama from the previous night. None of us discussed it much, apart from asking after Paulina. Trystan told us that she was in a coma, and the doctors weren't able to give a prognosis. She'd be in intensive care for a while.

Gino was arriving at lunchtime, and had told Gray that he'd be going straight to the hospital. I'd hoped to finally meet him under happier circumstances, but fate had played it's hand, and I just prayed that he wouldn't be bereaved and distraught when I eventually got to shake his hand.

It was Michael's day off, but he turned up anyway, telling us all that he was happy to man the desk for the day, save us sacrificing our one good junior, or even the sly, rubbish one, who nobody trusted around cash at the best of times. With everyone in, we painted on our salon faces, and began our day.

The only high point was a text from Mum to say that her firm had received a copy of the lease for the Mayfair salon, the day before, and were going through it. She'd got the secretary to send me a copy too, so that I could read through it, and check to make sure everything was as I expected. ***Get Julian to read it for you*** was her final text.

I sped through the day, thankful that it was busy enough to take my mind off everything. My final client was at six, just a cut and finish, nothing too complicated. I was in the loo when Michael called out; "Susan Ward's here Lily."

I finished up, and followed him through to reception, where I got a shock at coming face to face with one of Julian's exes, the one from the coffee shop. *What the fuck is she doing here?*

"Hi Lily, nice to meet you properly at last. Julian recommended you, said you were a great hairdresser, and goodness knows, I need one," she said, smiling at me.

Wary, I smiled back, and greeted her in my professional way. I took her through to my styling chair, and sat her down for her consult. Grudgingly, I had to admit that she had great hair, really thick and glossy.

"I've not had the chance to get it cut for ages, so it's well overdue. It's too long, and my split ends have gone rampant," she explained, "I'd quite like a change too, maybe a fringe, maybe a bit shorter. That's what us women do isn't it? Heartbreak haircuts..." She trailed off.

"Why are you heartbroken?" I asked.

"Another one bit the dust last week." She said. "All men are bastards, well, apart from Julian of course." *He can't have told her I'm his girlfriend.*

The concept irked me. She clearly didn't know that Julian and I were involved. I sent her off to be shampooed, and busied myself getting my equipment ready, laying out everything I'd need in advance, so I could get her done, and over with quickly.

I'd just begun to cut the base line of her hair, when she started to tell me about her latest, failed relationship. Apparently, he'd turned out to be married with a child, a

Salon Affair

fact he'd managed to conceal for around three months. "That's terrible Susan, how'd he manage that?" I gasped.

"Call me Susie, everyone does. I don't know how I didn't spot it. Suppose I didn't want to really. He lived in town during the week. Bastard told me he went off at the weekends motor racing. The truth was that he was playing happy families, while I worked my arse off in the café."

"How awful, bet you're devastated," I said, my 'professional sympathy' face on.

"I'm definitely having a run of bad luck at the moment," she told me. "I don't know how much, if anything, Julian's told you about our business partnership, but it finally ended about a month ago. I thought I'd be loaded, not having to pay him a half share, but all that's happened is a horrible, big rent hike, and a deluge of paperwork, which he used to do. I almost wish we were still partners."

"Rent hike?"

"Yeah, my lease has five yearly rent reviews, upwards only. Coincided with Julian's contract ending. I asked him to help negotiate it down, but by then, he'd ceased to be a director, so the landlord wouldn't talk to him." She gave a large sigh. "I'm no better off than I was before, plus I have double the workload."

I was puzzled, as I was under the impression that anyone, acting as an agent could negotiate rent. My Mum had seen the solicitors at work do it. I decided on a little fact-finding as I worked on her layers. It was breaking all my rules about 'air-time' with clients, but I figured it was more important than selling her a bottle of shampoo.

"You were involved with Julian?" I prompted.

"For a while. Once we set up the coffee shop, I suppose the pressure of working together made it fizzle out. That man can love for a day, a month, a year, and then just revert to being friends. One minute he needed me to breathe, the next, he didn't. We stayed good friends though, there's no hard feelings. He doesn't have an issue with me having boyfriends, and I never had issues with him having girlfriends. He's like that, just an easy-going, likeable person."

I was filing all the information, for consideration later. Her comment about him needing her to breathe echoed a line he'd said to me. *I couldn't breathe if I needed you any more than I do.* As I worked on her blowdry, I asked her about the coffee shop, how it was doing, finding out that Julian had set it up to be immensely profitable, with great suppliers, and his usual attention to detail regarding layout and equipment.

"If it wasn't for this bloody rent hike, I'd be sitting pretty," she said mournfully, as I tweaked her new fringe into position. "That looks amazing, I love it."

"Who is your landlord?" I asked, as I helped her into her coat.

"Just some company. Beta limited, I think it's called." *Holy shit.*

I didn't see Julian that evening, as he said he had some work to do. Instead, I took a deep breath and called Lisa. Our stand-off had gone on long enough, and I missed her. She answered straightaway, "Are you cross with me?"

"I was. I've calmed down now. Why did you tell Matt what I was up to?" It'd been bugging me.

"Because I knew he cared for you, and I thought at the time you were making a mistake, dumping him. He's a nice guy."

"He wasn't nice, Lise. He was a selfish, greedy beggar, who behaved as though I was after his money. I paid for absolutely everything, while he kept hold of every penny."

"I know that now. Your Mum told me what had happened. I just thought he was being truthful, you know, that you kept pestering him to take you out, buy you stuff. I'm sorry."

"I had one meal out, on my birthday, which he said was my present. Even then he bitched about the bill so much

Salon Affair

that I offered to pay. Tight git ordered tap water, and scowled at me for asking for a glass of wine." We both began to laugh.

"Not like my Tony then, that man can certainly pack it away. We've been to every carvery in a ten mile radius."

"*Your* Tony? So you're an item now then?"

"Yeah," she admitted, "he's a sweetie, a real gentleman. Your Mum told me that your new fella's a real dish."

"He is indeed. He's got a killer body, abs and everything."

"I drew some on Tony's gut the other day, for a laugh," she admitted. We both howled with laughter. It felt so good to talk to her again. I'd really missed her. Nobody could make me laugh like Lisa. We arranged to meet in town on Sunday. Before I ended the call, she asked about the new salon. No doubt Mum had been boasting.

"It's gorgeous, slap bang in the middle of Mayfair. I'm going into partnership with Julian, so I'll have plenty of help," I told her.

"Sounds great. Are you buying the shop?"

"No, leasing it for fifteen years. It's a new lease. Mum's colleague, Mr Vizier is checking it over for me. My job for tonight is to read through it myself. It's a bloody long document, so I'm not looking forward to it." I glanced at the thick wad of paper on the coffee table, which had arrived in that day's post. One word on the front page jumped out at me, *Beta*.

"Lise, is there a way to find out who runs a company?" I asked.

"Yeah, companies house. I do it at work sometimes, why?"

"Could you do me a favour tomorrow please?"

"Sure."

"Find out who is behind Beta Limited. It keeps cropping up."

"Will do, and I'll bring it all on Sunday. Ten o'clock, Victoria, outside Coffee Republic yeah?"

"Can't wait."

I was just finishing off a client the next day when Gino arrived. I could tell it was him the moment he walked in. He was a distinguished, charismatic man, with immaculately groomed, pure white hair, and an elegance about him. He greeted a couple of the clients, who he clearly knew well, before wandering over to my client, who was beaming at him. "Gino, how lovely to see you again. Just wish it was under happier circumstances, Lily told me about poor Paulina. How is she?"

"She's poorly Margery, still unconscious. Terrible business. She's all the family I have left, so I feel very responsible. You're looking well, younger than ever. How's the family?" He had a trace of accent, and a deep, melodic voice. I could understand straightaway why all the ladies of the West End had thrown themselves at him, he must have been quite a looker in his day.

I left them to it, while I prepared Margery's bill. Gino still chatting as he escorted her through the salon to where I was waiting at the desk. I took her payment, and rebooked her. When she'd gone, he turned to me, "So you're the new talent Gray's been raving about. It's good to meet you at last."

I swelled with pride at the revelation that Gray rated me. "I've heard a lot about you too. I just wish the circumstances had been different. How is she?"

"Bad, very bad," he shook his head, his eyes downcast. "Even if she survives, she'll probably never be the same again. There was a lot of brain damage."

"That's....terrible," I didn't really know what else to say. "I'm so sorry."

"Thank you," he replied, "it must have been a terrible shock for you all, seeing it."

We were interrupted by Tomme seeing his client out. "GINO!" he screeched, "I'm so glad you're back, I've been traumatised. Poor Paulina, I heard you telling Marge that she was still in a coma." I watched as he hugged Gino hard. "Lil, would you take Lesley's bill for me please? She just had a cut and blow, needs some shampoo too." He turned to his client, "I'll leave you with Lily, ciao babe." He air-kissed her, then disappeared with Gino.

He held court on the staff room for the following few hours, chatting to each of us in turn. Unlike other salons, where the boss is normally hated, everyone seemed to genuinely adore Gino, who dispensed wisdom and encouragement to all the team members. He had a way of focussing while you spoke to him, as though what you had to say was of utmost importance. He'd patted my arm, and said that he hoped that the recent dramas hadn't put me off working for the salon.

"Of course not, I love it here. I'm very happy, apart from being sad for this week's events," I told him.

"And are the men all treating you well?"

"Absolutely. I adore them."

"That's good to hear. They all seem to love you too. Until this disaster, it seemed that Gray was running a very happy ship. He told me you designed the colour for the L'Oreal competition this year. I was very impressed when I saw the proofs. You showed a lot of skill and creativity, as well as innovative technical knowledge. I think it'll do well." He paused for a moment. "Gray also told me how supportive you were at the news of his illness. It breaks my heart to see him struggling, he's the son I never had..." he trailed off.

"We all promised to help Gray, we can cover any sickness, or time off between the rest of us." I was a little surprised that he'd told Gino; I'd half expected it to be a secret.

"You're a good woman, Lily, and I'm glad you found us. All the great hairdressers have heart, without it, our craft is just mechanical. Never let circumstances suck the joy out of your art." His eyes glistened as he spoke.

He left an hour later to visit Paulina in hospital. "Waste of time, from what I heard," said Tomme, "Apparently she's pretty much brain dead. If she survives, she'll probably be a vegetable. I'm going to trauma counselling because I'm so upset," he announced.

"Stop clutching your pearls Tomme," said Michael, "Gino won't give you her iPad however much fuss you make." Tomme stomped off to do his next client, throwing Michael a filthy look on his way out. "Such a drama queen," Michael muttered.

Julian came over late that evening, telling me they'd had a staff issue at the South Molten Street wine bar, which he'd had to sort out. "Caught a waiter stealing out of the till. Even when I showed him the CCTV footage, the bastard denied it," he said. I could see that he was angry, his lovely face belied his annoyance. "I had to wait half an hour for the police, then give a statement. Two fucking hours, just because that greedy lowlife couldn't keep his sticky fingers out of the till." he scrubbed his hands over his face. I placed a glass of wine on the table in front of him.

"The wanker even tried to justify himself, telling me I was rich, and wouldn't miss it." He thumped his hand on the sofa, making me jump. He was barely holding onto his self control, and it was kinda...hot.

"I know just the antidote for stress," I purred seductively, "and you're sexy as hell when you're angry." I watched as his face softened, a hint of a smile tugging at the corners of his mouth.

"I might be a bit rough," he murmured, "but then again, I think you like it that way."

He led me through into the bedroom, leaving me standing by the bed while he closed the blinds, and

Salon Affair

switched on the bedside lamps. "I think you like to really feel the passion, Lily. Feel how much I want you." His voice was low, and edge of danger to it. I shivered in anticipation as he circled me like a predator.

In a swift movement, he grasped the bottom of my shirt, and yanked it roughly over my head. My jeans followed soon after, dragged down my legs with none of his usual grace. He thrust his finger into me, followed by another, pumping them to feel my wetness. With his free hand, he yanked down one of the cups of my bra, freeing a nipple, which he suckled hard. I gasped at the intensity of it. I arched into him to try and relieve some of the pressure, but he carried on, his hot mouth tugging mercilessly.

He slipped his fingers out momentarily, leaving me bereft, until I felt a tugging at my hips, followed by a ripping noise, as he tore my knickers right off my body. "I have to fuck you right now," he said, his voice ragged and breathless. I undid my bra, as he quickly stripped off, his erection springing free, straining for attention. "Get on your knees," he ordered. I knelt down. "I'm gonna fuck your mouth."

His hands fisted in my hair as he held my head, thrusting his cock repeatedly into my eager mouth. I loved watching him lose control, surrender his cool, calculating manner, for those rare moments when I could glimpse the hot, passionate man within.

My eyes flicked upwards to gaze into his, as I swirled my tongue over the wide crest of his dick, concentrating on relaxing my throat so that he didn't choke me.

"Doggy style," he barked, pulling out of my mouth, and flipping me onto the bed. He plunged into me, gripping my hips, digging his fingers in, as he fucked me at a punishing pace. He slapped me twice, the noise ringing in the quiet, punctuated only by our breathing, and the noise of our bodies crashing together.

I could only hang on for dear life as his thrusts got ever harder, and faster, pushing my entire body up the bed, until only the pillow prevented my head from banging against the wall. "You want it rough? I'll fuck you rough," he gasped, before landing another resounding smack on my flesh.

I came with a scream. Best.Fuck.Ever.

Julian followed suit, calling out his climax like a wild animal. I felt him swell inside, as he let go, slumping forward onto my back, his slick, hot body pressing me into the mattress. We stayed silent for a few minutes. I could feel his heart hammering wildly in his chest. Eventually, his cock softened, and slid out. He rolled off me, and lay on his back with his arm over his face.

I shuffled onto my side, and pulled his arm down. "Hey you."

He opened one eye, and turned to face me. "Did I hurt you?"

"No, not at all. I loved it." I cringed inside slightly at using the 'L' word, but he didn't seem to notice. He rolled onto his side and smiled at me.

"You're beautiful, you know that?" Some unknown emotion clouded his face. "You're too good for me."

"Don't be daft," I said, brushing his hair back from his face, "I think you'll find it's the other way round." I took a deep breath, "Susie came into the salon today. She's very pretty."

"Did she?" His tone was mild, indifferent. "Yes, she's a pretty girl." A pang of jealousy hit me square between the eyes.

"Tell me about her. Were you together long?"

He screwed up his face. "Should we really be discussing my past relationships in bed after we've just had amazing sex?" I stayed silent. "We were together about six months, but it was over five years ago. She's a nice girl, we stayed friends, but thats it. What did she tell you?"

Salon Affair

"Not much, we didn't really discuss you. I don't think she knows we're together."

"Yeah she does. I told her you were my girlfriend when I recommended you. She was moaning about her hair the last time we spoke."

A strange relief washed over me. I'd been worried that he was keeping me a kind of dirty secret. "She's having trouble with her landlord. Do you know who runs Beta Limited?" *You must do as it's my landlord here.*

"It's a consortium I believe. My friend John is one of the many directors. They're just professional investors. I've always found them to be pretty good landlords. Susie's just pissed because she had a rent review, and won't get her own way. Her rent only went up by five grand a year, yet the way she's behaving, you'd think they were robbing her blind. A rent increase after five years is pretty normal. She asked me to get involved, but I fobbed her off, as I thought she'd got away light."

I relaxed. Susie had portrayed it as a huge amount, not just a hundred a week. With the way property prices in London were shooting up, her increase was chicken feed. "I forgot to tell you, I'm away this weekend. I promised my parents I'd attend my Godmother's birthday dinner. I'm combining it with a visit with them, I'd have asked you, but I know you're working tomorrow." He looked a little anxious.

"It's fine, I'm seeing Lisa on Sunday, so it suits me. Surrey isn't it? Where your parents live."

"Yeah, near Oxshott. I've not seen them for about two months, so I'd better show my face. I'll take you next time."

Lisa had really made the effort, wearing a smart, loose top, and a long, flowing skirt. She'd clearly been shopping for more than onesies. We hugged tight, "I've missed you, she said, standing back to look at me.

"You look wow. Guess being in love suits you," I exclaimed. She'd blowdried her hair straight, and was wearing full makeup, besides all that, she was glowing in the way only a woman in love can. She beamed at me.

"You look so sophisticated Lil. I feel like country mouse visiting the city mouse."

"Well you don't look it. Now, do you want to go for breakfast? or just a coffee to start with?" I led us out of Victoria station, and onto the street.

"Just coffee. I have something to show you." She sounded hesitant, a little unsure. We found a Starbucks, and she sat down while I fetched two lattes. She placed a file on the table between us. "I did that search for you, and I also called Matt, I hope you don't mind, but he can find out stuff that I can't." She fell silent, and pushed the file towards me. I opened it, and read the Companies House report.

Beta Limited
Formed: 18th August 2001
Company Number: 345768
Directors: Mr Julian Alexander
       The Meadows
       Oxshott Park
       Oxshott, Surrey
       OX3 4RY
Company Secretary: Mrs Margery Alexander
       Braden House
       Oxshott, Surrey
       OX4 5TG
The assignation of 100 ordinary shares are:
Mr J Alexander 99
Mrs M Alexander 1

I didn't really read the rest of the blurb, as my eyes were swimming with the revelation. Lisa leaned in, "Matt got hold of all the company accounts, I'm not sure how, but it appears that this Julian is pretty loaded. His company turns over a couple of million a year. Over two and a half million come in from rents alone. The company assets are listed in the millions too."

I felt the coldness prickling up my spine. "Why didn't he tell me?" I asked her.

"I don't know," she replied softly. "Maybe he didn't want you to know how rich he really is, in case, you know, you were a gold-digger?"

I stared at her with hurt eyes. "It's not just that, he's lied to me. Told me his friend John was one of the directors behind Beta." I flicked through the rest of the file. Matt had spelled out quite clearly all the properties he'd found on their books. I saw my flat, the Mayfair shop, and the South Molten Street wine bar, amongst a load more. *bastard.*

"I gather he found them all on the land registry," she said. "Lily, there might be a perfectly good explanation."

"Such as?"

"I don't know. I don't really understand about leases and stuff. It's him you need to talk to."

"What I really want to do is find this address in Surrey, and wring the truth out of his lying arse," I blurted, the flames of my anger burning me up inside.

"Is that really a good idea? I mean, you might find out something that you don't want to. He might have a wife, kids, anything."

"All the more reason to find out now. Jesus Lise, I was just about to go into business with him. I could be financially tied to him for years. I need to know."

We abandoned our day out, and walked back to Victoria, to get a train back to pick up Lisa's car.

Chapter 11

The closer we got to Oxshott, the worse I felt. Lisa tried her best to distract me, telling me all about her romance with Tony. He sounded straightforward, honest. *A bit like Matt was*, I thought wistfully. I felt homesick, for Bromley, for Matt, and for my boringly normal life. Anxiety was gnawing at my stomach, worsening as we passed a sign telling us we were in Oxshott. It was a leafy, affluent area, with huge houses which could only be glimpsed through the iron gates which seemed to guard every property.

I used the map on my iPhone to find Oxshott Park. It was a little like Keston Park, near home. Luxurious, large houses, on wide, beautifully kept plots, all displaying their owner's success in life in an extravagant, ostentatious way. Lisa whistled through her teeth, impressed.

The Meadows was every bit as large and impressive as its neighbours. It was a kind of faux-Georgian McMansion, newly built, and pristine. We stopped at the end of the drive. I spotted Julian's bike, parked neatly by the garage.

"So we're here, now what?" Lisa asked.

"I don't know," I admitted, losing my nerve somewhat. Part of me wanted to bang on the door and confront him, another part wanted to slink away quietly and forget all about it.

"Well, we've come all this way..." Lisa pointed out.

We both jumped out of our skins when someone knocked on Lisa's window. Some old bloke was staring into the car. Lisa wound her window down a bit. "Can I help you?" she asked.

"Neighbourhood watch. Can I ask why you're casing the joint?" he said in a posh accent.

"I'm looking for a friend, and wasn't sure if we've got the right house," I said.

"Who're you looking for? Perhaps I can help you," he replied, eyeing us warily.

"Julian Alexander. Does he live here?"

"Oh yes. You're at the right house." to my horror, he looked up and waved. "And here he is, the gentleman himself." I saw Julian walk towards us. He was clearly in weekend mode, wearing jogging bottoms and a jersey. It didn't escape my notice that he had slippers on his feet.

"Julian!" he called out. "These two young ladies are looking for you." Pleased with his good deed for the day, he wandered off, leaving us to face Julian, who had gone pale at the sight of me.

"What are you doing here?" he asked. He didn't sound angry at my stalking, just curious. My heart was in my mouth, and beating a frenetic pace. I felt stupid for going there, and panicked at what I'd discovered.

"This isn't your parent's house is it?" I demanded. "Are you married?" *I need to know, and seeing as I've already made a fool of myself, I may as well find out the truth.*

"Don't be daft, of course I'm not married. You'd better come in."

We followed him into an enormous entrance hall, beautifully decorated in rich creams and golds. It was a million miles away from his flat in London. At precisely that moment, I twigged. "The flat is just your office isn't it?"

He couldn't meet my eyes. "Yes, yes it is. I'm sorry for not telling you." My heart lurched. He was still the beautiful man whose body I craved with a passion, only now he couldn't look me in the face. *What have I done?* I glanced over at Lisa, noting that she couldn't take her eyes off his gorgeous body.

We followed him through to an enormous kitchen. It was lavishly fitted, a million miles away from his London flat/office/whatever. "Tea, coffee?" he asked. We both shook our heads. Lisa placed the file in front of him, on the kitchen island. I watched as he opened it, and flicked through it.

"Explains how you found me," he muttered, "how did you get hold of the accounts and property details though?"

"A friend of mine is a forensic accountant," Lisa told him. He scrubbed his hands over his face.

"Why did you lie to me?" I asked. "Did you think I was some sort of gold digger or something?"

"No, oh god no, I never thought that, not for a moment."

"So tell me, why?"

"Why what?" he asked. *Are you shitting me?*

"Why you lied about where you live? Why you lied about Beta? Why you invented this fictitious John?" I was shouting, my anger and humiliation getting the better of me. "Did you seriously want to set me up in a salon, be tied to me financially for five years, when you couldn't even be truthful about who you are?"

"Lily, it was his salon all along," said Lisa quietly, "He owns the freehold, it's on the list of properties." She threw him an accusing stare.

"I needed a hairdresser," he admitted, "but it was just pure luck that we met. I could've asked Anthony, or Trystan. Both of them have cut my hair before."

"But you wouldn't have got the extra benefits that I provided," I spat, "well, maybe you would. Either one of them would've been happy to lay back and think of England."

"Hang on," Lisa interjected, "did you only go for Lily because you needed a hairdresser?"

Salon Affair

"No, no, it was just luck," he replied rather weakly. With both of us quizzing him, he was struggling to defend himself.

"Forgive me for being suspicious," I said, "but there's a pattern here. You meet a girl, back her in a business housed in a property that you own secretly, then when you bow out of the business, having made a profit, you whack the rent up. Am I wrong?" He looked down at the black marble of the worktop, not meeting my eyes. "Answer me," I barked, "am I wrong?"

"Yes you are. I'll admit that it was my intention when I met you. I'll admit that I've done it before, but I need you in a way that I've never needed anyone before. That's the truth. I told you, I couldn't breathe if I needed you any more than I do."

I gave a hollow laugh. "You fed Susie that line too. She told me." I watched as he sucked in a breath. "Come on Lise, let's go. Our deal's off Julian. I'll vacate your flat at the end of my tenancy agreement." We stood to leave.

"Lily, this isn't what you think," he began. I didn't hang around to hear the rest of his excuses, sweeping out, dragging a rather lumbering Lisa behind me. She didn't really do fast exits terribly well. "Wait," he called out behind us.

We jumped in the car, well, I jumped, Lisa squeezed in quickly. "Just drive," I commanded. She floored the accelerator, and the little Fiat lurched away. We drove along in silence for a while.

"You ok?" she asked. The dam burst, and my tears flowed. She pulled over, and fished a tissue out of her bag. "Let it out babe, let all the disappointment out."

"I'm not upset about the salon," I said between sobs, "I just can't believe...." I couldn't get the words out.

"Can't believe what?"

"That I wasn't good enough for him to tell me the truth. Like I'm just a stupid, common little hairdresser, and not good enough to live in his world." At this point, I had a mixture of tears, makeup and snot dripping down my face. I glanced in the vanity mirror. No wonder he'd kept me away from his real life, there was no way I was millionaire's girlfriend material.

"Come on, let's go back to London, and drink ourselves silly in a posh hotel."

So we ended up in the Mandarin Oriental. "This is just like Hotel Babylon," Lisa remarked, sipping on her kir royale. I looked around.

"It is a bit," I agreed. It was a relief to just indulge in telly talk, away from business plans, problems, and dramas. It was always a habit of mine, pushing problems I didn't want to face to the back of my mind, and concentrating on the mundane."What's happening on Eastenders? I've not seen it for a fortnight."

By the time Lisa went home, we were both laggin drunk. She honked up purple sick outside Victoria station, which made me laugh so hard that I wet myself. In turn, she laughed so much at me, that she threw up again. God, I'd missed her.

It didn't really hit me until I was laying in bed that night, alone, missing Julian's warm body next to me. He hadn't tried to call, and in my heart of hearts, I knew full well that I'd been well and truly played. It hurt, actually it was agony, knowing that the man I'd fallen in love with so totally had only been interested because of how he could use me. I cried myself to sleep.

"You look rough babe, good weekend?" Trystan said as I walked into the staff room next morning wearing dark glasses.

"Not really, well, I dumped Julian, and got pissed in the Mandarin Oriental with my best mate Lisa." All ears pricked up.

"Dumped Julian? Why?"

Salon Affair

    I'd actually given a lot of thought as to what to tell my workmates. I couldn't tell them about the new salon, because even though the deal was off, I'd have been sacked, so instead I told them that I'd found out that Julian was my landlord, and that he really lived in Surrey.
    "I knew it!" Trystan exclaimed. "I knew the man had to be spending his money on something."
    "It was when you said that, I decided to dig a bit. Deep down, I knew you were right." He beamed triumphantly.
    "So what's his place like?" Tomme asked.
    "Huge, gorgeous, like wet-your-knickers stunning," I told them. "I only saw the hall and kitchen, but they were to die for."
    Tomme looked thoughtful. "So let me get this straight, you found out that he was loaded, and had kept it secret from you, for reasons unknown, and yet you dump him? Are you mad or stupid? Or both? It's not like he was a secret gay, mores the pity, or worse still, married with crotchfruit."
    "He might have felt embarrassed at being so rich, didn't want you to be with him for his money," added Michael.
    "Hmm, well, I don't know about that. All I know is he lied to me, blatantly. Whatever his reasons were, he's a liar."
    "All men lie Lily, It's kind of built in. You need to get over that," Tomme told me.
    "I've already dumped him, so it's too late. He didn't call me after we left."
    "He'll call," said Trystan. The others all nodded in agreement. "Don't you dare speak to him, or reply to any texts until you've had some coaching from one of us though."
    The next bit of excitement that day was a handsome, Mediterranean man walking into reception, then being taken through to the staff room by Gray. Tomme said hello

as he walked through, so I sidled up to him while he was mixing a colour. "Who's that?"

"Pierre, top stylist at Ten," he whispered, "Must've approached Gray for a job."

"How on earth will he squeeze in? It's not like we've got tons of space."

"He's got a vast clientele too. Maybe Gray'l install another mirror on the back wall. It'd be tight, but do-able. He's not gonna miss a chance to nick Pierre, been after him for ages."

Half an hour later, Gray introduced me to Pierre, telling me he'd be starting with us in two days time. I beamed a smile, and welcomed him. His accent was adorable. Only Anthony didn't appear too happy at the news that he'd be joining us.

"What's up with you?" I asked. "You've got a face like a smacked arse."

"I've been flirting with him for ages at Mancave. Off limits now," he muttered. I frowned, not understanding. "You don't shit on your own doorstep Lil. None of us shag each other. We work together; it'd be too awkward." *Oh, I geddit.*

I was in the middle of a blow dry when a bouquet arrived. "For you," Lottie muttered, sloping out to the staff room with it. I finished my client, and wandered through to see them. "Told you," whispered Trystan as I walked past him. Lottie had dumped them rather unceremoniously on the floor. I found the bucket, and added some water, before placing them upright.

This time they were pink lilies, all tied up in a pretty, pink bow. I pulled the card off its little holder, and opened it. I recognised Julian's handwriting immediately.

I'm sorry, I screwed up. Please meet me and let me explain. I can't bear to lose you

"Good first start," said Tomme over my shoulder, making me jump about three feet into the air. "Don't answer him though. Let him stew." With that, he skipped back out into the salon. I checked my phone. There was a couple of missed calls from my Mum, due to me texting her that the salon deal was off, and her colleagues didn't need to check the lease. She probably wanted to know what had happened, and I just didn't feel up to explaining it all. Lisa would probably fill her in. I was still holding it when it began to ring, Julian's name appearing on the screen. I declined the call, and put it on silent. I'd deal with it later.

By lunchtime, there were seven missed calls from Mum, and four from Julian. I ignored his, and called Mum back. "I heard what happened," she said, "Lisa told me."

"Glad I don't have to go through it all again," I said, "He's sent flowers and been trying to call, but I just don't feel up to talking to him."

"I know," she soothed, "must have been a shock. Listen, why don't you come to dinner tonight? I'll do a nice roast." It was my day off the following day. The thought of some down time in the safety of my family home sounded wonderful.

"Count me in. I'll be at Bromley South around seven."

With Mum all happy, I went out to reception to check my schedule for the afternoon. I frowned when I saw that a staff meeting had been booked at half five, just as we were finishing. *Damn, needed a quick exit.*

"Apparently Gino requested it. Dunno why," said Gray, who was taking his client's bill. "Still, it shouldn't take long."

Gino arrived just after five, bearing two bottles of wine. He disappeared into the staffroom, presumably to get everything ready. By the time I'd finished my client, all the others were in there. I locked the door, and trotted through.

Gino handed me a glass of wine, and motioned me to sit down. "Right, now that we're all here, I'll begin." He paused as though he was trying to find words. "Paulina is gravely ill, as you all know. If, and it's a big if, she wakes up, the doctors expect the brain damage to be severe and debilitating. Whatever happens, she won't be coming back to work.

This happened in *my* salon. It was, in effect, *my* fault. I'm struggling to come to terms with that. I have made a promise to both Paulina, her mother, my late sister Crocetta, and myself, that I will look after Paulina for the rest of her life. Because of this, I've made a difficult decision. I'm going to put the salon up for sale."

There was a collective gasp.

"Please don't Gino," Tomme begged. "We'll all help you. We won't be any trouble, I promise."

Gino smiled indulgently. "Tomme, it's not that simple. Paulina will need round the clock care, and I need to make sure there is enough money for that after I'm long gone. Besides.....it's time."

"No it's not," Tomme argued, "we make you good money, and that'll pay for Paulina's nursing."

"Tomme," Gray placed his hand on Tomme's arm, and shook his head. "His mind's made up."

"It is," agreed Gino. "Before I put it on the open market, I'm going to offer it to all of you. I'm looking for a million. I had it valued at one point two million, so I'm prepared to offer it at a preferential rate if you want to do a buyout. If you don't, or can't, then I'll place it on the open market next week."

"It'll go to some horrible corporate buyer," Tomme wailed, "they'll make us all be employees on minimum wage, and use cheap shampoo...and, and, do fifteen minute haircuts."

"I won't sell to Supercuts Tomme, don't worry." With that, Gino left.

We were all reeling from the shock. "Can't you buy it?" Trystan asked Gray.

He shook his head. "Not with the divorce looming, and being ill, I mean, nobody will lend money to an HIV

Salon Affair

sufferer. I'll need to use all the proceeds from the flat sale to buy a little place to live. There wouldn't be enough anyway by the time Chris has had his share."

I looked around the room. None of us could do it, even collectively. "Corporate buyer it is then," spat Trystan, "I suppose all good things come to an end."

"Can't you get back with Julian and ask him?" Michael said.

"No I can't," I snapped. "He'd be a worse snake than Supercuts." It was actually a great idea, although I wasn't sure how to go about it.

After such a dramatic few days, it was bliss to be back home in the comfy, familial bosom. Mum fussed round, making her special gravy, while Dad was dispatched to pick up Doris to make it a family occasion. Even Mark seemed quite perky, looking up from his new iPad from time to time.

Dad had to help Doris up the steps to the front door, she was definitely getting wobblier as time went on. He parked her at the dining table, and placed a glass of wine in front of her. "Linda, do you need any help?" She called out.

"No, just dishing up. You enjoy your wine," Mum yelled back. I sat back and soaked up the normality. It was comforting.

"I hear you pulled out of that Mayfair salon?" Doris said.

"Yes. Julian hadn't told me the whole truth. He owned the freehold. Made out someone else did. I don't know whether he went for me because he needed a hairdresser, or because he actually liked me," I explained.

"I see. Very wise not to get involved until you know for sure one way or another," she agreed. "What else has been happening?"

Telling them all the dramas of the past fortnight took the entire dinner. During dessert (one of Mum's famous baked Alaska's) I told them about our staff meeting that day.

"It might get sold to someone who'll keep things on an even keel," said Dad.

I shook my head. "Only a hairdresser would do that. I watched the way Julian squeezed profit out of his businesses. Any non-hairdresser would cut back on stock and stuff, they wouldn't understand that we need huge ranges to have the confidence to be creative. It's the creativity that clients come to us for. I saw what the bean counters did to Gavin Roberts. Cheap colour ranges, basic products, and tightly controlled staff management. It's completely different where I am now. We work longer, harder and faster than anyone ever did at Gavin Roberts, and we make more money than any stylist there ever did. Trying to control hairdressers with HR rules just doesn't seem to work."

"Like herding cats, I should think," Mark piped up.

"Well, yeah. For instance, at Gavin Roberts, if you finished at six, and someone walked in at ten to, wanting a haircut, they'd be turned away, because the staff member would only be paid until six on the dot. At Gino Venti, we'd do it, because we'd get our forty percent. Gino would also be getting forty percent too. So rather than a hundred percent of nothing, the salon earns forty percent of something. It works."

"And there's six of you there?" Doris asked.

"Soon to be seven. Gray managed to lure the top stylist from our rival to come and join us. He starts day after tomorrow."

"How come?" Mum asked.

"His salon joined up with some company that fits out your salon free, in return for using their manky products for five years. I looked at that deal for the Mayfair salon until Julian pointed out that it was a scam."

"This Julian sounded quite a clever chap." Doris said.

"Yeah, he was. Had lots of successful businesses, all with his exes at the helm though," I told her.

Salon Affair

"So he picked his women according to what business he wanted to set up?" Mark asked. "That's actually pretty clever."

"Might be clever, but it wasn't very nice being on the receiving end. I'll never know if he just wanted me for my hairdressing skills, or because he liked me." I suspected it was for my hair skills.

"Maybe it's time to discuss the kids' inheritance?" Doris said to Mum, looking rather pointedly at me.

"Oh, I'm not sure about that Doris. It's a bit early, hopefully you've got a lot more years in you yet."

"Don't be daft Linda. Better that they have it when opportunity strikes than when they've got nothing better to spend it on than holidays and rubbish."

"We inherit something? Cool!" Mark exclaimed.

"Not yet you don't," snapped Mum. "Don't go getting ideas."

"Linda, you must agree that you had help when it was needed. If you had it now, would it have made the same difference to your lives?" Doris asked. Mum shook her head.

"You're thinking of doing the same for Lil?" Dad said. I held my breath, thrilled with the way the conversation was going.

"I am. This is a great opportunity, and to be fair, if a good businessman such as this Julian thinks she could do it, I'm prepared to trust his judgement, and back her myself." She turned to me, "Lily, this would take up your entire inheritance. Is it what you want? There'd be nothing left over to buy a home with."

"I don't mind working to buy a house," I declared, my insides fizzing with excitement. "Gino wants a million quid though, I'm not sure you heard that bit."

"Of course I heard that bit," Doris snapped. "I might be old, but I'm not deaf yet." She beamed at me, the smile of proud, loving family. "I'd suggest you call this Gino, and make sure nobody else buys it."

After dinner, when everyone was settled in the lounge watching Masterchef, I took my phone upstairs to my room, and with slightly trembling hands, phoned Gino. "Hello Lily, what's up?" He answered.

"I was wondering if we could meet tomorrow?" I said. "I'm in a position to put in an offer for the salon."

"Is it family money?" He asked.

"Yes, yes it is."

"You have no idea how happy this will make me, knowing that my life's work will carry on. Where and when shall we meet to discuss this?"

"Ten ok? Where would work for you?" I had no idea where he lived or stayed.

"Ten o'clock in the Savoy? We can have brunch."

"Super, I'll see you then."

I hugged myself with glee. I wanted it so badly, both for myself, and knowing that the boys would be happy too. I went back downstairs. "I'm meeting him at ten tomorrow. He's delighted."

"Good."

Doris went home after Masterchef 'to get settled', as she put it. I promised to call her as soon as I had some news. I decided to go back to my own flat, as I needed to be in town for the next day. Mum took me to the station.

"You're not angry about Doris' offer are you?" I asked.

"Not at all. I'm surprised, but you know, they did the same for us when we were young and struggling."

"I can't believe she's got that much money. She's quite frugal."

"Well what's she gonna do with it? Go travelling? Hang-gliding lessons?" We both laughed. "All she wants is to see her family happy."

I hugged Mum tight, then hopped out of the car to get my train. Pulling my phone out of my bag, I could see

Salon Affair

another four missed calls from Julian. *Points for persistence*, I thought. Thanks to the events of the evening, I'd had a few hours of respite from the crushing misery of missing him. I debated calling him, but noting that it was gone eleven, decided against it.

I strolled into the Savoy lounge at two minutes to ten the next morning, to find Gino sitting there waiting. *Typical hairdressers, always on time.* He stood to greet me, kissing both my cheeks, as is the Italian way. We were shown straight through to the elegant morning room, all starched white tablecloths and gleaming silverware. "I'm having poached eggs on toast, what would you like me to order for you?" Gino asked. *Such a gentleman.*

"I'll have the same please, and a latte, thank you." I waited quietly while he ordered from the immaculate waiter. It was all so civilised. When the waiter disappeared, Gino turned to me.

"So you have the backing of your family?"

I nodded. "They've agreed that I should have my inheritance early. I'd like to preserve and build on what you achieved."

"That's comforting. The boys will be relieved. I brought the last three years accounts for you to look at. I want you to be happy that this deal is a good investment for your family." He handed me three bound pamphlets. Each one was a year's balance sheet and accounts. I read through, not really understanding them. One item jumped out though.

"How come the rent's so low?"

"It's a long lease, it was 99 years, there's 89 years left. It's why the price is so high. It's not a large shop, but it's well situated." *Surely he realises it's worth more than that?*

"Who valued the salon?" I asked.

"A friend who's into property and businesses. I asked him."

"Oh ok. Do you know how he came to the figure?"

"Julian took the profit, multiplied it by three, then added the value of the building I believe." *Julian?*

"Was it the fella who has the wine bar down the road?"

"Yes, comes in for haircuts. I take it you've met him then? Nice fella, very successful."

"Yes, I've cut his hair." *Naked...*

I changed the subject, and asked about Paulina. Instantly I saw regret and worry cloud his face. "She won't really recover, if she wakes up at all. The doctors say there was a lot of brain damage. They won't know just how much until the swelling goes down, but they've told me to prepare for the worst."

"I'm so sorry..." I trailed off. "One of the boys said she was your only family?"

"Immediate family, yes. My sister died when Paulina was twelve. Her Dad had died in an accident when she was a baby, so she regarded me more as a father than an uncle. I have some distant cousins, but that's about it. Tell me about your family. You have brothers? sisters?"

"I have one younger brother, Mark. He still lives with our parents."

"And they're happy to buy you a salon?"

"It's actually my Great Aunt giving me my inheritance early. She's a widow, but lives nearby and is very much part of our little family."

"Families should always help each other. When we have nothing else, we can always rely on our blood relatives."

We spent the next hour chatting about hair, the salon, and gossip surrounding the other celebrity hairdressers. Gino was a hoot, full of wicked stories, and happy to dish the dirt on a few famous stylists who had originally been trained by him. "I said to Nicky, you can't let her leave my salon like that. It looks like you cut her hair with a knife and fork. It was the wonkiest cut you've ever seen; a full inch longer one side than the other. The poor boy just had no sense of symmetry. I gather he's improved a lot now

Salon Affair

though. He'd cry in the staff room after every haircut back then."

I giggled at the thought of it. Gino glanced at his watch. "I really need to go. It's visiting time soon."

I picked up the accounts, and Gino's solicitors details, and we hugged goodbye, with a promise to speak again in the next couple of days. I sat back to finish my coffee, and debated what to do. I really needed someone to take a look at the accounts, and I didn't trust Julian's valuation. Sucking in a deep breath, I called Matt. He answered straightaway, "Lily."

"Hi Matt. I know it's not terribly appropriate, but I wondered if you'd do me a favour?"

A hour later, I was treating Matt to lunch in a bistro near his office. I watched as he went through the balance sheets meticulously, tapping away on his calculator, and scribbling things down on a notepad. "While I'm doing this, google 'commercial property W1, and see if you can work out what that shop's worth." I did as he asked, as we both ate one handed.

"I've found one," I told him, "It's not on South Molten street, but close enough, and it's got eighty years left on it. It's up for eight fifty." *Wow.*

"Sounds about right," he murmured.

I'd finished my sandwich by the time Matt had worked through his calculations. "Gino had a good accountant by the looks of it. The person valuing the business took the end profit figure, and quite correctly multiplied it by three. What they didn't do was strip out the depreciation, amortisation and directors loan accounts first."

"I don't know what that means," I confessed.

"They're just legal ways to reduce your tax bill." He explained them in simple terms until I understood.

"So, in effect, I'd say you were getting a really good deal. It's definitely worth more than he's asking for it."

"Thank you," I said. I was grateful for his help. "How's the flat?"

"It's nice," he told me, "but it wasn't worth losing you over." He paused, "will you reconsider?"

I felt so sorry for him, but in truth it was all I felt. Matt was a nice guy. He deserved a nice wife, two kids, and a white picket fence. Julian had ruined me for the Matts of the world. "You deserve a good woman who doesn't work weekends, doesn't spend a thousand quid on a dress, and shares your dream of a comfortable middle class life. I'm not that girl. I'm sorry." I was genuinely sorry, as he represented all that was comfortable and familiar. It wasn't his fault I'd tasted a sex life that was a million miles away from his indifferent, 'efficient' shags. I wanted explosive orgasms and a bit of kink in my future, and I knew it wouldn't come from him.

I'd just got home that evening, after a bit of shopping, when my buzzer went. I pressed the intercom gingerly, fully expecting it to be Julian. I was delighted to hear it was Tomme. "Can I come up?"

He arrived wearing a tiger print onesie, complete with little ears. He was also bearing Hagen-Daz choc chip ice cream. "We need comfort food," he announced, before plonking himself down on the sofa, and switching on my telly.

"What's up?" I asked.

"I'm depressed. My life is a wreck. I'm gonna end up working at Supercuts, nobody loves me, and I may as well get fat. That's why I came round here, you're a worse mess than me. It makes me feel better."

I laughed, and grabbed two spoons. "I can make you feel better," I told him.

"Lily, don't start all that. I'm strictly batting for the home team. No offence, but I don't like fannies."

I smacked his arm. "I didn't mean that, idiot. I agreed to buy the salon today. Gino and I shook on it." His head whipped round to stare at me.

"You're not lying are you?"

"Nope, its 100% gods honest truth."

"You made up with Julian? Did he buy it for you?"

"No, my aunt gave me my inheritance early."

"Fuck me."

"I'd rather not, if you don't mind."

"Do the others know?"

"No, not yet. I only met up with Gino today to agree it all. We instructed solicitors this morning. It'll all take a while to go through."

He sat, spoon poised above the ice-cream. "I really don't want to get fat. Are we gonna stay Gino Venti?"

"Yep. I'd rather not change the name if I don't have to." *I must ask Gino about that..*

Tomme put his spoon down, and flipped down the hood of his onesie. "I feel so much better already. Everyone'll be relieved, especially Gray. You won't sack him for being poz, will you?" I shook my head.

"I'm not changing anything. I like how it is. I've never known such a happy salon." Tomme pulled me into a fierce hug.

"We'll all be good, I promise Lil. We'll make you loads of money, and you'll be famous, especially if we lift the trophy this year. Just don't have anything to do with that Sugar company. Pierre told me they took George, his boss, to some nasty fetish club, and asked him to whip and fondle that Charlie fella while the wife watched. George doesn't swing that way, and was horrified at the thought of touching another man's dick. He's desperately trying to get out of his contract with them, especially after losing Pierre." *Ah, so he's the perv. Thought so.*

"I definitely won't be going over to the dark side that is all things Sugar," I reassured him. "I'm sure the annual

Sugar colour trophy would just be various shades of beige. I've seen their range, and beige features heavily." We both giggled.

    We snuggled up to watch Eastenders, comfortable to just hang out. I opened a bottle of wine, and made some pasta. "When you're our boss, do you think you'll change?" he asked.

    I paused, a forkful of pasta hovering in the air. "I genuinely don't know. Gray will still be manager, and I'll still do hair. Beyond that, I haven't given it much thought. I hope not."

    "I hope not as well. You're alright....for a girl."

Chapter 12

As soon as Tomme told the guys at work the news, the whole atmosphere perked up enormously, despite Gray being a bit green around the gills because of his new tablets, and the news that Paulina was still in a coma.

Gino popped in to see us all, and confirmed to everyone that it was all agreed, and the solicitors had started. He also confirmed that I didn't need to change the name, if I didn't want to, which was a relief. He also gave me the details of his accountant, a small firm in Holborn, in case I wanted to use them.

Mum called mid-morning to tell me that her firm had received the lease and stuff from Gino's, and would try and push things through as fast as possible. Doris had already given her a cheque for the money, which would be paid into the solicitor's client account, so that everything was ready.

The day flew by, as we were exceptionally busy, plus we were still short of a receptionist, so Tula had to cover the desk, leaving us with just the sullen, and rather slow Lottie, who seemed to disappear into the loo whenever one of us needed a client shampooing. *Lazy little cow.* Gray had to switch them over before the rest of us mutinied.

I was just finishing my last client, dressing out a bouncy blowdry, when Michael sidled up. "Julian's in reception, asking to speak to you. What do you want me to say?" My stomach fizzed slightly with excitement. I was missing him dreadfully, and was looking forward to rubbing his nose in the fact that I didn't need his precious money.

"Tell him I won't be long," I replied. I finished what I was doing, and showed the client the back of her hair. He stood up as I walked through to reception with her, to sort out her products, and take her bill. "I won't be long," I said to him, before switching my attention back to the client.

She was one of those indecisive ones that took ages to decide which products she liked best. I'd made my recommendations, which she'd smelt, looked at, and read the leaflets on. In the end she bought a different range, on the basis that it matched her bathroom colour scheme. I disguised my contempt, and scanned it into the computer. We then had to spend another five minutes waiting for her to decide which card to use, wondering out loud whether hairdos came under her household budget, or luxury expenditure. *Couldn't you have thought about that while I was doing it?* Eventually, she paid and left, and I had to deal with Julian.

"Hi," he said.
"Hi," I replied.
Silence.
"Can we talk?" he asked. He looked like shit, with dark circles around his now dull, blue eyes, and about four days worth of stubble, which on him, wasn't a good look.

"I'll just get my things, and say goodbye. I won't be long." I left him there while I pulled on my jacket, and walked into the staff room to get my bag. Gray was berating Lottie for her appalling attitude, while she just had her bottom lip out in that unpleasant, sulky way. "Oops, sorry, I just need my bag," I said, grabbing my handbag, "See you tomorrow."

Julian didn't say much at first, as we walked down South Molten Street. "Where are we going?" I asked.

"Something to eat? Somewhere quiet where we can talk. There's a lot I need to explain to you."

Salon Affair

"Really? Why's that?" I asked, rather snarkily. Although events had taken my mind off him, I hadn't forgotten just how shit I'd felt at his house. There was no way I was just forgiving and forgetting, as much as I wanted to. I needed to make him sweat a bit, work hard to get me back. At least that was what Trystan told me, not that he was a good advert for 'how to get and keep a man'.

"I need to tell you about myself, tell you the truth."

This was too good an opportunity to pass up, just to maintain my 'bitch' persona, so I let him lead me into a small Italian restaurant just off Oxford street. He clearly knew the owner, greeting him by name, and asking for their most private table, which turned out to be a small booth near the back of the room. We sat down, and Julian asked for a bottle of Chianti, while I read the menu. "I think I'll just have the sole please, when you order," I said to him.

I sat back while he placed our orders, watching his familiar face, his lovely smile, as he thanked the waiter. I was expecting him to come out with excuses as to why he'd lied, so I braced myself for them. "Not working tonight then?" I asked, mainly to break the ice. The nervous energy was flowing off him in waves.

"I've not been into work since last week. After Sunday, I've not felt like it."

"Oh? Why's that?"

"Isn't it obvious?"

"Not to me it isn't, no."

"Now you're just being obtuse Lily. I lost you, through my own stupid fault."

"You only wanted me because I was a hairdresser, to head up your salon. It'll be easy to find another one, London's full of hairdressers who'd bite your hand off."

"That's not what I'm upset about. I can let that shop out for anything, I don't care if it stays a salon or not."

"You cared enough to seduce me in order to start you a salon." I wasn't about to give in gracefully. He hadn't even confessed anything.

He steepled his fingers in front of his face, and stared at me intently. "Ok, I'll confess that I was on the lookout for a hairdresser, and when I saw you with the boys from across the road, I asked Anthony who you were. You fitted the bill perfectly, and I asked you out for that reason. What I didn't bank on was the way you made me feel." He sucked in a breath. "You were this funny mix of naivety and intelligence, and you made me feel as though I could look at the world through your fresh eyes, with your optimism and enthusiasm."

He stopped speaking while the waiter served our food. "I'm not very good at this," he muttered when the waiter had disappeared.

"Not good at what?"

"Explaining my feelings. You're a closed book, and I'll never forget how horrified you were, seeing me at home. I feel terrible about that."

"It wasn't good, still, I'm feeling better now...thanks for asking." I knew I was being sarcastic, but he hadn't really told me anything much. I began to eat, ignoring him to concentrate on my dinner, which was delicious.

"I'm sorry, I just want you to know that," he murmured. I put down my knife and fork.

"What I don't get is why you don't just rent out these shops. Why do all the fake seduction thing, and have the hassle of setting up the businesses? Why go to all that trouble when you could just rent 'em out and forget about them?"

He chewed thoughtfully for a moment. "If you saw the figures, you'd understand. When I bought my first shop, I struggled to let it. It just wouldn't let, even offering three months free. I chatted up some girl in a bar, who desperately wanted a coffee shop, it was her dream, you know, to have her own business. I had her in that shop within two weeks, and I made more than double what I would've made had I just rented it out. I saved the money, as I was still working in the city back then, and bought another shop. I suppose once you've done something once, it seems the easiest way to get a property filled."

"Isn't that just using those women?"

"Not really, they got what they wanted, which was a profitable business."

"No, Julian, they wanted you. Can't you see that? What were you going to do? Go through life seducing women to get tenants? Don't you think that's a bit....sick?"

"I have shops let out to men too, and I can promise you I didn't seduce anyone for those. I don't play a part in their businesses though. I'm friends with all the women involved. I wouldn't have done it with someone I didn't get on with."

"They're friends with you because you lied to them. They have no idea that you're their landlord. That's kind of false pretences, isn't it. What's even more insulting is that you assumed I'd be too stupid to figure it out."

"Well none of them have worked it out yet." He was becoming defensive. "Those women weren't perfect Lily, Gemma didn't fancy me, Susie got bored with me, I can list them all out with the reasons they each rejected me. The only one who didn't was you."

"I'm sorry, I don't believe you. All those women are affectionate towards you, and let's face it, you've not been hit with the ugly stick." I was getting annoyed. "I thought you were the most gorgeous, sexy man I'd ever be lucky enough to meet. I liked your geeky side, all the knowledge and details that you soak up, it fascinated me. Then when I find out it was all an act, because I'm just a dopey hairdresser, not fit to live in your world, yes, it bloody hurt. Yet here I am, sitting like a mug, because I actually believed, no, wanted to believe, that you had something to tell me that would actually change things." I could hear my voice rising, and a stupid tear rolled down my face. I swiped it away angrily.

"I'm in love with you," he barked, "does that change things?" he added, more softly.

I blinked, not quite sure I heard him right. His face held a sadness, a yearning expression. " I don't know," I said. "I truly don't know what to believe."

"I was following my usual pattern, I met you, chased you, made myself interesting. All the things I've done before. I deceived you into thinking that the office was my home. It should have been as straightforward as the others, only it wasn't. That first night, when I put you to bed, I watched you sleeping for hours. It was like you were sent to me, to show me, you know, that I can love." He kept his eyes firmly on his meal, which he wasn't eating. "When I made love to you, it seemed as though your orgasm took you by surprise, that you'd never experienced it before. Am I right?"

I was struck a bit dumb, and could only nod in agreement. "When you ran out on me that night, it was because I snapped at you, wasn't it?" Another nod. "I was furious that I'd let you get under my skin like that, angry that I'd lost control of my own emotions. I don't do stuff like that, I don't fall in love."

"Why not?"

"Because the one time I did, she upped and left me. I was in a black pit of despair for months. I vowed never to put myself in that position again. I kept my life simple, had my businesses to keep me occupied, a nice home, a good social life. I was happy. Then boom, you walk in, and yet again I'm crawling around trying to find some air to breathe." *Hang on pal, I'm not the liar around here.*

"Perhaps, if you felt that way, honesty would've been the best policy," I pointed out, "then you wouldn't be trying to talk your way out of this."

"I know that now."

We ate in silence for a while. My mind was racing. I wanted to believe him, wanted him to make things right between us, but knowing he'd lied so easily before, made me wary. "Do you hate me now?" He asked.

"No." I could say quite truthfully. "I desperately want to believe you, but right now, I've a lot to take in, and I'm not entirely sure if I could ever trust you again."

"I'll take a solemn vow never to lie to you again." He held three fingers up in a scouts honour sign. I giggled. "That's a lovely sound," he said, smiling. I smiled back, tentatively.

He insisted on walking me home. "So will you drive to Surrey tonight?" I asked.

"No, not if I spend the evening in town, or if I've had a drink. I just stay at the office. Any chance of a coffee before I go home?"

"No, it's late, and I'm tired. I'm not ready to jump into bed with you again, you know that don't you?"

"What's it gonna take to convince you?"

"I don't know, time I suppose."

"When's your next day off?"

"Next week now, why?"

"Because I'm gonna take you home to Oxshott, and introduce you to my parents."

"Ok." *Shit! What am I gonna wear?*

He gently grazed my cheek with his goodnight kiss, soft and chaste, but still close enough for me to inhale his lovely Julian-scent. It'd been a hell of a day, but I went to bed with a smile on my face.

I floated into work the next day with that same stupid grin on my chops. "Here she comes, bet you shagged him," screeched Tomme as I sauntered into the staff room.

"Nope, I took all your advice on board, and said 'not yet'. You'd have all been proud of me."

"You won't be able to say things like that to her when she's the boss you know," Michael pointed out. Both Tomme and I rolled our eyes.

"I won't be having a personality transplant you know," I muttered.

"Spose not. Ok then Lil, did you at least give him a blow job to keep him going then?" Michael was back to normal. I breathed a sigh of relief. The last thing I wanted was for anyone to be scared to be themselves around me.

"Nope," I popped the 'p' sound. "I listened to my inner bitch, and left him with blue balls."

"Attagirl. You're learning."

I made a coffee, and changed into my heels, ready to start the day. Pierre was joining us, and I beamed a smile at him, and shook his hand when he arrived. His accent really was adorable. I had a cancellation that morning, so worked the desk. I marvelled at the sheer number of clients booked in with Pierre in advance, he clearly had a vast clientele, which would probably rival Trystan's.

News must have spread fast, because the phone was ringing off the hook all morning with people trying to book in. It was handy having another stylist, as Tomme and Anthony were out doing the regionals for the colour trophy. It wasn't deemed important enough to be a whole salon event, which we'd have to close for.

They came back at five, looking extremely pleased with themselves. "Head and shoulders above the rest," Tomme screeched, "We're finalists!"

"Well done," said Gray, "looks like we're closing for a day then. Have they given you the date of the final yet?"

"Sunday 4th May. We need to get there at ten," Anthony told him. "The only close contenders were Toni and Guy, but they did a copper block effect, not a patch on ours. The judges were fascinated by how we discovered how to make that lilac. I just told them that we had a very geeky colour expert who experiments all the time." I beamed at him, and

Salon Affair

hooked my arm around his shoulders to give him a squeeze. Gray blocked that day out on the computer.

"Everyone needs to make sure they have fresh haircuts a day or two before. Lily, Tomme, make sure your roots are done please. We need to blow the competition out of the water in every possible way." *I'll wear my Prada dress and shoes.*

With that all settled, we got back to our clients. I worked fairly late that evening, still finishing before Pierre, who I'd barely spoken to as he'd been so busy. The odd bits of his work I'd seen had been good, but relatively ordinary, well, ordinary for a salon such as ours. I realised that I'd very quickly got used to a superlative standard of hairdressing. A stylist like Pierre would've had jaws dropping in Gavin Roberts. Up against the finesse of Trystan's cutting, Gray's styling, and Antony's colouring, he was a little.....meh.

We all gathered in the wine bar for his welcome drink. "I can't believe how busy you were for a first day," Michael told him.

"Yez, I have lotz oz ladieez, who followz me."

"How did they know where you were?" I asked, frowning slightly.

"Ze word, it gets around quick you know. My clientz, they all friendz of friendz. Zey tell each ze ozzer."

"Oh, I see, well that's good."

"George, my old boss, he not think zo. My Mama, she tell a few people, zey spread ze word. George, he pizzed at me for leaving, but you know, I cannot work wiz the nasty productz. My clientz, zey like ze best, you know." *I could listen to that accent all day..*

We all drank a toast to welcome Pierre into the family, then another to celebrate getting through to the finals of the colour trophy. Michael noticed that I kept looking around the bar.

"He's not here tonight Lil, relax, I asked the barman, and they're not expecting him," he said.

"He said he was working tonight in a text earlier, which I haven't replied to yet. I thought he meant he'd be working here. Must be one of his others."

"Lily, stop worrying about that man," Trystan huffed, "he's not going anywhere. We're doing the work thing tonight, remember?"

"Yeah, sorry," I said. I leaned in to listen to the conversation.

"So when are we getting a new receptionist? I'm certain that sly bitch, Lottie, isn't putting it all through the till. A gap appeared in my schedule yesterday that shouldn't have been there. I worked solid, and didn't run behind, yet a forty five minute gap appears. She was on the desk then." Michael was annoyed.

Gray groaned, "Another bloody thing to deal with. Gino asked me not to make any changes, with all that's going on. I'll speak to him tomorrow. I'll put Tula on the desk instead, it's just that she's a far better assistant than Lottie."

"Will we get a new receptionist when you take over?" Tomme asked me.

"Of course," I replied, "I just don't know who yet."

"Shame you don't have a sister. It's such a position of trust. Gino always said he preferred family to be handling the money, rather than a stranger," Gray told me.

"I couldn't see my little brother fitting in, mind you, my Mum always wanted to be a hairdresser, maybe she'd like to do it." *Actually, that's a great idea.* "She's glamorous and young looking. She's a receptionist and book-keeper at a solicitors office at the moment."

"You wanna work with your mum?" Tomme was incredulous.

I frowned, "My Mum's great, a real laugh. You'd all adore her." I made a mental note to discuss it with her. "Anyway, it's family money buying the salon, so it might not be a bad thing for her to help look after it."

Salon Affair

"Will she be all Mother Hen with you though?" Tomme sneered.

I shook my head. "No, she's not like that, she's pretty laid back, and if she starts telling me off in front of you lot, she'll be out on her ear." They all laughed.

I called Mum when I got home that evening, to run the idea past her. To my surprise, she was delighted, and really excited at the prospect. "Just remember there'd be no 'being my mum' in front of my workmates, as they'll be my employees by then," I warned her.

"Don't be daft, I wouldn't do that. It'll be weird to have you calling me Linda though. Will I get to go on any product courses?"

"Oh yes, you'll have to learn to flog 'em too, and learn the computer system."

With Mum beyond excited, I debated whether or not to call Julian. I'd had a few texts from him during the day, but nothing that evening. Eventually, I decided against it, and went to bed a bit horny and lonely.

The next day, I was trotting down to the sandwich bar to get my lunch, when I spotted Julian and Pierre chatting outside the wine bar. I pretended to look in Prada's window, so that I could duck into their doorway, and watch without being seen. The two of them appeared to be deep in conversation, both smiling and laughing. I watched Pierre touch Julian's arm in a friendly gesture.

I stood spying for a full five minutes, wishing I could hear what they were saying, when I saw Julian hand Pierre a business card, and gesture in the direction of Mayfair. *Oh no you don't lover boy.* Infuriated, I broke cover, and marched over. "Hello you two. I didn't know you knew each other?"

"We don't," said Julian, "I just heard he'd joined you in your salon. I was just being a friendly neighbour."

"I better git my loonch," said Pierre, pocketing Julian's card, and wandering off.

I narrowed my eyes. "Don't get any ideas about poaching him for your salon," I snapped, "he's not up for grabs."

"Lily, I don't know if you're aware, but Gino has sold your salon under your nose. It's gonna have new owners pretty soon, and they may well want to make changes. You really should look after number one."

"I'm fully aware that the salon has been sold. I'm also aware that you valued it. Tell me, did you want to buy it?" I was seething.

"I wanted to, yes, but Gino told me yesterday that he'd already accepted an offer on it. He wouldn't tell me who though."

"Are you trying to poach Pierre for the Mayfair place?" My teeth were gritted.

"I'd have preferred you, but Pierre would be interested. I'm not sure why you're so angry, it's not as if it would affect you, unless you were regretting turning my offer down?" *Cocky little git.*

"I'm not regretting turning it down at all, but I am regretting the fact that you're now clearly a rival."

He looked confused. "How do you work that one out?"

"Because fairly soon I'll be the new owner of Gino Venti. Yes, he's sold it to me. Thank you for the low valuation by the way. You clearly forgot to strip out the depreciation, amor, amor" *Damn, what was it?*

"Amortisation." He smirked. *Bastard.*

"Yeah, that, and the director's dividends, before you got your figure."

"Getting to be quite the clever hairdresser aren't you?" he sneered. "Well Lily, if it means that much to you, I'll step aside where Pierre Le Frog is concerned. Can I ask how the hell you got the money to buy that place though?"

"My inheritance." I saw the shock on his lovely face. "Aw, did you think I was a penniless hairdresser? You made a lot of assumptions about me Julian. The difference

Salon Affair

was that I never lied, you just didn't ask the right questions." With that, I turned on my heel, and stomped back to work, leaving him standing on the street. *Damn, I've missed my lunch. Can't really go back there now either. Bugger.*

Back in the staffroom, I reconciled myself to going hungry, and had just switched on the kettle to make a drink, when Pierre, who had just finished scoffing a sandwich, sat and told Anthony and Tomme that he'd been chatted up by a gorgeous man, who wanted to give him a salon. I tensed.

"So this gorgeous man, who was he?" Tomme asked.

"His name waz Julian, heez a sexy biznizman. He waz soo flirty, cute, you know. I might let 'im take me out. He promizzed me a salon." He leaned forward, "I probably have to suck 'is cock, but you know, iz no problem."

It was all I could do not to laugh.

"Erm, mate, that's Lily's boyfriend you're talking about," said Anthony.

"No! Surely not! Ee waz flirting, I promiz. Ee 'az a salon, ee told me," Pierre protested.

"Well, he's a lying toad," I said, more forcefully than I meant to. "He'll tie you into a rotten deal, one that makes Sugar look like a charitable trust, then he'll bleed you dry for years to come," I spat.

"That's why you dumped him, wasn't it?" Tomme said, catching on pretty quick.

"Yep. Tried to promise me the earth, but when I checked the small print, and all the stuff he'd covered up, well, I'd have been practically a slave. Do yourself a favour Pierre, and steer clear."

His face fell. "I probably suck 'iz cock anyway," he said, which made us all laugh.

I walked home with Tomme that evening. It was one of those warm spring twilights which give the promise of lighter nights to come. "Why didn't you tell me, you know, about Julian's salon?" Tomme asked.

"I didn't want to get the sack, which, if it was common knowledge that I was setting up, would've happened. I'm just pleased that I learnt enough from him to research all the details. He was really a good liar, and had shafted plenty of other women in business before. It was his ex who alerted me, although she didn't know it."

"You're quite clever really, aren't you?"

"Not really. I didn't do terribly well at school." We walked along in companionable silence for a while. Tomme was out that evening with his friend Julie, so I carried on home to spend an evening alone.

There was an enormous packet waiting for me in my post-box in the lobby. I saw straightaway that it was from Mum's firm. I opened it while my ready-meal was heating up, and began to go through it. They were clearly pushing the boat out to get things done quickly. I'd just made myself comfortable to start reading through the lease, when my buzzer sounded. Thinking it was Tomme, I pressed the button for the intercom. "Hiya, were you stood up?" I trilled.

"Not that I know of," replied Julian's voice, "were you expecting someone else? Can I come up?" I pressed the buzzer to let him in. A few minutes later he was in my flat. "Who did you think it was?"

"Tomme, he's out with his friend Julie tonight, only he hates her, at least that's what he told me…What are you doing here?"

"Just seeing how the competition's doing," he said nonchalantly, glancing at the pile of documents on the coffee table. "Is that your lease?" I snatched it away, and stuffed it back in the envelope.

"Did you want something? Or have you just come round to spy on me?"

He beamed his film star smile. "I'm here to win you back, remember? Remind you how good we are together. We shouldn't ever be rivals, so I propose a merger."

Salon Affair

"I'm not merging our salons," I told him angrily, "you can get that idea straight out of your head."

"I wasn't thinking about that type of merger, my mind was on a far dirtier sort." He trailed a finger down my face. I shivered slightly at the contact, my body still reacting to him, even if my brain was screaming at me to take a step back. I could feel his hot breath on my neck as he leaned in to press tiny kisses up the side of my face, working their way slowly to my lips. His hands grasped my shoulders, as he kissed me urgently, his tongue grazing my lips to meet mine again. I was rooted to the spot, torn between my physical reaction, and my desire to punish him. *Damn, he tastes good.*

Breathless, I pulled away, my brain momentarily winning the battle. He seemed surprised, leaning forward to kiss me again, his hands holding my shoulders a little more firmly. "I told you I'm not jumping back into bed with you," I said, while every cell in my body screamed otherwise. He released my shoulders, which instantly felt bereft at the loss of his touch.

"What's it going to take? Tell me so I can make this right. Being without you...it's driving me crazy."

"You tried to poach one of my soon-to-be staff today. I can't have you anywhere near my salon. I need to be able to make it work, and sleeping with the enemy, well, don't you think that's kind of dangerous?" To my surprise, he started laughing.

"First off, I didn't know you were the person buying it, and second, I wouldn't ever steal off you. I'm not your enemy, and I never will be. To be honest, I wasn't so keen on that French fella, he seemed a little over-friendly to me."

"You didn't hear what he said about you in the staffroom afterwards. Plans to give your dick a nice suck in exchange for that salon." I giggled at the memory.

Julian pulled a face. "Jesus, did he think I was...?" he trailed off. I nodded, laughing at his look of horror. "I'll definitely give him a miss. Don't fancy being chased round that salon by a sex crazed Frenchman. Who on earth would mistake me for one of them?" I didn't answer. "Lily, I don't bloody believe you find that funny. I hope you put him right." His voice had risen an octave.

Stifling my amusement, I poured us each a glass of wine. Julian flopped down onto the sofa, making himself at home. "Would you like me to go through that lease with you, explain it all for you?" he offered, eyeing the envelope.

"It's alright thanks, my solicitor will do it all."

"I can do you a business plan?"

"I'm ok for that too."

"Find you a good accountant?"

"Got one already."

He huffed slightly as he sat back on the sofa. "Please don't be pig-headed about this. I want to help, and I'm pretty damn good at setting up businesses." He watched me warily, as he waited for my response.

"I know you are, but you're also a shark, and not to be trusted." As soon as the words were out of my mouth, he exploded.

"For fucks sake Lily, how many times are you gonna rub my nose in it? Yes, I lied to you, yes, I tried to make money off your back. I'm trying to make amends, and you still want to throw it back in my face. If you really can't stand the sight of me, then tell me now, rather than giving me false hope."

I sipped my wine as I considered my response. "Perhaps you're not aware that since Sunday, you've actually only talked to me about business? If, and it's a big if, I'm your girlfriend, then surely we'd be talking about other things too? Like how upset I was Sunday? What I've been up to this week? You don't even know that my colour got through to the national finals of the colour trophy." I kept

Salon Affair

my voice quiet and controlled as I spoke. He stared at me for a moment, then scrubbed at his face.

"You're right. Sometimes I wonder what's wrong with me, why women get bored. I guess you just nailed it."

"So what are you going to do about that?" I asked. What I really wanted was for him to pledge undying love, apologise, and take me out to dinner, as my tragic little lasagne smelt as though it was burning. I jumped up to pull it out of the oven, and switch everything off.

"I thought I could smell burning," he said, as I examined the remnants. "Don't eat that, it smells rank. Come on, let's go out." *Yay, telepathy works!*

I didn't need asking twice. I pulled on my jacket and heels, and grabbed my handbag. "What do you fancy?" Julian asked when we were in the lift. *You actually.*

"I don't mind, surprise me." He pulled out his phone, and booked us a table at a place called Roca.

Pretty soon we were in a cab heading towards Mayfair. "I'm taking you for Japanese. I discovered this restaurant a few weeks ago, during a business lunch, and decided I'd like to try it in the evening for dinner. Do you like Sashimi?"

"No idea, I'll let you know soon enough."

Julian ordered a load of dishes, so that we could both try a bit of everything. He fed me fluffy tempura, while I fed him tiny crab cakes. It was a lot of fun, and the food was divine. He made me laugh by doing a funny impression of Pierre's flirting. I made him blush by doing my own impersonation of him talking about Julian in the staffroom. "I can't believe he thought I was one of them. Guess I need to butch up a bit."

"I happen to think you're butch enough. Those boys really do think straight men are just deluded fools who put up with women, because of societal demands. Tomme told me that only another man can give a decent blowjob. He even demonstrated his technique on a can of mousse, to show me how it should be done," I giggled, my tongue loosened by all the wine we'd drunk.

"And?" Asked Julian, fascinated.

"It was no bloody different to how I do it. I think the ability is instinctual."

"You're making me even hornier for you than I was already. That could be dangerous..."

"I told you," I said primly, "that I'm not jumping into bed with you. You have to work for it."

Half an hour later, we were banging like bunnies.
No.Bloody.Willpower.

Chapter 13

I woke up to a pair of twinkly blue eyes gazing into mine, and a beaming film star smile. I stretched my slightly stiff and overused muscles, and yawned loudly. "Morning beautiful," he said, his smile broadening.

"What time is it?"

"Early, six o'clock. Shall I make you a coffee? Toast?"

"You're still on best behaviour then? Alright, I'll have some coffee please." I watched as he slipped out of bed, and out to the kitchen, his lithe, fit body glowing with health and vitality. He really was the most gorgeous specimen of a man.

"Stop looking at my arse," he called out. I lay back to contemplate the night before. The sex had been amazing, of course, and somehow it had been different, more intimate, sort of closer. I was still smiling when he came back in bearing our drinks. "Happy?" He asked.

"Very. You?"

"Totally ecstatic. I missed you so much. Did you miss me?"

"Yes, yes I did," I admitted.

"I want you to promise me something.."

"Go on."

"If I'm ever being a bore, or an arse, tell me. I'll promise you that I'll never lie to you again, and I'll never do anything to harm your business. Is that a deal?"

"Ok, it's a deal." I spat on my hand and held it out. He did the same, and we shook. Then he jumped me. Again.

I was walking bandy by the time I made it into work. We had a fairly straightforward day ahead, and I wasn't planning to work late. Gray collared me as soon as I walked into the staffroom. "Are you free this evening after work? I'd like a chat if that's ok. We could go out and eat if you like."

"That'd be great. I've not got anything planned." I was a little puzzled, and hoped that Gray didn't intend handing in his notice.

I had a call from Mum, telling me I had to see the solicitor, so that he could explain the lease. I made an appointment for the following Monday morning, early, so that Julian and I could still pretty much have our day together. "You might even be signing that day, if everything's in order, and the searches are back," she said. "Make sure you read all that stuff, and write down any questions you have. I booked a surveyor for tomorrow, to come and check the property, he'll arrive about eleven. Won't take long, as it's a small shop. He'll do a condition report, and make sure it's not falling down."

"We've got a bit of damp in the staff room," I told her, suddenly nervous.

"He'll just tell us why then Lily, no building's perfect, especially one that old. Nobody ever looks after commercial property as well as their home."

The rest of the day passed quickly, and one by one the boys all left for the day. I waited while Gray cashed up, and put the takings in the safe, ready for banking the following day. "You're going to have to learn to do all this part," he pointed out. I didn't reply.

Salon Affair

We locked up, and walked down towards Brook street, where I followed Gray into a little bistro. We sat down, and looked at the menu. "Treats on me," he said.

"I don't mind going halves," I said. Before we could argue, the waiter came and took our orders. When he'd gone, Gray sat back slightly, and fiddled with his napkin.

"Just spit it out," I said, sensing he was nervous.

"Are you gonna get rid of me? You know, when you take over? I mean, you won't need a manager, as you'll be there all the time." His words came out in a rush. I watched as he twisted his napkin repeatedly.

"Of course I'm not getting rid of you. I'm gonna need you even more than Gino did. I was more worried that you'd want to leave, you know, with having a new boss." He let out a breath.

"What with everything that's going on right now with the divorce, Chris was taunting me, saying I'd be unemployed. I mean, who'd employ me now, with this disease?"

"I'd employ you any day of the week. You're a great manager." I told him. He relaxed, and smiled. "These...difficulties you're going through, they're temporary. One day you'll be divorced from Chris, and your virus will be under control. We all meant what we said, that we'd all help you. I'm sure you'd feel the same if the boot was on the other foot."

"Of course. When Trystan was diagnosed, I worked his clients until he'd got his medication right." *What??*

"I didn't know that Trystan had it too?"

"Yeah, had it for a few years now. He didn't want people to know, so he only told me and Gino. Please don't let on that you know. He'll probably want to tell you himself." I recalled his reaction to Gray's diagnosis, it all made sense.

"How's the drug therapy going?"

"Not too bad. I feel a little better. My coughs starting to clear. They try different drug combinations until your T-cell count lowers. Trystan's is so low now that it's almost as though he doesn't have the virus. It's called 'an undetectable viral load'. It takes a while on the drugs to get to that point."

"And how's things with Chris?"

"We're not speaking. I saw a solicitor and began the dissolution of our civil partnership. The greedy bastard wants three quarters of our flat, on the basis that I earn more than him. My lawyer will argue that my earning power's been curtailed due to Chris' actions, and is arguing for three quarters to me. It's all pretty nasty and bitter. Our friends have cut him off, and, without me subsidising him, he's racking up his credit card. Think he's banking on our flat selling quickly to get him out of trouble. Serves the leech right. He lived off me for years. Mind you, I feel like a mug now, when I think of all the stuff I paid for."

"At least when he's out of your life, you'll be comfortably off. You have that to look forward to."

"Very true. I can't wait. I take it you won't mind if I take a holiday once all this is done?"

"Course not." I paused. "Do you think the others will be put out, you know, by me buying the salon?"

"No, no I don't. I think they're relieved, I know both Trystan and I were. I'm even more relieved now that we've talked."

"So am I."

With difficult subjects out of the way, the rest of our meal was a delight. Gray was urbane, and great company, dishing gossip on some celebrities he mixed with, who the public would be shocked to find out were gay. "But he's married!" I exclaimed at the news that a fairly famous actor was in their circle.

"Bearding. She's gay too. She gets his money, he gets to stay in the closet. He gets all those tough-guy roles by being straight. Nobody would have a limp-waisted faggot as a hardman character, now would they?"

"Spose not. Who else?"

Salon Affair

After my salacious gossip fix, Gray and I said our goodbyes, and I walked home, calling Julian on the way. "I'm in a meeting babe, someone replied to my advert about renting the salon. We've viewed it, now just thrashing out the details. I might be late."

"That's ok. I'm just on my way home now. Are you coming round to mine tonight?" I purred.

"Depends how late I am." *What?*

"Oh, ok." I tried to hide the disappointment in my voice. Businessman Julian was clearly back. I walked home via the salon, smiling at it as I passed. I couldn't wait for the moment it became mine. I made a mental note to buy some champagne to celebrate.

Passing the wine bar, I glanced through the window, out of habit. What I saw stopped me in my tracks. I could clearly see Julian, seated at a table, in animated conversation with a familiar dark-haired woman. As she turned her head slightly, I recognised Holly-the-über-bitch straightaway. *No!* My stomach sank into my boots, and I went cold. *This just can't be happening.*

I debated what to do. I felt too sick and shaky to go marching in, and demand that he didn't speak to her. All I could do was stand rooted to the spot, and watch them. I nearly threw up when Holly touched his arm, in a flirty way, beaming at him with her ultra-whitened smile. *They look like a perfect couple*, I thought, in my jealous meltdown.

I was still standing there watching, when Julian glanced over, paling when he saw me. We held eye contact for a moment, before I ran for it.

Yep, I ran. I needed to get away from the situation. I knew he'd say it was just business, and I'd feel stupid for being jealous. As I pegged it across Oxford street, my phone began to ring. I ignored it, and carried on. All I wanted was to be locked indoors, safe from everything. People jumped out of my way, probably assuming I was some sort of criminal running from the police. I got back to the flat in record time, locked myself in, and threw up.

He rang another four times, all of which I sent to voicemail, before a banging on my front door made me jump. "Lily, open up. I've been trying to call you," he shouted.

By that time, I was a juddering mess. I'd sobbed my heart out, so had makeup sliding around my face, and a bit of sick in my hair where I hadn't got it out of the way fast enough. I didn't want to face him. "Lily, this is ridiculous," he yelled, "I've got no idea what's wrong. Talk to me...please. I'm not leaving until you do......I'll sit here all night if needs be."

I debated what to do. My jealousy was irrational, and borne of years of Holly making me feel inferior. I wouldn't even know where to begin, trying to tell Julian why I'd reacted so strongly to seeing him with her. Rationally, I was going to be the owner of London's premier salon, and she was gonna be shafted by a shark, yet I still felt small and pathetic next to her. I made a decision.

My thoughts were interrupted by Julian banging on the door again. Worried that he'd upset the neighbours, I unlocked all the bolts, and opened it. "Lily, what on earth is going on?" He demanded as soon as he saw me.

"I don't want to see you anymore," I told him, the words tumbling out in a rush, before I could change my mind.

"Why? Because I was meeting with a possible tenant?" He was incredulous. "I meet with women every day. It's just work....what's wrong with you?" I could see he was panicked.

"This isn't going to work. I don't want to go into my reasons, I just know. I know how you do business with women, and I'm not prepared to wait around to see if she finishes with you early enough to come round and see me."

Salon Affair

"That's not how it was." He looked distraught. "She's already got a backer, someone else. I was just helping her with the property side."

"My arse," I said. *Mature, I know.* "Listen, I can't go through this every time you have to deal with a woman. Knowing what a liar you are, and what a bullying bitch Holly is, you can count me out of your life. Now please leave me alone." I was yelling by then, and I didn't care.

"You know her?"

"Unfortunately, yes. Now GO!" I shoved him out the door, and slammed it in his face.

"You're nuts," he yelled through the door, shocking me. Not really knowing what to do, I made a cup of tea, and sat on the sofa. He'd obviously gone home. *Either that or back to Holly.*

I barely slept all night. It seemed that every time I closed my eyes, I could see the two of them together, with Holly giving me one of her fake, pitying looks. At four in the morning, I gave up trying to sleep, and sat going through all the paperwork the solicitor had sent over. It was all fairly straightforward, and actually a little boring. By seven, I was done, and had made some notes ready for my meeting on Monday.

I was working the desk, several hours later, when Holly stormed in. "Demoted to receptionist Lily? Did they discover you were just a mediocre stylist after all?" *Fucking bitch.* Tomme, who was standing nearby, overheard it.

"What're you after Cruella?" He asked, referencing her slightly dominatrix-like appearance.

"I'm here to see this little bitch," she spat, gesturing in my direction. "I gather you're trying to put the kibosh on my new salon. Just because you weren't up to being a salon owner doesn't mean you've got to be some sort of mean bitch to those of us who are. Julian told me that you have a problem with our deal. God only knows why he listens to you though."

I struggled to find the words to defend myself against her onslaught. Holly had always been able to intimidate me. Luckily she didn't have the same effect on Tomme, who went into full bitchslap mode. "Oh my god, the cheek of you, coming into the salon Lily owns, and spouting off because poor Julian found you so revolting, he was looking for an excuse to get rid of you. Sounds to me as though you are one deluded little loser. Now fuck off slag, and don't come back."

Hearing the commotion, the others peered round the wall dividing the reception from the salon. "You own this? Oh please, don't make me laugh. I'm shocked you even got a job here. Maybe they were desperate, or are you the new junior?" I felt my anger begin it's unstoppable rise.

"Yes I'm the owner, you stupid bitch. And yes, I told my ex, Julian that you were a nasty little shit, and a total nightmare to work with. Now before you start calling other people names, you should take a good look in the mirror, and see what an unpleasant bitch you really are. You lost that salon through your own actions, not mine. I'm sure if Julian's in any doubt about what a bully you are, he can watch our CCTV coverage of you right now, and see it for himself." I gestured to the camera. "Now get the fuck out of my salon, and don't come back, stupid cow." I could see all the boys grinning. They were clearly enjoying the show. All it needed was for them to all start chanting 'fight, fight,' and it would be handbags and fisticuffs. She must have realised she was at a disadvantage, as she flounced out with a face like a slapped arse, to much laughter from the others.

"Whoa, Lily, you sure you haven't got a pair of bollocks hanging down there?" Tomme asked, laughing. Shakily, I made myself a cup of tea in the staffroom, and pulled my phone out to check it. There were two missed calls from Julian, and a text. I opened it.

Salon Affair

I'm sorry about last night. Can I see you tonight?
I was debating what to do when Anthony walked in.
"Who on earth was she?" He asked, before plonking himself down in a chair.
"She's the girl who pretty much bullied me out of Gavin Roberts. Now she's making eyes at Julian, cos she wants his shop in Audley Street. I saw the pair of them having a meeting in the wine bar last night. She was all flirty with him."
"So do you think he's doing the same to her as he did to you?"
"I don't know. I dumped him last night, I was so upset. Just seeing him with her..." I trailed off.
"We all thought she worked in a sex club, not a salon," he said, which made me smile. "Bit fierce isn't she? You gave her a good dressing down though."
"I hate confrontation," I admitted.
"We all do, apart from Tomme, who loves it. Think he was quite impressed with you."
"I impressed myself," I said, "although it sounds like Julian's fucked her off."
"Anything for you," Anthony sang. *Pisstaker*

He was rudely interrupted by the arrival of the surveyor, who spent precisely ten minutes in the shop, took a few measurements, and buggered off.

I practically crawled home from work that night, totally exhausted from lack of sleep, and too much excitement. I switched off my phone, and all the lights, and spent my Saturday night in bed watching Britain's got talent on the telly. *So much for my exciting London life.*

It was my Sunday to work, so I got there bright and early, stopping off to pick up a latte on the way. I'd decided to go straight to Bromley after I finished, spend the night there, ready for my appointment with the solicitor the next morning. I called Mum to say I'd be over for dinner that evening, and got on with my day.

We were packed out, as there was only three of us working. It was lovely to have a bit more space in the salon, but Trystan, Michael and I worked like dogs to get everyone done. Lottie was our junior that day, and she'd clearly been out on the lash, having been paid the day before. Getting her to do anything was generally tricky, but that day she was hopeless. In the end, we stopped asking her to help, and just did everything ourselves, including tidying the salon at the end of the day, while she made a meal out of washing up a couple of tint bowls.

Trystan called me out to the desk, where he was running out the takings printout. "Look at this." He gestured at the screen. Sure enough, each of us had gaps appear in our schedules. We went through our columns. I had a cut and blow dry missing, and Trystan had a regrowth tint disappear. We called Michael in, who identified a gents cut missing from his.

"The cash all adds up, so those people must've paid cash, and she pocketed it, and deleted them," Trystan said. I got Michael to keep her talking while I called Gino, and told him what had happened.

"Call the police. Keep her there until both the police and I get there. If she doesn't admit it, we can tell which clients were in, and how they paid from the CCTV footage," he said. I called the police straightaway.

Trystan locked the door before confronting her. At first she denied it, then she accused us all of nicking our own takings, then, when I pointed out that it was all on digitape, she broke down and confessed. *Sly little bitch.*

She was still crying when both Gino and the police showed up. I watched Gino treat the whole incident in an extremely matter of fact way, sending the footage from the camera to the police email. He sacked the little ratbag on the spot, telling her it was a gross misconduct, so she wouldn't get any paid notice. *Good.*

Salon Affair

I watched her being led out by the two burly coppers, and a funny thought struck me, *I'm gonna have to do all that stuff next week.*

Gino must have read my mind, "Thank god I've not got much longer having to do this kind of thing. Let's keep our fingers crossed it's soon eh?" He waved goodbye as he followed the coppers out to go and give a statement.

He'd only just left when Julian barrelled in, "I saw the police just leave. What happened?"

"Just a thieving junior, nothing to get excited about. It was more entertaining yesterday when your new girlfriend came in to pick a fight," I told him.

"Holly? She's not my new girlfriend. Why did she come in?"

"She decided it was my fault you didn't give her that shop. Mind you, you can do what you like now that you're a free agent," I said, all sarcastic.

"Do you want to see the footage? Michael said. "It was brilliant. Lily put her in her place good and proper. I'm surprised at you though Julian, wouldn't have thought you'd go for a tranny..."

"I didn't 'go for her' at all. I mentioned I knew you, and she was all bitchy. Said you'd got above yourself, and shit like that. Besides that, she failed her credit check. Got two CCJ's for unpaid credit cards, so I said no. For your information, Michael, she wouldn't have been my type." I could tell he was barely holding onto his temper.

Michael played the footage of Holly's visit. I watched as the corners of Julian's mouth twitched, he was clearly trying not to laugh. As soon as it finished, I grabbed my bag. "I've got to go, I promised I'd be somewhere by six."

"Where?" Julian demanded.

"None of your business," I told him, as I walked out of the door. He didn't try and follow me.

It was a huge relief to get to Bromley. I zipped round to see Doris for half an hour, before strolling home, enjoying the unseasonably warm weather. I parked myself at the kitchen table while Mum cooked, telling her about all the events of the week.

"Sounds like a stressful week," she observed. "Well, you've got two days off now, and apart from this meeting in the morning, your time's your own. Do you want to go shopping?"

"Could do, couldn't we? Are you off too then?"

"Only till two tomorrow. I'm doing the two till six shift. I thought I'd come with you for your appointment, then straight to the shops afterwards."

With a plan in place, I relaxed that evening. Lisa popped round, saying she had a night off from Tony, as he was playing for the darts team in his local pub. She looked different, glowing. *Maybe because she's in love?* I mused.

We spent a fun evening chatting, laughing, and generally being daft. As much as I loved my London life, nothing could beat the comfort and familiarity of home. After a late night, I was still up early, fizzing with anticipation of the day ahead.

Mr Vizier was one of those old fashioned family solicitors, who exuded a comforting presence. His office was mahogany panelled, and filled with large legal books. Mum and I sat down in front of his desk.

He droned on for a while about the lease, the searches, and the contract of sale, which all seemed ok. I asked him my list of questions, which he answered concisely. There didn't really appear to be any problems. All the shops in the street were owned and administered by a charitable trust, which published annual accounts, and had no record of dodgy dealings. The ground rent was fixed at two hundred pounds a year in the lease, and the sale contract for the business was standard, and included a clause preventing Gino opening another salon for five years, not that there was any danger that would happen. With everything in order, I signed all the contracts with a flourish.

Salon Affair

"We'll exchange today, and as the money is already available in cleared funds, we can complete tomorrow, if you're in agreement?"

"Perfect." It made sense to do it on a day off for me, as I'd have a lot to do, changing over utilities, and speaking to my new accountant about payroll.

"Well, I wish you the very best of luck Ms Hollins, and do let me know if you need any other services from us." We all shook hands.

Stepping outside into the cool air, I felt a sense of anticipation, as if the world had shifted, yet Bromley High Street was still the same as ever, people bustling around, unaffected by the seismic shift in my world.

We meant to go shopping, but ended up in Costa instead, discussing Mum's change of career. I was astonished at how nervous she was, and how much research she'd been doing via the Internet. "You don't think I'm too old to do this?" She asked nervously.

"Of course not. You're only 47, not 67," I told her. She looked fantastic for her age, still having the trim figure that thankfully, I'd inherited.

"I'm stressing about what to wear," she admitted, "I'm guessing my Marks' suits won't cut it?"

"Definitely no polyester suits from Marks," I laughed. Think about the outfit you bought me from Karen Millen, that type of thing will do until I can introduce you to Claudine in our local Prada. Have you put your notice in yet?"

"Yes, I did it the day before yesterday. They've agreed to let me go a little early, and I've got some holiday left over, so I'll be free in a week. That gives me some time to shop a bit. I think I'll get three outfits to be going on with."

She was so excited, it was a joy to see. I knew the boys would adore her, and I felt a little less terrified knowing she'd be around. Mum was great with figures, having done bookkeeping for years, so would keep the books in perfect order.

    We spent a couple of hours mooching round Bromley. I helped Mum choose an outfit, and treated myself to some new makeup. I was just walking her to her office, when my phone rang. It was Mr Vizier's secretary telling me I'd exchanged contracts. My stomach lurched with excitement. She informed me that completion was all set for the next day, and would happen before three o'clock. I thanked her profusely, and clicked off my phone. Turning to Mum, I said simply; "It's happened." She pulled me into a fierce hug.

    "It'll be brilliant, Mrs West-End salon owner."

Chapter 14

After waving Mum off into work, I trotted down to Bromley South, and hopped on a train back into London. I called Gray to let him know that the exchange had occurred, only to find out that Gino had already told him. "It's brilliant news, congratulations," he said. "By the way, I booked you to meet the L'Oreal rep tomorrow, hope that's ok? Anything else you need me to do?"

"I can't think of anything. I'll be in tomorrow, as I need to sort the utilities, read the meters and stuff. What times my rep coming?"

"Ten, is that ok?"

"Yep. Apparently it'll be mine by three, so Gino and I agreed that the day's takings will come to me, and He pays everyone until the end of today, and will clear the till. That reminds me, I need to get some change for the float."

With practicalities taken care of, I went home via the mini-mart, and filled my fridge. I was determined to be organised. I'd just got in when my phone rang again, this time, the insurance broker confirming that the new salon insurance would begin in the morning, and detailing all the various clauses. By the time I'd dealt with him, it was five, and I hadn't even begun my laundry. Another call interrupted me, this time it was Tomme, asking if I was cooking that evening.

"Wasn't planning to," I said, laughing.

"Never mind, we'll bring Chinese. Have you got wine?"

"Yes, hang on, who's we?"

"Only Anthony, Michael and Pierre, oh and me of course. Thought we'd celebrate your last night of freedom, bit like a bridal shower, only you're marrying the salon."

"Hen party more like. Alright, come over."

"Hang on," I could hear him talking to someone in the background, "can Trystan and Gray come too?"

It ended up a hilarious evening, with all the boys on good form, I laughed until my sides hurt. I think we all felt the same relief that our salon was secured, and the good times would keep on rolling. Even Pierre seemed to have fitted in easily, being totally relaxed about all the frog jokes, and the gentle teasing about his devotion to his 'Mama'.

"Your first day of salon ownership Lil, and all your staff'll be wrecked," said Gray, draining another bottle.

"You forget that I've seen you all work with hangovers, they'll be no pulling the wool over my eyes." They all groaned.

"First day, and she's already a little hitler." Tomme announced. I smacked him. "That's assaulting the staff, that is." I poked my tongue out him. "You'll have to learn to be more mature than that Lily." *I.Can't.Bloody.Win.*

They all left at midnight, promising to turn up for work the next day. I was clearing up all the plates, when I remembered I'd left my phone in my bedroom. There were twelve missed calls, all from Julian. Tentatively, I called him. "Lily, I've been trying to call you all evening."

"I just saw. What is it you wanted?" I sounded a bit cold, but I was still struggling with his meeting with Holly. I just...didn't trust him."

"I miss you."

"I'm sure Holly would've kept you occupied." The words were out of my mouth before my brain could engage, and prevent me from sounding like a jealous child. I cringed.

Salon Affair

He sighed. "I don't want her, or anyone else. I keep telling you that, and you don't believe me. What's it gonna take to convince you?"

"She bullied me. Drove me out of Gavin Roberts. I threw up when I saw her touch you."

"I wondered what that was in your hair." His voice was soft, gentle. "Oh Lily, I'm so sorry, I'm sorry you saw that, I'm sorry I ever agreed to meet her, I'm not sorry that she made you move on from Gavin Roberts though, as she did you a huge favour."

"True."

"Did you know they've gone bust?"

"WHAT? When? How?" I was shocked. I knew things had been a bit shaky there, but I hadn't foreseen bankruptcy.

"Last week apparently. That's why that Holly woman's looking for a salon. Said she's fed up with working for minimum wage, and found some fella to back her."

"She was on minimum wage? Lying bitch used to say she was on far more than I was." I could feel the familiar anger rising. Even the mention of her name seemed to rile me up.

"Lily, why on earth are you letting a dozy little tart like her upset you? I mean look at you, you're beautiful, talented, and about to own the best salon in London. I'm not sure why you aren't looking down your nose at her instead."

I relaxed, his words diffusing my anger. His voice had a soothing quality, and in a moment of clarity, I realised that he was still chasing me, still calling, stalking, and trying to be with me. If it had only been about his salon, he'd have moved on to someone else. Maybe I'd got him a bit wrong.

"Are you in Oxshott?" I asked.

"Yes, I came down this morning. You were meant to be coming with me, remember?"

"I know, but I had a meeting with the solicitor this morning, so it would've been difficult. I've had a bit of a mad day."

"Why's that?"

"I exchanged contracts today, I complete tomorrow."

Silence.

"How'dya do that so quick?"

"My Mum works at the solicitors. It's amazing how fast they can go when they want to."

"Well, congratulations. You got a bargain."

"I think so. I'm going to be in the salon tomorrow. If you want to see me, that is." I tentatively held out an olive branch.

"I'll be there. I want to celebrate this with you. Go get some sleep."

"Yes, sir."

The next morning was a blur of meetings, calls, and admin tasks. Gino came in to collect the previous days takings, and present me with all the keys. "Take care of my baby, please," he asked with glistening eyes.

"I will, I promise," I told him, hugging him back, "just you take care of Paulina, and send her our love." After lots of hugs, and promises to keep in touch, he gave the salon a final glance, and left, blowing a kiss over his shoulder as he went.

The next surprise was a visit from Mum, Dad and Doris, who tottered into the salon on Dad's arm. "The lady herself," I announced. "This is my great aunt Doris everyone."

"Just aunt will do dear, especially in front of all these lovely young men," she quipped, making them all laugh.

They made the most enormous fuss of her, doing her hair for free, and more besides. She was in heaven having them all fussing over her. I couldn't have loved those boys any more than I already did for the way they looked after her. Anthony coloured her hair a pretty pastel blonde, and

Trystan cut and blow dried it into a pretty decent interpretation of Gloria Hunniford's style. Doris was delighted.

Dad walked around with his hands in his pockets, commenting on what a 'top class finish' the salon fittings were, in that sort of Dad way, while Mum was shown the computer system by Gray, who she seemed a little dazzled by.

At one, my mobile rang, the solicitor's number flashing up. I answered nervously, praying that nothing had gone wrong. It was Mr Vizier's secretary. "Hi Ms Hollins, just a call to confirm that you've completed. I trust that you've made arrangements to collect the keys?"

"Got them already, thanks."

"Excellent, well, congratulations, and I wish you every success."

After ending the call, I must have looked a little shell-shocked. Around me the salon was buzzing, busy and happy. Every chair was filled. Tomme noticed, and asked if I was alright.

"Yes, I just completed. It's all done."

Choruses of 'congratulations' and 'well dones' went around the room, from clients as well as the boys. Dad followed me out to the staff room to organise the champagne. "You alright?" He asked.

"Yeah, a bit shocked. Too late to be scared now eh?"

He pulled me into a hug, and kissed the top of my head. "You'll be fine Lil. You've enough good people around you. I can't believe how busy it is out there though. How on earth do you all stand it all day?"

"You get used to it," I said, smiling. I loved it when it was packed and manic, as it was when we were at our most creative. "And it's not that busy today. Sometimes it's like a madhouse."

"I dread to think," he laughed. I watched as he opened two bottles of champagne, and poured them into flutes.

We'd handed them round, and Gray raised a toast to the salon, to my success, and to Aunt Doris, who was having the time of her life watching proceedings with a head full of foils.

"Visitor Lil," Tomme called out from reception. I hurried through to come face to face with Julian, bearing an enormous bouquet of lilies, and another bottle of champagne.

"Hi," I said.

"Hi," he replied.

"Are those for me?" *Duh, stupid question.*

"I thought we should celebrate." He saw the flute in my hand. "You started already?"

"I completed about half an hour ago. Mum and Dad are here doing the proud parents thing, plus Doris of course. She's having a whale of a time, getting her hair done."

"Oh where are they? I'll say hello." He craned his neck to look into the salon.

"Before you do...there's something I need to ask you."

"Ask away," his eyes bored into mine, two pools of bright blue, sparkling with happiness.

"Is it true? I mean, were you telling me the truth? You know....what you said," I was rambling a bit, but I couldn't bring myself to ask him the question directly.

"What? That I'm head over heels, stupid in love with you? Of course it's true. I know I didn't start off too well with you, but never, ever doubt my feelings for you Lily. I love you desperately."

"I love you too," I told him. We stood silent for a minute, just grinning stupidly at each other. Lost in the moment. With the flowers in the way, he couldn't do the passionate kiss like they do in the movies, so we made do with a slightly awkward peck, both trying to avoid getting covered in pollen.

He followed me through into the salon, where Tula relieved him of the flowers, and champagne. "Hello Bob,

Salon Affair

nice to see you again," he said, shaking Dad's hand warmly. "Linda, how lovely to see you. Keeping well I hope?" He kissed Mum's cheek affectionately. She went all stupid. I groaned inwardly.

"And this is my Aunt Doris," I said as I introduced them. By then Doris had had her hair washed, and was sitting waiting for Trystan to finish his client.

Now Doris is an absolute doll, but she's also an old lady, and does that old girl thing of saying exactly what's going through her mind, no matter what the consequences. I seriously think the brain to mouth filter withers away as women age.

"Linda said you were a real dish," she said, causing Mum to groan and blush furiously. "And he's got a cracking body by the looks of him Lily, as well as a pretty face. You look after this one girl, he's quite a catch."

Ground, open me up.

Julian just laughed in his good natured way, and told Doris how lovely it was to finally meet her. He didn't seem at all fazed by her gushing assessment of his attributes. "Would you like to join me in the wine bar for some lunch and a drink?" He asked Dad.

The two of them escaped, happy not to have to sit and wait in the salon. Gray had told me that he'd cash up and lock up, and that I should enjoy the rest of my day off. Mum and I waited for Doris, before trundling her down to Julian's wine bar, where he'd organised some tapas for us all.

Glancing around the table at the people I loved most in the world, knowing that thanks to them, I'd achieved my dream, I don't think my smile could've got any wider.

"To Lily, the best hairdresser in London," said Dad, raising a toast.

"To Lily," Julian agreed. We all clinked and drank. "I forgot to tell you, I have some news about the Mayfair shop," he began. I tensed straightaway, thinking he was about to burst my balloon. "I shook on it this morning. It's going to be an antiques shop. The fella wants to be in super-quick. I might recommend your solicitor, as he seemed pretty efficient." I relaxed. Knowing that he wouldn't be a rival, or anywhere near Holly-the-über-bitch just sealed my happiness. I prayed that the family weren't planning to make a day of it, I needed to get him alone....

Mum, Dad and Doris left around four, mainly to get Doris home in time for her tea. I waved them off happily, then practically dragged Julian home. We'd been sort of flirting all afternoon, a look here, a touch there, in a sensual tease.

We barely made it into the foyer, before he was kissing me hard. The lift dinged its arrival, and had Julian not caught me, I'd have fallen straight through the doors as they slid open against my back.

In the lift, his hands roamed over me, pulling at my clothes, as he kissed me, his tongue pressing deep into my mouth, dominating me completely.

We fell into my flat, both desperate to get naked. Julian kicked the door closed, and grabbed me. He flung me over his shoulder, and carried me, giggling into the bedroom, before throwing me onto the bed, and pulling down my jeans.

"I've got to taste you, reassure myself that you're real," he panted, as he pulled off my shoes and threw them on the floor.

Once my bottom half was naked, he slowed down, and took his time with my shirt, carefully undoing all the little buttons, then unclasping my bra, and sliding it off. His hands roamed over my entire body, sending sparks through my skin.

"Why are you still dressed?" I asked, my voice husky with desire.

Salon Affair

"You want to see my cock? Dirty girl," he teased. He undid his trousers, and pulled the tip of his cock out of the waistband of his pants.

"All of it," I said, greedy for more. I pounced on him, and yanked at his clothes, freeing his cock completely. I stroked it for a moment, before taking it in my mouth to taste it, sliding my tongue around the wide crest repeatedly.

"Oh god," he gasped, "If you keep doing that, Im gonna spank that pretty little arse of yours until its glowing." I wiggled my bum provocatively, and glanced up at his face, his cock still in my mouth. He was gazing down at me, smiling, his intense blue eyes sparkling with happiness.

He moved his hips back, causing his dick to exit my mouth with a pop. He shrugged off the rest of his clothes, and dived onto me, pushing me back onto the bed, pinned by his weight. He kissed me hard, his hands holding each side of my face, fisting into my hair. He needed to be close, I figured. We both needed to feel skin against skin.

He drove me nuts, kissing and licking almost every inch of me, exploring my body with his mouth, biting, then soothing my flesh. "Patience baby," he cooed, as I tried to pull him on top of me. *Two can play at this.*

I rolled him over, and did the same to him, fighting my desire to take him hard and fast. I ran my hands, lips and tongue over his silky, golden skin, teasing him until he couldn't take any more.

He thrust into me hard. I was so turned on that he slipped in easily. He began to move at a primal pace, his hips slamming against me, pushing me up the bed.

I could feel the orgasm building, the delicious fizzing inside that signals a soul shaking climax approaching. Julian must have felt it too, as he reared up onto his knees, grabbed my ankles to lift them up onto his shoulders, and deliver a resounding slap on my arse.

I came so hard that I saw stars. I was barely aware that he was coming at the same time, his expletives hardly even punctuating my orgasmic daze.

Eventually, he slipped out of me, and lay down beside me, pulling me close for a cuddle. It felt amazing to be back in his arms after all that'd happened. " Can we never fall out again please?" he whispered. "I don't think my nerves could take it."

"Then we'd miss out on the make-up sex," I pointed out.

"Fair point. God you're clever," he said, beaming his film-star smile. *Will I ever get tired of that smile? Never.*

Another kiss led to another, and pretty soon he was pulling me onto him. Again. *Insatiable.*

Epilogue

"For those of us who expressed doubt that young über-stylist Lily Hollins could step into the shoes of former hairdresser of the year, Gino Venti, following her shock buy out of his salon, we were well and truly answered. Watching her and salon manager, Gray Parker, lift the colour trophy at the prestigious event at the Savoy last night, saw the Gino Venti artistic team, led by her, assert their total superiority over all the competing teams.
The glitterati of the hairdressing world may have wondered what hit them when Gino Venti turned out an immaculate ombré in shades of violet, showing that, despite her tender years, Ms Hollins is indeed a force to be reckoned with, in the echelons of top hairdressing. We can only imagine the heights she'll reach if she's already leading the hairdressing world at just 26 years of age. Read her exclusive interview in next month's Hair World magazine. Not a bad write up," said Julian, after reading it out loud to me. We were sitting on his patio in Oxshott having our breakfast. It was delightfully warm for the middle of May, so we were making the most of the beautiful weather. It was also my first day off since we'd won the trophy. Our phone had been ringing off the hook with both people trying to book in for an 'Ethereal Ombré', and also press requesting interviews. It had been a mental week. I'd even been on breakfast telly. Purple and lilac ombré was deemed

to be the new 'in' look of the summer. I'd started to see quite a few people sporting it.

I thought back to the competition. It had been held on a Sunday. We'd all been included. Even Pierre had come along even though he wasn't strictly involved. It had been a fairly intense day, especially for Tomme, who was up on stage doing the finishing. The tension had been broken by Pierre coming out of the gents, with a rather sheepish face, only to be told by Tomme that he 'had a bit of jizz on his chin'. An equally sheepish little Italian fella from the Di'Alba art team sneaked out behind him, to much hilarity. *Bloody hairdressers, can't take 'em anywhere...*

We'd been the hands down winners. Toni and Guy had come second with a copper block effect, deemed a little dull by the hairdressing press, well the ones who bothered to even mention them. In comparison, everything about our entry, our team, and our salon just shone.

"It appears you're the new darling of the hair world. Even Vogue has a piece on you, look," he said, thrusting another magazine into my hands. I glanced at the now familiar image of the ballet dancer. All the write-ups had gushed about it. Julian had googled it, and discovered it was being discussed in detail on every salon forum around the world, with people desperately trying to figure out the formulas we'd used. The publicity alone was worth an absolute fortune to us.

"I've been doing some research," Julian began, snapping me out of my trance. "It would be a great time to start thinking about franchising the Gino Venti brand. It's secured the top spot, so it'd be a shame not to leverage that."

"Stop right there," I murmured. "I've been working eighteen hour days for the last three weeks. I need to just listen to the birds singing, and spend a lazy day making love."

"Noted. Was I being a.."

"Yep."

"Best I make love to you here, now. Then you can listen to the birds tweeting at the same time. Kills two birds..as it were."

I giggled, then gasped, as he pulled me onto him. Again.

If you enjoyed this book, please consider leaving a review, as it helps other readers discover my work. Oh, and say hi to your hairdresser for me.
Dawn x

About the author

D A Latham is a salon owner, hairdresser, and mother to two Persian cats and a dog called Ted. She is also the devoted partner of the wonderful Allan.

Other books by D A Latham

The Beauty and the Blonde

A Very Corporate Affair Book 1

A Very Corporate Affair Book 2

A Very Corporate Affair Book 3

And it's offshoot

The Taming of the Oligarch (Book 4)

A Very Corporate Affair Book 1

CHAPTER 1

    I stood on Welling station shivering in the cold, and trying to calm the butterflies fluttering around in my stomach. Today was the day of judgement at work. The day I would find out if my training contract would turn into a fully fledged job at Pearson Hardwick, one of the big four law firms in London. If today went well, I would become a qualified, and gainfully employed, corporate lawyer. If today went badly, then six years of studying would be down the drain.

    It had been a real slog to get this far. I came from a working class family, who didn't believe in social mobility, and thought I was wasting my time. I had worked hard at Bexley Grammar to get top grades and secure a place at Cambridge to study law and business. I had kept my head down through university and had put in enough effort to gain a first. A year long legal practitioner course led to my traineeship, and another two years of intense concentration at Pearson Hardwick had followed, as I threw myself into the opportunity they had given me.

    I looked around the grey, featureless platform. At six thirty in the morning, only the early bird commuters were present. Pale, pasty looking men in badly fitting suits looked resigned to another miserable day in mundane jobs.

There was not one exciting or interesting looking person there. Suburbia doesn't really breed the people who make you sit up and take notice, I thought to myself. All the more reason to escape as quickly as possible.

I'd enjoyed Cambridge as it had been a huge relief to be around intelligent, informed people who had been passionate about academia. My mum had never understood a thirst for knowledge, and had tried to get me to lower my aspirations and take a 'nice shop job' at sixteen. The thought of returning home tonight unemployed and a failure, confirming all her warnings about 'getting ideas above my station', made the butterflies ten times worse.

I arrived at the offices at quarter past seven, pausing in the stunning wood panelled lobby of the ancient law firm, and wondered if it would be the last time I would walk through on my way to work. I ducked into the cloakroom to change into my heels and shed my coat.

"Good morning Elle," said Roger, the security man who was based in the lobby, as I waited for the lift up to my floor.

"Morning Roger, today's the day."

"I wish you the best of luck. I'm sure you'll be fine, the time you get here everyday must have shown them how conscientious you are."

"Thanks. Hope so." I smoothed the front of my neat pencil skirt, and gripped my handbag a little tighter.

Once I had reached my floor, I made my way straight to my desk to switch on my computer, check my emails, and just wait. All the cases I had been assigned to work on had been completed, and as my traineeship had been near its end, they hadn't given me any new ones. For the last week or so, I had just been assisting the other trainees with their cases, doing their drudge work, and helping out in the filing room. I had felt that the lack of new cases being put my way was a bad omen, and if they were keeping me, they wouldn't have worried about giving me fresh work.

Salon Affair

    Checking my emails, I saw one from Mr Lambert, my line manager. I opened it.

From: Adam Lambert
To: Elle Reynolds
Subject: Interview
Date: 28th March 2013

Dear Ms Reynolds,
  Your interview today will be held at 11am in room 7 on the 4th floor. In attendance will be Ms Pearson, Mr Jones, and myself.

Kind Regards
Adam Lambert

    I stared at the email for a minute or two. It wasn't giving anything away. I decided I need a cup of tea. In the small kitchenette area, I realised that my hands were shaking as I filled the kettle. I needed to get a grip. The last thing I wanted to do was show nerves or weakness when the rest of my workmates arrived. Cool, calm and collected was the image I wanted to project at work, not needy, insecure or scared, no matter how I felt inside.
    As the other trainees filed in, I could see how rattled they were. It was interview time for all of us who began in 2011, and usually only a quarter of the intake would be offered permanent jobs. Scanning the faces, I tried to figure out who had screwed up, who had excelled, and who would be a tough call.
    "Why are you looking so pensive?" Lucy demanded, standing in front of my desk, "we all know you'll be ok, miss perfect," she teased.

"I don't know about that, they could easily decide I'm not posh enough to fit in," I said, fully aware of my lack of private schooling and accompanying posh accent.

"Don't be daft, the fact that you have a perfect record and are a bloody genius will easily outweigh the problem of a glottal stop." She smiled to let me know she was teasing.

"Wha times yuh mee-ing?" I said, in full south London accent, taking the piss.

"11.30. You?"

"11. Good luck."

"You too. If it's good news, I'll treat us both to lunch in Bennies." Lucy came from a wealthy background and didn't have to watch the pennies as I did. She sauntered off, seemingly unconcerned about her fate being decided upstairs.

At ten to eleven, I rinsed my hands in cold water to avoid a sweaty handshake, and made my way up to the floor above. The secretary directed me to take a seat just outside the meeting room to await my turn. The door swung open, and a fellow trainee, John Peterson, came out looking as white as a sheet. I caught his eye, and he gave an almost imperceptible shake of his head. He had been one of the 'sure things' I had judged earlier that morning. My stomach sank into my boots.

"Miss Reynolds, you may go in now," said the secretary. I plastered on my best fake smile and entered the room. The three interviewers sat behind a long table, with a single chair placed in front of them. Mr Lambert smiled at me, and asked me to take a seat. I shook their hands, and sat down.

"Good morning Miss Reynolds, I'm sure you must be nervous, so I won't waste time on pleasantries," began Ms Pearson. My heart sank. "You have the highest work output rate of your year group, the best attendance and punctuality rate, and the best report from your superiors." My heart

Salon Affair

hammered, and I tried to stop myself blushing at her compliment. Ms Pearson was a managing partner, so remaining in control in front of her was extremely important.

"So I'm delighted to be able to offer you a permanent position at Pearson Hardwick. Now your report states that you would like to specialise in corporate law, is that correct?"

I pulled myself together quickly enough to answer her, "yes, that's correct."

"Good. We have an opening in our corporate department at Canary Wharf. You can begin there on Monday. For the rest of this week you will be on paid leave, as Mr Lambert has indicated that you have taken no holiday at all this year. The salary will be eighty thousand per year, plus the grade 3 benefit package. Do you have any questions?" Ms Pearson looked at me intently.

"No questions, and thank you Ms Pearson, I won't let you down," I said, barely able to take it all in.

"I'm sure you won't. Now, please head over to HR, where they have your new contract ready for you to sign, and sort out your package, then I suggest you have some rest until Monday."

I smiled widely at the panel, "thank you for this opportunity," I said before heading out.

Over at HR I signed my new contract, collected the details of my new workplace, and perused the list of benefits I could choose as part of my package. As I didn't have a car to be subsidised, I chose gym membership, private health care and an enhanced pension. The HR lady assured me that the gym at the Canary Wharf building was superb, and useful for showering and changing facilities if I needed them. On my way back to my floor, I bumped into Lucy, who was sporting a wide grin

"Great news Elle, I got family law, just as I wanted. What about you?"

"Good news for me too, I got corporate, so Canary Wharf here I come," I replied with an equally big smile.

"Wow! They are the most prestigious offices in the firm, you must have done really well. I'll come and visit you there. Now, shall we meet by your old cubicle as I have to see HR before we go to lunch?"

"Great, see you in a bit."

I went back to my cubicle with my shoulders back, and a lightness I had never felt before. Success felt fantastic, and for the first time ever I could escape my background.

Bennies was a bistro type bar tucked away down one of the tiny passages that characterised the city. Lucy ordered a bottle of Moët while we waited for our overpriced sandwiches. We clinked glasses and gossiped about who got kicked out and who was kept on. It turned out that out of a hundred who began the training contract with us, only fifteen had been offered full contracts.

"So, what's your next plan? Are you moving nearer work?" Lucy asked.

"Sure am, I have the rest of the week off, so it's a good opportunity to look for a flat share or a studio. Mum's boyfriend wants to move in, and it's too small a flat to have all three of us there, so it's time to move out." I hugged myself with glee. Escape from the moaning about my getting up early, use of hot water and aversion to junk food.

Lucy broke my reverie, "my brother's friend is looking for a flatmate, he lives near Canada square. Would you like me to call him?"

"Oh yes please, that would be great." She pulled her phone out of her bag and prodded the screen.

"Hi James, it's Lucy Elliott. Have you still got that room available? Only one of my friends is looking for a flat near Canary Wharf." She listened to the other person, injecting a 'mmm' every now and then. "Yes it's a she, and she is a nice, hardworking, quiet, corporate lawyer. Yes I

Salon Affair

work with her.....yes.....no......ok I'll send her along this afternoon. Text me the address yeah." Lucy ended the call.

"Room's still available then?" I asked.

"Yep. He's a bit fussy about who he shares with. James is a nice guy, and likes a quiet life. He works from home, so needs a flat mate who goes out to work, and isn't too noisy." Lucy's phone chirped as a text arrived with the address, which she forwarded to me.

A couple of other trainees from our year arrived to celebrate with us, nicking our champagne, much to my relief. I didn't want to view a flat half cut.

After lunch, I headed over to the docklands, taking the DLR. I had to double check the address, as the building looked way too swanky to be a flat share type of place. Pressing the buzzer, a voice came through, "who is it?"

"Elle Reynolds, Lucy sent me."

"I'll buzz you in. Take the lift to the fourteenth floor. My door is right in front of you." The buzzer sounded, and I pushed my way into a marble and glass lobby. I took in the silence, the deep carpet, and sense of restrained opulence. The lift was large, mirrored and silently sped straight up to floor fourteen, which I noticed, was the highest floor.

The door in front of the lift was open, and what could only be described as a bear was standing in the doorway. It was hard to gauge his age with all the facial hair, but I took a guess at early thirties. He was tall and broad, dressed in jeans and an old t-shirt which showed off muscular, hairy arms. Through all the long, curly hair and copious beard, a pair of twinkly blue eyes reflected a smile. "You must be James? I'm Elle," I said, extending my hand out to him. He shook it warmly and invited me in.

"Did you find it alright?" he enquired, "and would you like a coffee?"

"Yes it was easy to get here, and yes I'd love a coffee if you're having one." He showed me through to what could only be described as a state of the art kitchen. James pulled two cups out of a cupboard and pulled two pods out of a drawer.

"What sort of coffee? I can do americano, espresso, latte or cappuccino."

"A latte would be lovely," I said, awed that there was a choice. If my mum remembered to buy fresh milk it was an event, and yet this hairy, bearded, bear-person had fresh coffee and fresh milk. I was impressed.

I found out that James was an app developer, and had built a few hit apps, which had enabled him to buy the apartment. He was working on a new app, and worked from home, so needed some peace during the day. I told him all about my promotion, and we toasted my success with fresh coffee, which made me giggle. He explained that Canada Square was quite literally round the corner, and my walk to work would be around five minutes.

"So why do you want a flat mate?" I asked.

He squirmed slightly, "I work from home, and sometimes barely speak to a living soul from one day to the next. I guess I get a bit lonely here on my own." He looked a bit sad.

"No girlfriend?" I wanted to make sure there was nobody to get jealous that a woman was moving in. The last thing I wanted was to put anyone's nose out of joint.

"Nope. My last girlfriend went to live in Australia, so don't worry, nobody to get arsey about a girl living here. I have to ask, any boyfriend?"

"No. I've been working like a demon for the last few years. No time for a man." Much to my mother's disgust, I thought.

Salon Affair

"Well, I have no issue with you bringing friends back, but I'd rather not have a man move in here, so if you get serious with anyone, please bear that in mind."

"Will do. Can I see the room?"

"Sure, this way." James led me down a short corridor and opened a door. The room was enormous, with floor to ceiling windows covering one wall. There was just a large bed and a cabinet with a TV in the room. It looked a bit sparse. I walked over to the windows and stared at the view of the Thames.

"There's a dressing room through here, and an ensuite through that door," said James, pointing at two doors. Looking in the first one, I found a beautifully fitted out walk in wardrobe, with acres of hanging space, shoe racks and a dressing table. My paltry clothing collection would take up about a tenth of the space.

The ensuite was lovely. It had a large, deep bath, a separate shower, and a heated towel rail. It all looked brand new and pristine.

"How much is the rent?" I asked, suddenly nervous that I wouldn't be able to afford to live in this luxury.

"A thousand a month, but that includes all bills. Does that suit?" I breathed a sigh of relief.

"Fantastic, it's a deal." We shook hands. I arranged to pay the deposit and first month's rent into James bank account via my laptop, and he gave me a key.

We bonded over another cup of coffee. I really warmed to James. He was just the right mixture of intelligence, geekiness and humour. We had thrashed out some basic house rules which, thankfully, didn't include hot water usage or rationing the gas. He also mentioned that he was an early riser, and hoped that it wouldn't be an issue for me to be quiet late at night. We both laughed when I pointed out that ten pm was staying up late for me.

I headed back to Welling with a spring in my step, eager to begin my new, London life. As predicted, my mum could barely contain her excitement at my moving out. She dug out the News Shopper and found an ad for a 'man with a van' who would be able to move all my belongings at short notice. He was able to do Thursday, so that left Wednesday to pack up, and get everything ready. I would still have a few days to unpack, settle in, and explore before starting work.

Mum was eager to help pack my belongings, and I actually didn't have much. The whole lot took us a morning to box and bag up. I had invested carefully in good work clothes, but apart from that, I didn't really buy a lot. Plus I had used the money I earned during my training contract to pay off my student loans, and build some savings, rather than blow it on clothes and makeup.

That afternoon, I decided to hop on a bus to Bluewater and treat myself to a haircut and some new work outfits ready for Monday.

I went into the swankiest salon there, and booked in for a trim. I kept my hair long, but the stylist added layers, and the whole effect was classy and grown up. Delighted with my new hair, I wandered round the boutiques trying on clothes until I found a fabulous navy dress and jacket combo which fitted like a dream, and projected just the image I was aiming for. I stocked up on tights and toiletries and bought a pair of navy heels to match my new dress. In a mad moment of optimism, I even bought a box of condoms before heading home.

The next morning a slightly grubby van pulled up outside the flat, and an even grubbier, skinny man got out. He wasted no time flinging my stuff in the back while I wrote out my new address for mum.

"You have fun, and don't work too hard," were her parting words of wisdom. No doubt Ray, her boyfriend was

Salon Affair

waiting round the corner for my van to pull away before rolling up with his bags.

As we pulled away from Welling, the excitement rose in my belly. This was the moment I had worked towards for six long years. My life could finally begin.

James helped van man with my bags and boxes, so with the three of us, it didn't take long. It took a further two hours to unpack and neatly hang my clothes in the closet.

"You don't have much stuff for a girl," said James, wandering in with two glasses of wine.

"I'm not a great shopper, and I've not had much spare cash to spend on clothes and stuff," I replied, a bit embarrassed by my meagre use of the dressing room. I aimed to spend 10% of my new salary on clothes every month to make sure I looked the part.

"Not criticising, just saying. I've got even less clothes than you," he said in a good natured way. He sat on the dressing table seat sipping his wine as I checked all my shoes for dirt before stowing them on the rack. He told me all about the new app he was working on, which sounded great, and described the other occupants of the building.

"The only unfriendly one is the fella on the floor below. Never says hello, and seems to bring lots of different women back. I saw one crying in the lobby once, said he threw her out. He's definitely one to stay away from."

"Thanks for warning me. He sounds delightful, not. Now is there a grocery store around here? I need to pick up a few bits."

"There's a small mart round the corner. What do you need?"

"Milk, bread, that kind of stuff."

"I had it all delivered today. There's loads in the fridge. I get everything ocado'd in. I have everything sorted for dinner tonight, thought you might be too busy with the move to worry about it."

"James, that's really kind of you, thank you. I'll pay you back."

"Nonsense, it's only a few groceries, and besides, I love to cook, but I never have anyone to cook for, so indulge me and let me prepare something." He smiled warmly, and wandered back to the kitchen area.

I hugged myself with glee. Sipping wine in a gorgeous apartment overlooking the river, with a new friend, and a new job. It was everything I'd imagined it would be.

"Elle," James yelled, "foods ready." I hurried into the kitchen as he dished up a pasta and tiger prawn concoction. He poured another two glasses of wine, and pushed one over to me.

"Bon appetite little Elle, and welcome to Canary Wharf. I hope you'll be very happy here." We clinked glasses.

"Thank you big James, and I'm sure I'm gonna love it." I took a bite of my pasta, it was all lemony and buttery, and delicious. "Wow, you are a great cook, this is gorgeous."

"You look like you need a bit of feeding up."

"I'm not a great eater. My mum only ever heated stuff up out of the freezer, so it was often better to go without than suffer the nightly unidentified breadcrumbed fare."

James laughed, a rich, deep, hearty laugh, "no wonder you're skinny. You need good, healthy, hearty food, especially with a pressurised job. Will they have you working all hours of the day and night?"

"Probably. I'm going in there as the lowest in the pecking order, so I'm in no doubt that I'll get the donkey work. Law is like that, hierarchy is everything. I'm pretty certain that I'll be given a cubby hole next to the bogs for my office, and the secretaries will be sly bitches. I don't mind though, I'm prepared to earn my stripes."

"I hated corporate life," James confided, "glad to be out of it. Hated sucking up to a useless wanker of a boss, and attending endless meetings. If I need a status meeting nowadays, I just look in a mirror."

"Do you always work alone? Or do you sometimes collaborate?" I asked.

"Always alone. I did one app a few years back with a designer, and it was a bit of a disaster, all style over substance, so since then, I do it all myself. So what made you go into law?"

I pondered his question. "Money really. Corporate law is a well paid profession, and I wanted to escape my background. I wanted to aim high, and I enjoy the intellectual rigour of law. I didn't want to be involved in criminal law because I hate grisly stuff, and family law is often emotionally draining. I like the detail of contract law, and the fact that it's usually done in shiny, neat offices rather than police cells or prisons."

James smiled at me, "I admire your ambition, I wish I had more of it. I'm happy just sitting coding apps and dreaming up games."

"You did ok out of it," I said, sweeping my hand to indicate the apartment, "this place is fantastic."

"Yeah, I'm pretty lucky," he agreed.

I spent the first evening in my new home watching telly on the big flat screen in the living area. James had shown me how to use the coffee maker, and dishwasher, so I insisted he sat down while I cleared up after dinner, and made us both coffee. By nine, I was yawning, so bade him goodnight, and went to bed.

The next morning I was up at my normal time of half five. I wandered through to the kitchen to make tea, and discovered James boiling a kettle.

"Morning Elle, sleep well?"

"Morning, yeah great thanks. Is there enough water in the kettle for two?" James nodded. He looked even more dishevelled in his dressing gown and pyjamas, with his beard sticking out like bed hair. He pulled out another cup and threw a tea bag into it.

"So what's your agenda for today?"

"I'm gonna check out my new gym, pop into my new office to say hi, and explore my surroundings. Anything you need me to bring in?"

"Don't think so, I'll text you if I think of anything. I've got stuff in the fridge for dinner tonight, so don't worry about food."

"Ok, thanks, just let me know. I'm gonna take a shower now and head out." I took my tea back to my room and drank it while staring at the view from my window. After a luxurious shower, I dried my hair as I watched the stylist do, and applied a touch of makeup. I decided that trousers and flats were best bet for the day I had planned, so dressed in neat but trendy trousers and a simple cashmere jumper. As I wasn't sure what time the gym would open, I went back to the kitchen and made another tea. James wasn't around, so I sat quietly at the island and read through the bumf on the gym that HR had given me. It all looked pretty straightforward. I would have unlimited use of the facilities, and only pay for personal training. I checked the opening hours, finding that it opened at six. I would be able to do a workout in the mornings and still be at my desk by seven thirty, perfect. I finished my tea and placed mine and James cups in the dishwasher before heading down.

The lift stopped and the doors slid open while I was looking at my map of the area, and I automatically began to walk out, bumping straight into someone stepping in.

"I'm so sorry," I began, before noticing we were not in the lobby, and I had just bumped into Adonis himself. "I thought I was on the ground floor." I said lamely.

"Just be more careful," he snarled, before studiously ignoring me for the rest of the journey down. Must be the man James warned me about I thought. James didn't tell me he was sex on legs though. I surreptitiously studied him as

Salon Affair

he exited the lift. Short dark hair, bespoke suit, and a face that would be handsome if he smiled.

I was indeed five minutes away from the Canary Wharf tower, which rose majestically to top the surrounding skyscrapers. I followed the directions to the gym on the lower ground floor. It was a health enthusiasts dream, row upon row of state of the art equipment, complimentary towels, pristine changing rooms, and a full list of fitness classes. I booked in for an orientation session the following day, and picked up a class timetable. I exchanged my voucher from HR for my gym pass at the desk, and wandered around for half an hour, checking out the changing room and the machines.

My new office was based on the 34th floor of the tower, so at nine, I went up there to introduce myself. The receptionist was a pretty Asian girl, called Priti, who seemed efficient and welcoming. She introduced me to a few of the other lawyers, all of whom seemed friendly enough.

"I can show you where you'll be working," said a geeky, skinny man who introduced himself as Peter Dunn. "They told me you were starting Monday, so your desk is all ready." He showed me through a large open plan office full of people to a corridor of glass fronted offices. Pushing a door open, he revealed a large office with four desks. Two desks were occupied by men. Peter explained that he sat at the far end, and the final desk was earmarked for me. I introduced myself to the other two.

"I'm Adrian Jones, and he's Matt Barlow. So you're the ex trainee we have to get up to speed then?"

"That's me. I hope you don't mind having a newbie around," I said, hoping to disarm them. I knew that nobody liked babysitting newbies.

"I'm sure we'll cope, and it'll be nice having a bit of eye candy around, eh boys? This firm has an ugly secretary only policy," Adrian sniggered.

"I'll do my very best to look pretty gentlemen, just don't forget I'm not a secretary." I smiled to make them think I was teasing.

"If you wear a tight blouse I promise I won't get you making tea," quipped Matt.

"I'll see what I can do," I laughed, "as long as you'll be able to concentrate on your work if I'm in here with my cleavage on show."

"She's gonna have every hotshot in the tower salivating over her, you have no chance," laughed Peter, looking amused at the adolescent behaviour of his colleagues. I had fully expected sexist banter, and it all seemed quite harmless. Certainly my office mates seemed friendly enough, and I was confident I'd be able to handle them.

I didn't hang around long, as I wanted to explore the whole area. I discovered the vast shopping complex beneath the tower, looking out for decent lunch places and a dry cleaners. I found wine bars, restaurants, and pubs for evenings out, and a gorgeous deli for supplying food for evenings in. I stopped off at a Starbucks for a coffee, and settled into a sofa to check my map.

"May I join you?" My head snapped up at the masculine voice. Adonis from the apartment block was standing in front of me.

"Sure," was all I could manage. I went back to my map. I could do rude too. He coughed slightly, which made me look up. He was staring intently.

"You just came out of Pearson Hardwick," he said.

I stared back, "yes," I replied, giving nothing else away. He unnerved me, which I didn't like. I hoped he didn't work for them as well. He blew on his coffee before sipping it. I watched his mouth. He had the sexiest mouth.

"So what were you doing there?"

Salon Affair

"I beg your pardon?" How rude was this man? Out of all the ways to frame a question, he had to pick the worst.

"Are you a secretary?" I almost spat my coffee at him.

"No I'm most certainly not. It's none of your business why I was there." I watched as his eyes flashed. I couldn't work out if he was laughing at me or angry.

"I suppose it's not, I just saw you in their offices. I was in there signing a contract," he said.

"Are you a client?" I asked, suddenly wary of upsetting him.

"No, I was there with my own legal team, they had drawn up a contract for the other party. So are you going to tell me why you were there?"

"I start work there Monday, I'm a lawyer for Pearson Hardwick, just moving over to corporate. Went there today to introduce myself."

"So are you going to introduce yourself to me? Seeing as you nearly knocked me over at home and work two floors below me in the tower?"

"I'm Elle Reynolds. I just moved into the apartment, James' new flatmate. Have you lived there long?"

"About two years. I'm Oscar Golding, and it's very nice to meet you Elle." He leaned forward and shook my hand. His hand was surprisingly warm and soft for such a harsh looking man. I wanted to get a smile from him to see if I was right about him being more handsome. I gave him my best beaming smile, hoping he would reciprocate. He just about managed to turn the corners of his mouth up when his phone rang. As soon as he saw the screen, he scowled and excused himself. I went back to my coffee and my map.

I picked up a box of Krispy Kremes before heading home. James came out of his study when he heard the front door.

"Thank god you're back. I was going boggle eyed at my screen in there. What you been up to?" He made coffee and set out the box of doughnuts while I told him about the gym, my office, and the shopping mall.

"I bumped into our downstairs neighbour this morning, quite literally. He really is a strange one. Snarled at me in the lift, saw me in Starbucks this afternoon and managed to piss me off again."

James laughed, "how did he manage to piss off a jolly little thing like you?"

"Said he saw me in the Pearson Hardwick offices and asked if I was a secretary." James' eyebrows shot up.

"Why did he assume you were a secretary? Stupid man."

"Quite. He really is quite unpleasant. Never smiles either." I sipped my coffee, and smiled at James demolishing the pile of doughnuts. "I did make sure he wasn't a client though."

"Clever move. Never a good idea to make a client feel like an idiot." We both laughed.

James made fajitas that evening, which were delicious. Afterwards I had a long hot bath before putting my pyjamas on and joining him for a bit of telly and a glass of wine before I turned in.

Thank you for reading this excerpt from A Very Corporate Affair Book 1, available at all e-book retailers, and in paperback.

Printed in Great Britain
by Amazon